REWIND

BOOKS BY JOY KLUVER

Detective Bernadette Noel Series:

Last Seen
Broken Girls
Left For Dead

About Joy Kluver

Joy Kluver has been an avid reader and writer since childhood. More recently she's been escaping the madness of motherhood by turning her hand to crime novels. A book blogger, she also organises author talks for her local library. Joy lives in SW London with her husband and three children. She has written three DI Bernadette 'Bernie' Noel books – 'Last Seen', 'Broken Girls' and 'Left For Dead', and the series has been shortlisted for Best New Kid on the Block (best new series) in the Dead Good Reader Awards 2022. 'Rewind' is the fourth book in the DI Bernadette 'Bernie' Noel series.

Joy is represented by Anne Williams at the Kate Horden Literary Agency.

REWIND

JOY KLUVER

Published by Marchant Press 2024

ISBN: 978-1-0686873-1-0
eBook ISBN: 978-1-0686873-0-3

Cover design by Michael Watermeyer

To my husband, Phil

PART ONE

CHAPTER 1

Monday

Thwack!

Bernie started. The punch had come from nowhere. In the dim light, she focused on the fist as it came in for a second blow and caught it in her hand.

'Oi, Little Miss Mira, hitting Mummy is not allowed. I could arrest you for ABH.' Bernie kissed her daughter's hand. 'And what are you doing in our bed anyway?'

Bernie glanced over at a sleeping Dougie. She already knew the answer. Maternity leave was swapping for paternity leave and Dougie had fallen at the first hurdle – settling Mira in the middle of the night. Bernie sighed. It had taken her weeks to get her baby girl to sleep in her cot in her room.

Mira tugged at Bernie's pyjama top. Glancing at the clock to read five fifty-two a.m. – they didn't need to set the alarm any more – Bernie moved Mira into position to nurse. While her daughter fed, Bernie thought about the day ahead. Her return to work had finally arrived. In some ways she was desperate to get back – she missed seeing her colleagues and having adult conversations. And it would be nice to wear smart clothes again, even if they were a little on the tight side currently. But she'd also miss being with

Mira all day. At the time, splitting parental leave between them had made sense. Now, though, nine months seemed too soon to leave her. At least Detective Chief Superintendent Wilson had given her good working hours to make sure she could be home to feed Mira at night.

'Mama.'

Bernie smiled. 'Yes, Mira?'

'Nana.'

'You want banana for breakfast? OK.'

Mira was shoving banana slices into her mouth when Dougie appeared at the kitchen door, looking sheepish, his dark hair tousled.

'I know,' he said, 'but she wouldn't settle. She wanted you. And as soon as I put her in bed next to you, she went straight off to sleep. She's a mummy's girl.'

'Oh, I don't know about that. She's got you wrapped round her little finger.' Bernie kissed him on the cheek. 'I need to get showered and dressed. Can you take over here?'

'Sure. I'll need to shower and get dressed too.'

Bernie laughed. 'How many times did you let me do that when you were working?'

'Ah. Sorry.'

'Look, you shower when I get dressed. I want to leave by seven this morning but we still have time.'

Thirty minutes later, Bernie waved goodbye to a screaming Mira as she drove away. Tears pricked her eyes. She needed to pull herself together before she got to headquarters.

The sky was slowly brightening, clouds covering the rising

March sun. The narrow country lanes with their high hedges were empty as Bernie made her way to Devizes. It wouldn't be long before leaves appeared on the hedges again, protecting the nesting birds. Spring was breaking through with pockets of crocuses and daffodils. After a cold, wet winter, they were a welcome sight.

It had been a long time since Bernie had been on the roads this early. It seemed quieter than she remembered. Going round a bend, she discovered why. Ahead of her, blue-and-white tape blocked the road. A white BMW had smashed into a tree. A police car was parked beyond it, its blue lights flashing. Bernie pulled up and got out. She recognised the officer.

'So, what have we got here, PC Barton?'

The young man looked up and smiled. 'DI Noel. I thought you were still on maternity leave.'

'First day back. On my way to headquarters when I spotted this.' She nodded to the car wreckage. 'I assume you've checked for signs of life.'

PC Barton wrinkled his nose. 'Yes. Driver's been dead for a while, I'd say.'

DI Bernie Noel raised an eyebrow.

Barton blushed. 'Although, obviously, that's for the pathologist to decide. Back-up and Forensics are on their way.'

Bernie ducked under the tape and walked around the car, keeping her distance. She didn't have any forensic overalls with her, not even gloves. The car only had one occupant – the driver. He appeared to be male but the deployed airbag hid his face. Barton had done the right thing in checking for a pulse before sealing off the scene. Tyre marks on the road suggested the car had swerved, probably at speed judging by the damage done to the front. What had caused him to swerve was another matter.

An animal? Another vehicle or cyclist? If Barton was right about the man being dead for a while, then this happened in the middle of the night. Something felt a little bit off.

Bernie circled back round, slower this time, her eyes covering the whole of the car. She spotted something on the saloon boot. There was a rust-coloured smudge.

'Barton, did you check the car for any other occupants? Any indication that there was someone else in there?'

'Yes, I checked. There were no doors open and nothing obvious on the rest of the seats.'

'Then how did that get there?' She indicated to the smudge. 'I think that's blood. Got any spare gloves?'

'Yes, in the car. I'll just get them.'

Returning a minute later, Barton passed over two pairs of forensic gloves. 'Wasn't sure if you wanted to double-glove? Would it be better to wait for Forensics though?'

'What's the first rule of approaching any scene like this?'

'Check for signs of life.'

'And that's what we're doing,' said Bernie, snapping on her gloves, knowing full well that Lucy from Forensics would be cross with her for not suiting up first. But she had to check. She stood back as far as she could while she reached for the catch to open the boot. Barton's radio crackled in the background.

'PC Barton responding. DI Noel is here at the scene...'

Bernie clicked the catch and the boot creaked open.

'... One fatality,' said Barton into his radio.

Bernie took a shallow breath as she stared into the boot. 'Make that two,' she said.

CHAPTER 2

'I know how keen you are to get back to work, Bernie, but I didn't expect you to pick up a case on your way in this morning. I take it you want to head it up.'

Bernie smiled. 'It wasn't on my agenda, sir, but yes, I'd like to work this one.'

She'd missed her boss, Detective Chief Superintendent Wilson. He appeared even balder than before, and tired. His face was thinner. Retirement wasn't far away now and he seemed ready for it. In theory, there should be other ranks between them for Bernie to report to but Wilson had been her personal mentor since arriving at Wiltshire Police.

'Well, you'd better go and start the investigation with your team. I know they're looking forward to having you back. But a couple of things before you go. Your finishing time of six thirty is non-negotiable. If I find you here five minutes past that time, I'll be kicking you out. You may, of course, leave earlier if needed. And secondly, it's time to be a proper detective inspector. Delegate tasks. You don't need to do everything yourself. Dougie led the team like that in your absence and they really rose to the challenge.'

Wilson gave her a stern look. Bernie felt chastised. She was an unconventional detective inspector. Sitting back and delegating wasn't her thing but maybe, for Mira's sake, she needed to change tack.

'Yes, sir. I'll do my best.'

Bernie bumped into Jane Clackett, the media officer, as she left Wilson's office. She looked the same – dark suit, white shirt matching her pale skin, her signature razor-sharp black bob without a hair out of place and bright red lips, basically like a vampire – but she had a huge smile on her face.

'Bernie, it's so great to see you. Place hasn't been the same without you.' Jane linked arms with her. 'Let me walk you to your department.'

Bernie frowned, looking at Jane's arm. She wasn't normally this tactile. 'Nice to see you too, Jane, but I can manage to walk on my own.'

'I know. I just want to come with you.'

'Hang on a minute, is there something planned?'

'No idea,' said Jane as she pulled Bernie down the corridor to MCIT – Major Crime Investigation Team. Jane opened the door and pushed Bernie through.

'Surprise!' came a shout from within.

Party poppers were popped and streamers covered Bernie. She saw a 'Welcome Back' banner hanging up and on a desk was a large white box.

'Oh guys, thank you. You've even been to the bakery,' she said, looking around at her team – DS Kerry Allen, DC Matt Taylor, DC Alice Hart and DC Mick Parris.

'That was Matt's task this morning,' said Kerry. 'Welcome back. We've missed you.' She stepped forward and hugged Bernie.

The others followed.

'I hear from the super that you've managed perfectly well without me,' Bernie said.

'I wouldn't say that exactly,' said Kerry.

'No,' said Alice. 'I mean we have managed but it's not been the same. Mick's got away with more inappropriate jokes than he would have done otherwise—'

'True,' Mick piped up.

Bernie laughed. 'That doesn't surprise me.'

'And we've all lost weight,' said Matt, 'because DI Anderson never seemed to have time to go to the bakers in the morning.'

'Ha! Me too, although there's a bit more still to go,' said Bernie, patting her tummy. She pointed to the box. 'What's in there?'

'Probably too much but Danish pastries, doughnuts, yum yums, Malteser cake,' said Matt, lifting the lid. 'You have first dibs, boss – sorry – ma'am.'

Bernie looked at Matt. 'Did you call Dougie "boss" rather than sir?'

'Yes. Said he preferred it.'

Bernie suppressed the shudder building in her. There'd only been one senior officer she'd called 'boss' and she didn't really want to remember him again. Wilson's words came back to her. She had to get over it. Time to be a proper detective inspector, like Anderson.

'Then let's stick with it.' Bernie spoke louder. 'Boss from now on, rather than ma'am. The super praised you all earlier. So maybe I need to follow DI Anderson's example and lead you in the same way. Delegate tasks and give you more free rein. But you still need to run everything by me first, OK?'

The team nodded in agreement.

'Great. If someone could get me a coffee please, then we can grab a pastry and start looking at this new case. Think I might go and wash my hands first. I can still smell the latex from the gloves.'

As Bernie left the room, she heard Mick mutter, 'I guess that's the end of Friday night drinks then. Shame.'

'As if that matters,' said Alice.

'It matters to me. It was good bonding time over a pint with DI Anderson. We're not going to get that with DI Noel. She'll be rushing home to feed her baby.'

'Personally, I'd rather bond over coffee and cake,' said Kerry. 'And you can make the coffee, Mick.'

Bernie sighed. Working with her team again wasn't going to be as easy as she first thought.

CHAPTER 3

'So, we don't know a huge amount right now, other than what I saw.'

Bernie took a sip of her coffee and winced slightly. She hadn't missed police instant blend.

'We have a white series 5 BMW that crashed into a tree. Tyre marks show that the car swerved, possibly to avoid something, and then maybe lost control of the car. I'm sure Traffic will analyse it better than me. One dead male driver. White. Airbag deployed but not enough to save him.'

Bernie paused. The image of the other body swam into her mind. She'd only seen it for a couple of seconds but it was long enough.

'The other dead occupant, and I'm not going to say passenger, was found in the boot. We'll have to see what the pathologist and Forensics say but I suspect he was already dead when he was put in there. He was black.' Bernie swallowed slowly. 'And he had not been treated well. But we need full details first. Just prepare yourselves though.'

Bernie looked at her team. Someone needed to go back to the scene and there was only one person who could handle it.

'Kerry, I'd like you to head down there and see what's happening. I can't go as I've technically compromised the scene but perhaps you could do a video call with me. Matt, Alice and Mick, start going through the information that's come in so far. In particular, see if you can get a registered owner for the car. It's probably too much to hope that it's the driver but maybe we'll strike lucky. Any questions?'

'No, boss,' they all said.

'I have one though – where's my desk?'

The rest of the team looked at each other. Kerry spoke up first.

'DI Anderson moved it into the small office next door. He preferred working there.'

'Ah. I see. He didn't tell me. Oh well, if I'm going to be a proper DI, I guess I'd better work in there too. Let's check back in an hour. See how far we've got.'

Bernie took her coffee and lifted the lid on the bakery box. One of the doughnuts had oozed bright red jam which definitely didn't appeal after what she had witnessed earlier. She grabbed a yum yum and headed to her new office.

She sighed as she went in. Painted light grey, it wasn't much bigger than a cupboard and only had a small window to let in light. There was room for a desk, two chairs and a filing cabinet. Not enough room to swing a hamster, let alone a cat. How had Dougie endured working here for nine months? How would she? She knew Dougie liked to have a bit of space from the team but Bernie preferred to be in the thick of it. There was nothing she enjoyed more than when a case was coming together and everyone was calling out what they'd found.

She sat down heavily on the chair. Apart from a monitor screen, a keyboard and computer tower, the only other thing on the desk was a photo of Mira. Dougie had left it for her. Bernie picked it up and looked at her daughter – a mass of dark curls on her head, huge brown eyes, olive skin and an infectious smile. She was so much like Dougie, there was no doubting who her father was now.

There was a knock at the door.

'Come in.'

Kerry popped her head round. 'I'm about to go to the scene. Do you want me to video call you for the whole time?'

'Yes, please, if possible. Kerry, it really is horrific. I'm sending you because I think you're the only one who could cope.'

Kerry nodded grimly. 'OK. I'll call when I'm ready.'

'Maybe do it on WhatsApp and then I can see it on the monitor rather than my phone.'

'No problem. Speak later.'

Bernie drank more of her coffee and wrinkled her nose. It was bad. She'd bring in her own tomorrow. She opened the desk drawers and found pens and other stationery. No chocolate at all. She'd remedy that later.

There was a key for the filing cabinet and Bernie opened it and pulled open the top drawer of three. There were files for cases that Dougie had worked on. If they were closed, then she could send the paperwork to the records department. The second drawer was the same. The third however was empty except for an envelope addressed to her and a large bar of chocolate. She opened the envelope and pulled out a piece of paper.

Let me guess. You checked the desk drawers for chocolate first. Enjoy your first day back. D xx

CHAPTER 4

Thirty minutes later, Bernie had her computer set up and was waiting for Kerry to message her. The crash site wasn't far out of Devizes and on a country lane but the road closure had still impacted traffic in town. Bernie's phone buzzed. It was Kerry.

In place. Are you ready?

Yes. Go ahead.

Bernie connected to the incoming video call on her computer. Kerry's face, covered with a white hood and mask, appeared.

'I'm ready to go in,' she said. 'Lucy's here, along with Nick White – your favourite pathologist.'

Bernie grimaced.

'I saw that. Going to turn the camera round so you can see the whole scene.'

The area was a lot busier than when Bernie had been there. She recognised some of the traffic cops who would be working out how the accident happened. There were three white-suited forensic officers around the car. One taking photos, one examining the driver and the other by the boot. Judging by the build of the third one, that was Lucy.

'Where's Nick White?' Bernie asked.

'He's getting kitted out now. Arrived the same time as me. Took him an hour from Salisbury.'

'And the private ambulances?'

'On their way. Two are coming. Hi, Lucy. You're on camera to Bernie.'

The figure by the car boot turned round. 'Oh hi, Bernie. Welcome back. Thank you for staying away from the crime scene after being here earlier.'

If anyone else had said that, Bernie would have thought she was being told off but Lucy was kind-hearted.

'I know. My bad. But at least I found you the second body.'

'Yes. It was good to be prepared.'

The camera tilted forward and Bernie heard a gasp.

'I guess you've just seen the body, Kerry.'

'God, yes. You weren't joking, were you.'

A close-up image on her screen brought it back to Bernie.

'What have we got here?' said a male voice that Bernie recognised as pathologist, Dr Nick White. They had a love/hate relationship, erring on the side of hate.

'Hi, Dr White,' Bernie said.

'Who said that?' he asked.

'It's DI Noel,' Kerry replied. 'She's on camera.' The angle turned and White came into view.

'Oh I see. Couldn't be bothered to come down yourself?'

Bernie decided to let the barb go. 'I've already been. Saw it first thing this morning, not long after it was found. It's my first day back so I didn't have a forensic suit. Technically I've compromised the scene so I'm not allowed on site. Hence the camera.'

'Right. Well, let's have a look. You'll need to step back though, DS Allen. You can do a closer shot afterwards. But I'll speak aloud for DI Noel to hear. Hmm. This is not pretty at all. I can give more details after the post-mortem but at first glance we have the naked body of an IC3 male, probably in the eighteen to thirty-five age range. He's been shot in the face so facial identification will not be possible. If his family is found, I don't recommend they view him. There are cuts across most of his torso, possibly a sign of torture rather than self-harm but I won't rule the latter out just yet.'

White paused before continuing. 'His hands and feet have been removed and don't appear to be in the boot. This might have been done to hinder identification. At present, I don't know if this was done pre or post death. We'll need to bag the stumps.'

White stood up and faced the camera. 'Well, DI Noel, I've had quite a boring time over the last few months since you've been on maternity leave. I can always rely on you to bring some gruesome entertainment my way, and on your first day back. How do you do it?'

The sarcasm was not lost on Bernie. 'It's a special gift, Dr White. A stupid question, I know, but am I allowed to come to the post-mortem?'

White glanced at Lucy.

'How much did you do earlier? Did you lean in at all?' Lucy asked.

'No. I opened the boot with my arm outstretched and with gloves on. Saw the body and then closed the boot again.'

'OK. Viewing platform only at the morgue. No closer.'

'Thanks. And what about the driver? I didn't go near him at all.'

'Let's have a look at him now.'

The camera moved past the side of the car to the driver's open door. A forensic officer stepped back and Dr White moved in.

'IC1 male. I'm not even going to hazard a cause of death until after he's been on my table. But judging by how smashed up the front of the car is, he was travelling at great speed. Will that do for now, DI Noel?'

'That's great, thank you, Dr White. What time for the post-mortems? It's just coming up to ten o'clock now.'

'Let's say two p.m. for our murder victim. Might leave the driver until tomorrow morning. I know you have a little one to get home for.'

'I do and she's quite demanding. Like her mother.'

'You said it, not me. I'll see you later.'

The camera view turned back to Kerry. 'Do you want to see anything else?'

'I don't want to see it but can we go back to the body in the boot, please?'

'Sure.'

The camera switched round again and the body came into focus. Kerry moved her phone slowly around, capturing the details Dr White had called out. Bernie shuddered as she saw the cuts on the torso. The man's face was horrifically disfigured by the gunshot. He definitely couldn't be identified that way. As for his missing hands and feet – was it about identification or was it torture? Bernie hoped for the young man's sake that it was the former.

CHAPTER 5

'OK guys, what do you have for me?'

Bernie perched on Alice's desk. Unlike some of the others, there was room on hers to sit.

'Car was stolen last night, around twenty-three thirty hours, in Hounslow West,' said Matt. 'Owner called it in six o'clock this morning. I've got the registration and I've just put it into ANPR. Hopefully we'll get some hits.'

'We have footage from a video doorbell of the car being taken too,' Mick said. 'The Met have sent the report over. Not that the footage helps much. Two people with balaclavas on, so can't see their faces.'

'Can I see it please?' Bernie asked.

'Sure. I have it here.'

Bernie made her way to Mick's desk. He pressed play. The footage was in night vision so colour was lost. Two figures appeared, their heads and faces covered just as Mick said. One of them was holding something up in front of the house.

'Relay box,' Bernie said.

'Yep. They're into the car pretty quickly.'

The other person stood by the car, waiting for a click.

Seconds later, he opened the door and they were away.

'Do we know if this was the only car they targeted?'

'Not sure. BMW have improved their technology to prevent this kind of theft from happening but it's an older vehicle.' Mick shrugged.

'They knew to target a vulnerable car. But it might not have been the only one they tried that night,' said Bernie. 'Car thefts happen every day in London so local neighbourhood sites might have more information. Putting up footage of crime seems to be commonplace now.'

'Yes,' said Alice. 'Normally with the title, "Does anyone know who these scum are?"'

'Exactly. Mick, go back to the Met and ask if there's any info on those sites. There's normally a police presence on there in the form of a PCSO. In the meantime, send that to Tom in Digital Forensics and see what he can come up with.'

'What are you looking for?' Alice asked.

'Anything that's going to tie these two people with our dead driver. We can't see faces but there might be something about their clothes or shoes that we can pinpoint. The little details.'

'You know who you really want for that, don't you?' Alice said.

Bernie nodded. 'Yes. Leigh.'

She thought about Local Crime Investigator Leigh Roberts who had joined them for a while. Not easy to get on with at the beginning, Leigh had won the team over with her incredible observational skills and her ability to think outside the box. Bernie had never viewed Leigh's autism as a hindrance but as a help. However, the changes in team and routine had put a burden on Leigh and Bernie didn't want to inflict that on her again. Plus, Kerry wasn't a huge fan of hers. They'd reached an understanding but Bernie wasn't sure if it would survive another big case.

'I'll have a think about Leigh,' she said. 'Mick, you've got your tasks. Matt and Alice, as the ANPR hits come in, map them and find out where this car went. I'm hoping it might lead us to the scene of the murder.'

As Bernie headed back to her office, she spotted an unfamiliar man walking towards her, pushing a trolley with post on it.

'DI Noel?' the man asked.

'Yes.'

'Hi, I'm Martin. I started working in the post room while you were away. I heard you got back today. I have a lot of post for you.' He nodded at a huge pile of envelopes on the trolley.

'OK. You could have sent them to me via DI Anderson. He's my partner. We live together.'

'Oh, sorry. I didn't know.'

'Never mind. Hopefully there's nothing important in there.'

Bernie spotted a few pink envelopes that might be baby congratulations cards. She'd have to explain to the senders why she was late in replying.

'DI Anderson is now on paternity leave so you can give me his post until he's back in three months.'

Martin sorted through some envelopes. 'That's good because I noticed a letter had arrived for him this morning. It looks important.' He handed it over.

Bernie looked at the logo marked at the top of the envelope. It was from the courts. Probably about a case he was involved in but normally they'd email.

'Let me open my door and then I'll pick up my bundle of post.'

'No worries. I can carry it for you.'

Martin scooped it up and followed Bernie into her office. He placed the letters carefully on her desk.

'Sorry again,' Martin said as he left.

'It's fine.'

Bernie looked at the mail and sighed. The last thing she wanted to do was go through it all, especially as they had a live case. Her phone buzzed in her pocket. She pulled it out and saw it was a text from Kerry.

Bodies are out and on way to morgue. Low-loader coming in to take car away for examination. Do you want me to come to post-mortem too?

Bernie thought for a moment. It made more sense for Kerry to return to headquarters.

No, come back here. Write up your report. You'll be in charge while I'm out. I'll take Mick to make it easier for you!

Seconds later, Kerry replied.

But I so enjoy the challenge of Mick!

Bernie saw this as her moment to ask Kerry something.

As much as Leigh?

It was almost a minute before Kerry's text arrived.

What are you really asking me?

This is a big case and I was thinking about extra hands.

Another wait.

Maybe. I'll let you know later.

CHAPTER 6

Bernie looked at the rough route that Matt and Alice were plotting out on a whiteboard.

'So, they headed out on the A4 Bath Road then, going west,' she said.

'Yes,' Matt replied. 'Got them as far as Donnington and then they disappear on the North Wessex Downs. Unless we can get private CCTV or doorbell footage, we've lost them.'

Matt zoomed in on a map on his computer and pointed to a large green area. "This is what we're dealing with. Far too big to search everywhere. A lot of it is farmland, as well as the Downs. Without more info, I don't know where to start.'

Bernie sighed. 'OK. Let's utilise what we do have. Get the description of the car out to the local neighbourhood teams and see if they can track down any local private CCTV that might have caught the car. Maybe we can narrow the area down. Mick, we've got an appointment with Dr White at two o'clock in Salisbury.'

'Oh, you're kidding. I hate post-mortems. Is it both of them?'

'No. Just our murder victim today. Dr White is conscious about me getting home in time for Mira.'

Alice stared at Bernie. 'Dr White is being considerate? That makes a change.'

'I know but we'll go with it. The driver will be tomorrow, Mick.'

'Great. Two days in the morgue.'

'We'll be on the viewing platform so we won't be too close.'

'Away from the smell then,' said Mick. 'Although this one is fairly fresh so it won't be as bad as some.'

Bernie tilted her head to one side. 'I see what you mean now, Alice, about Mick and his inappropriate comments. Let's remember that this man is part of someone's family, and when we find out who he is, I might take you with me to break the news.'

Mick flushed. 'Sorry, boss. I just find post-mortems really hard.'

'I'll go instead,' Alice piped up. 'I'm fine with it.'

Bernie looked between the two of them. 'OK. We'll leave at one p.m. to get there. Hopefully the traffic won't be too bad. Kerry will be back later and she'll be in charge while I'm out.

'Mick, have you heard back from the Met about any other car theft attempts?'

'Only to say that they have tons of stolen vehicle attempts but they'll scan the neighbourhood sites for us anyway. I know it's not the done thing but I have a cousin in Hounslow. I could ask her to look at the sites too. I know she's on them because she often messages me about stuff she's seen, asking me why the police aren't doing more.'

Bernie smiled. 'That might not be the best move at the moment. She might moan about doing your job for you. Let's leave it with the Met for now. If we don't have anything by tomorrow then maybe we'll contact your sleuthing cousin. In the meantime, I'm going to start the logbook and get our actions onto HOLMES. Let me know if anything else turns up.'

She returned to the small office. She hadn't even spent a whole morning in there yet but she was already feeling claustrophobic. Moving her desk out had freed up space in the Incident Room for the others. And if she did get Leigh back, it would be hard to fit two desks in there. It had been a tight squeeze when they'd done that last year. Maybe she should stay put for now.

Bernie pulled together the information she had and began the logbook. Normally, the pace at the start of an investigation was frenetic but she wasn't feeling that. Maybe it was because she was doing the admin rather than getting stuck in at the crime scene. But that was the role of the Senior Investigating Officer – to do the admin and not the running around.

She leaned back in her chair and closed her eyes. She'd been second on the scene, not long after it had been discovered. Surely, there was something else she could pick up on. Visualising her drive that morning, Bernie thought back. It had been cloudy but the sky was brightening. The hedgerows had been more twigs than leaves, the same with the tree the car had crashed into. The tree! Bernie's eyes sprung open. There weren't many trees down the lane but she knew that one marked the start of Ron Willis's farmland. They were tracking the car the wrong way. They needed to go backwards, not forward.

Bernie burst into MCIT.

'We're doing this all wrong. We need to work backwards from the crash. Matt, can I look at the map on the computer again, please?'

'Yes, of course.' He tapped on his computer and the map appeared.

'Thanks. Move over to the other side where we are. Look, there are a number of roads where he could have driven in from. Let's use our local knowledge and see if we can trace him backwards. And I suggest we start here.' She pointed at the map. 'Greenacres Farm. After all the trouble with the motorbike races, I'm pretty sure Ron Willis installed CCTV. Alice, if we leave now, we'll have time to do this before going to the morgue.'

CHAPTER 7

'You hate being in that office, don't you?' Alice asked as Bernie drove to Greenacres Farm. It wasn't far from the crash site.

'That obvious, huh? You know, if the road hadn't been completely blocked this morning, I'd have driven past the farm. I might have remembered then to check their CCTV.' Bernie shook her head.

'Boss, you've only been back a few hours. I'm sure you were expecting to ease back into the job rather than launch into a new case.'

Bernie bristled slightly at the term 'boss'. It would take some getting used to. She indicated right and then turned into the country lane that would lead them to the farm.

'Well, yes, I was hoping for at least a day to settle in.' Bernie thought about what Mick had said earlier about Dougie. 'So, what's it been like with DI Anderson? Don't worry, I won't tell him.'

Alice shuffled in her seat, 'It's been... different.'

'How'd you mean?'

'Well, if he was here now, running this case, he wouldn't be in the car with me. It would be Mick or Matt. DI Anderson would be in his office. He delegated tasks to us that played to our strengths and then we'd report back. We had a briefing in the morning and the evening. And that was fine. He managed us well.'

Bernie slowed the car as she saw the driveway for the farm. 'So maybe that's what I should do. Be a better manager and delegate, instead of driving to a farm.'

'In theory, maybe, but in reality, no. Please be you. We work really well when we bounce off each other. We're a team. There's no wrong or right way of doing it but, no offence to DI Anderson, I much prefer having you around. And both of you are miles better than DCI Worth.' Alice shuddered.

Turning the car in, Bernie nodded. 'I should hope so. Worth really was worthless. OK. I'll keep being me. The super might not be happy though.'

After parking the car, Bernie turned the engine off. 'I don't think you met the Willis family last time, did you? When we found Ria in the woods?'

'Not all of them. I saw Ryan at the station.'

'He'll probably be with his dad and brothers out in the fields but his mum and granddad are likely to be in. It's not so easy for Stan to get around these days. And don't be surprised if they're a bit wary of us. Although I don't think Ryan has had any illegal motorbike races since then.'

They got out of the car and the front door opened as they approached.

'Well, there's a sight for old, sore eyes. Hello, Bernie,' said a voice in a broad Wiltshire accent.

'Stan, can you see me?'

'Course I can. Had the cataract op last autumn. My other eye will always be blind.' The old man held his arms out to Bernie for a hug. 'Miss seeing you at the pub but I guess that baby of yours keeps you busy. Got time for a cuppa?'

Bernie glanced at her watch – eleven forty-five. 'Only if it's convenient.'

'Course it is. Janet, stick the kettle on. We've got visitors.'

Bernie and Alice followed Stan into the farmhouse. Janet came out of the kitchen, wiping her hands on a tea towel.

'Oh aye, it's you. Please tell me nothing's wrong.'

The wariness was still there. Bernie knew she had to tread carefully.

'Nothing's wrong, Janet. In fact, I need your help. This is my colleague, DC Alice Hart. Am I right in thinking you have CCTV?'

'Yes. Got a camera on the front of the house, two others covering the barns and one inside the lambing shed. Lot of action in there at the moment. Ron's on midwifery duty. I guess there's something you want to look for.'

'If that's all right. We can come back later if it's easier.'

'Makes no difference. Lambs will come out whenever they want, night or day. I'll get you both a cuppa and a piece of cake. Salted caramel OK? Ryan wanted something different this week.'

'That sounds wonderful, Janet. Thank you.'

'Go sit yourselves down and chat to Stan.'

Bernie led Alice into the front room where Stan was in his special worn armchair, the stuffing coming out, with a collie dog by his feet.

'Hello, Hollie,' said Bernie, stroking the dog.

'She's lovely,' said Alice.

'She's as old as me in dog years,' said Stan. 'And we're both still going. Now, Bernie, what's happened?'

Bernie and Alice sat down on a brown leather sofa opposite.

'There was a car crash last night, further down the lane. I'm hoping your camera might have picked something up. Did you hear anything?'

'Can't say I did. And nothing wakes Janet up. I tell you, those boys of hers soon learned to sleep through the night when they were babies. How about yours?'

'She's hit and miss. Alice has a little one too.'

Alice groaned. 'He's two and a half now but he's learned to climb out of his cot. I normally wake up to find he's in bed with us.'

Janet came in carrying a tray with cups of tea and cake. 'Do you mind helping yourselves while I swap with Ron? He knows more about the CCTV.'

'There was a car crash, Janet,' Stan said. 'Bernie was just telling me. Did you hear anything?'

Janet shook her head. 'You know me – I'd sleep through a bomb going off. But I was up at five this morning. Didn't hear anything until after seven and then there were sirens. You lot, I guess.'

'Yes. But that's helpful to know, Janet,' Bernie said. 'Narrows down the timeframe. I think it hit one of the trees that mark your fields. It's roughly half a mile from here. Maybe less.'

'Oh no. Ron won't be happy about that. Right, I'll get him. Back in a few minutes.'

Alice passed round the tea and cake. Bernie looked at the photos of the family on the walls and spotted a new one – a young, good-looking man with a pretty young woman.

'Is that Ryan with his arm around a girl?' she asked Stan.

'It is. He's changed a lot in the last eighteen months. Really grown up. Stopped smoking. Started taking better care of himself. And that's Casey. She's good for him. I know that business with him was difficult but it needed to happen. In a way, you helped sort him out. Janet wouldn't thank you but I will. Thank you, Bernie.'

'You're welcome, Stan.' Bernie took a bite of Janet's cake. 'Mmm. This is delicious.'

Alice nodded. 'It's fabulous.'

A few minutes later, Ron appeared. He was a tall, broad man with a ruddy complexion and he looked tired.

'Sorry to come at a busy time, Ron,' Bernie said. 'Were you up with the sheep last night?'

'I was. Janet's told me what happened. I didn't hear a crash as such but I did hear something around two forty a.m. I was dealing with twin lambs at the time so I didn't check it out. Come into the study. It's where the monitor and hard drive are.'

Bernie and Alice followed Ron towards a room at the back of the farmhouse.

'Excuse the mess.'

There were piles of paperwork on almost every surface in the small room. Bernie thought about the post back on her desk. She'd take it home tonight and go through it later.

Ron turned on the monitor and started to rewind the footage.

'I know it were two forty because I'd been keeping an eye on the time as the second lamb hadn't appeared after the first. I had to intervene. Not that you want to know that. Right. Here you go.'

Ron pressed play on the camera at the front of the house. A streak of white zoomed past.

'Was that a car?' Ron asked.

'Think so.' Bernie was about to ask Ron to rewind it when there was another streak.

'A second car,' said Alice. 'Looks a bit darker in colour. It's so fast though.'

'It's got to be chasing the first car,' Bernie replied.

'We hardly get any traffic down here in the middle of the night,' said Ron. 'Racing perhaps? It's nothing to do with my Ryan though. He was in the lambing shed with me, helping with the stuck twin.'

'Did you get it out?' Alice asked.

'Yes. Managed to save mum too. Do you want me to send you this footage, Bernie?'

'Please.' She put her hand into her pocket and realised she didn't have any cards with her. 'Alice, don't suppose you have a card with you?'

'Sure.' Alice pulled one out. 'Send it to my email and then I'll forward it to our tech team.'

'Matt, as well, Alice. I won't take your hard drive, Ron, because I know you need it,' said Bernie, 'but we might need to look at the rest of the weekend. Just in case the cars had driven through before. So, don't delete anything.'

'I won't. I'll just do this email and then if you don't mind, I need to get back to the lambing shed. But finish your cake and tea before you leave.'

Bernie and Alice chatted more with Stan while they ate their cake and drank their tea. After saying goodbye to the old man, they sat in the car. Alice forwarded the footage to Tom and Matt. Bernie pulled out her phone and rang Kerry, putting it on speakerphone.

'Hi, Bernie.'

'Hi. Are you still at the scene?'

'Yes, leaving soon.'

'Can you ask Traffic if there are two sets of tyre marks? I'm at Greenacres Farm with Alice and there were two cars caught on their CCTV last night around two forty a.m. I say cars – they were more like streaks of light they were so fast. I didn't notice any damage on the rear of the car but even a small nudge at that speed would be enough to cause a crash.'

'So maybe not an accident then.'

Bernie thought back to the feeling she had had when she first saw the car that morning. The feeling that something was off.

'Possibly not. I think we have a second murder on our hands.'

CHAPTER 8

After a pit stop to get a sandwich, Bernie and Alice arrived in plenty of time for the post-mortem in Salisbury. They were already on the viewing platform when the body was wheeled out. Bernie steeled herself. She didn't want to admit it to Mick but she hated autopsies too, especially as she already had an idea as to how this victim looked.

'Brace yourself,' she said to Alice but also to herself.

The morgue technician pulled back the cover and Alice gasped.

'Wowser,' Alice said. 'I'm not sure we're going to get dental records let alone facial identification. Poor kid.'

'You think he's young?'

'Maybe. I don't know. Hard to tell from up here. I've just got this feeling though.'

'I agree. I'd be surprised if he's over thirty. Even twenty-five. Might be gang related.'

'Especially with a possible second car involved.'

'Well,' said Bernie, 'despite our initial thoughts, we need to keep an open mind. Ah, here's Dr White.'

Nick White came through the door in green scrubs. 'Good to see you here early, DI Noel. I bet you've missed this.' He grinned.

'You know how much I love it. Before you start, we have reason to suspect that there might have been another car involved in the collision.'

'Right, I'll keep that in mind when I examine the driver tomorrow morning.' White glanced at his technician. 'Let's start.'

As much as Bernie hated attending post-mortems, she couldn't fault Nick White's commitment. She watched as he methodically worked his way through, from the initial observation to the Y incision to the scalp removal. He wasn't the most compassionate man but he did demonstrate dignity in all that he did.

'I know you want cause of death, DI Noel, but I want to wait for the toxicology reports. On first glance, the gunshot wound to his face would be a natural assumption but it's possible it was done afterwards to hinder identification. Same with the amputations of his hands and feet. All done post-mortem.'

'To hinder ID again?' Alice asked.

'If that's the reason then it's a bit daft. We have DNA and should get a result for that tomorrow if your boy's on the register. No, I think the amputations are for another reason but I'm damned if I know. But, I can tell you that a chainsaw was used and you don't always have one of those laying around your house. Plus, they've not been done equally. The right leg has been cut higher than the left and same with the hands.'

'Interesting. What about the cuts on his torso?' Bernie asked.

White turned back to the young man's body. 'They're recent but not as recent as I first thought. Some of them have started to scab. They've been done in the last few days – maybe a week – rather than hours. And I know what's coming next, DI Noel. Time. Last night. I think when you found him, he'd only been dead for a matter of hours.'

As Alice drove back to headquarters, Bernie collected her thoughts. She'd called a briefing with the whole team at six o'clock. She couldn't help but feel she hadn't handled this case well so far. It all felt a bit haphazard. Not as methodical as she would normally be. But then, she hadn't expected to be thrown into a possible double homicide on her way to work that morning. She hadn't even checked with Dougie how Mira was. She sighed.

'You all right, boss?' Alice asked.

That term again. She couldn't cope with being called that. 'Yes and no. I've been out of the game for nine months and I seem to have forgotten how to do this. And if I'm really honest, I don't like being called "boss". I do prefer "ma'am" but it sounds so formal and you've obviously had a different experience with DI Anderson in charge. Matt and Mick, in particular.' Bernie shifted in her seat to face Alice a bit more. 'This is going to sound so pretentious but I've been in the force for fifteen years now and I've had to work hard to get where I am. So, I feel I've earned the right to be called "ma'am".'

There was another reason why she didn't like 'boss' but she didn't want to go into that with Alice.

'Of course,' said Alice. 'You don't have to justify yourself to me, ma'am. We have to work twice as hard as the men to get recognised but maybe with our new female chief constable, things will improve.'

Bernie nodded. She hadn't met the new chief constable yet as the change had happened while she was on maternity leave. Maybe things would improve.

'Anyway,' Alice continued, 'as I said to you earlier, run the team how you want to do it. Forget what anyone else says. Especially Mick. You heard him, didn't you? Talking about drinks. That man would sell his soul for a pint. Please be you. You won't be at your best if you keep trying to fit into a mould that doesn't suit you.'

'Thanks, Alice. I'm putting you in charge of pep talks from now on.'

It wasn't long before they hit the commuter traffic in Devizes. Bernie could never get over how much traffic there was in town. It was almost on a par with London. They made it back to head-quarters with five minutes to spare.

'Thanks for driving, Alice. My wrist still aches a little. Shall we do this again tomorrow? Unless you don't want to go through another autopsy.'

'I'm fine to go again. Although I do think we should wind Mick up and tell him he's going.'

Bernie laughed. 'I agree. You know, when I first met you, I thought you were a bit of a mouse. I was so wrong.'

'That was the DCI Worth effect. He crushed my spirit. Now, I'm in a team that allows me to grow and that's all down to you, ma'am.'

'Thank you. Let's go and see what everyone else has been up to.'

CHAPTER 9

Bernie stood, whiteboard pen in hand, ready to write down what they had so far.

'So, thanks to the CCTV footage from Ron Willis, we have strong reason to believe that the car crashed sometime after zero two forty hours this morning. The footage also indicates a possible second vehicle, possibly giving chase. Tom, have you managed to get anything else from this?'

Tom, from the Digital Forensics team, looked up from his notes. 'I can't tell you make of cars from this but by slowing it down and going frame by frame, the first one is a light colour, more likely white. The second is darker. But, Matt and Mick have found some better footage.'

'Excellent, tell me more.'

Matt stood up, brought his laptop to the front and plugged it into the interactive whiteboard.

'After Alice sent me the other CCTV, Mick and I looked at possible routes for the cars. There was one obvious route that doesn't have council cameras so we drove around a bit and found a pub. They have an outside camera that covers their car park and the road. Plus, they leave a light on. We have some colour.'

Matt tapped on his laptop and a video appeared on the screen. The time stamp was for two thirty-one a.m. Matt pressed play and they all watched as the white BMW appeared first, clearly going a lot faster than the speed limit.

'The second car appears about a minute and a half later.'

Matt fast-forwarded and hit play just as the car appeared, there for a second before it was gone.

'Wow,' said Bernie. 'That's even faster than the white car. Have you been able to get anything from this?'

'Yes,' Tom said. 'It's black and possibly a Mercedes. If we can get some more footage then we can hopefully confirm make and model. Maybe even a registration.'

'Mick and I are happy to continue searching for more CCTV cameras in the morning,' Matt said.

Bernie glanced at Alice. 'I was planning on taking Mick to the post-mortem for the driver tomorrow morning.'

Mick paled.

'Only joking, Mick. Alice is made of sterner stuff than you. You two can carry on looking for cameras. Kerry, what do you have from the scene?'

Kerry picked up her notebook and stood up.

'Thanks to you mentioning the second car, we found tyre tracks beyond the crash on a corner. Second car would have had to brake hard to get round without crashing themselves. There's no obvious sign of damage to the back of the white BMW and no paint flecks either but the driver might have swerved to avoid being hit and lost control. The damage to the front of the car, according to the Traffic cops, indicates a possible speed in excess of seventy miles per hour.'

Bernie wrote up the details of the cars on the board. She then added 'driver' and 'victim' with question marks next to them.

'We'll know more about the driver's death tomorrow but the victim found in the boot of the car is still an enigma,' Bernie said. 'The only thing that Dr White could say conclusively, is that the scars on his torso are from the last week. Some have scabbed, suggesting that not all of them were done this weekend. At first look, you'd think the gunshot wound to his face killed him but White wants to wait for toxicology. The amputations were made post-mortem with a chainsaw and were done unevenly.'

'What do you mean?' Kerry asked.

'The right foot was cut higher than the left. Same with the right hand.'

Matt closed his laptop down. 'Was it all done to hinder identification then?' he asked. 'Fingerprint results are normally pretty fast.'

'Possibly,' said Bernie. 'Although, as Dr White pointed out, we can easily get DNA from the body.'

'But even that takes at least a day,' said Kerry. 'I think I know why the amputations were done and why they were uneven – tattoos.'

'Oh yes,' Bernie said. 'That would make perfect sense. And presumably tattoos that we might know about.' She added 'tattoo' with a question mark on the board. 'So, moving forward tomorrow, Matt and Mick, you're on CCTV search. Alice will come with me to the morgue. Kerry, can you keep focusing on the scene and forensics, please? I assume the road is still shut.'

'It is for the rest of today and definitely into tomorrow. Now we know there was a second car, there's more to examine. I might need some help though. I hope you don't mind but I've made some arrangements for that.' Kerry smiled.

Bernie knew what she meant. 'Are you sure?'

'Yes. Leigh will be joining us tomorrow morning.'

The rest of the team cheered. Despite the initial difficulties, LCI Leigh Roberts was a firm favourite with the rest of them and apparently even Kerry was now won over. Bernie looked around the room. Leigh would need a desk of her own. There wouldn't be room for her to move back in. Matt caught her eye.

'Don't worry, ma'am,' he said. 'We can make room for you both. I know a way we can do it. Leave it with me.'

Bernie smiled. Alice must have spoken to the rest of the team when she'd popped to the toilet after getting back from the morgue.

'OK. Thank you. One day, well, it wasn't even a day, in that office is more than enough for me.' She glanced at her watch. It was almost six thirty. 'I need to head home as there's a little one who wants a feed. I suggest the rest of you finish up too and I'll see you at eight a.m. tomorrow.'

Saying goodbye, Bernie headed into her cramped office, relieved she wouldn't have to stay in there any longer. She scooped up her post, including the one for Dougie with a court stamp. She couldn't think of any cases he was due to appear for, none that he had mentioned anyway. What did the court want with him?

CHAPTER 10

Bernie sighed with relief as Mira latched on. She hadn't said anything to her work colleagues but she was starting to feel uncomfortable towards the end of the day. Six thirty was definitely the latest she could leave, especially as she'd had to drive the longer way back to her cottage in Marchant. Mira had clung to her neck the minute she walked in. Dougie had her ready for bed and Bernie had gone straight upstairs with her baby daughter.

Mira's eyes were drooping as she fed, her long eyelashes almost brushing her face. It wasn't long before she was sleeping and Bernie placed her in her cot.

'Night, night, little one,' she whispered.

She crept downstairs where a delicious aroma met her. Dougie was the better cook of the two of them. He was stirring a pot when she came into the kitchen.

'Sorry I didn't get a chance to properly say hello when I arrived home,' she said, sliding her arms around Dougie.

He turned his head to kiss her. 'No worries. I think a hungry baby is higher than me in the pecking order. How was your day?'

Bernie told him about the car crash and the body she'd found in the boot, along with the developments throughout the day.

'God, Bernie. You hadn't even got to work before you picked up a case.'

'That's what the super said. I think I would have liked a few days to settle in though. Possible double homicide on day one was not on my "back to work" bingo card.'

'No, I guess not. Although, from what you've described, it smacks of gangs so Serious Organised Crime might want a look in.'

SOC was Dougie's normal team and Bernie knew there was a DCI there who would want to take charge.

'Yeah, well, murder is my remit so they can forget muscling in on this one.'

'I'm sure they'd be happy to leave you in charge but if this does turn out to be drug related, then a few DCs from there would be a useful resource. Try this.' Dougie held up a wooden spoon with tomato sauce on it.

Bernie tasted a little. 'Mmm. Your mum's recipe for Bolognese sauce.'

Dougie had picked up his cooking skills from his Scottish Italian mother, Elena, as well as her looks. Bernie had finally met Dougie's family not long after Mira was born and they had fallen in love with her and Mira. Elena stayed for a few weeks and helped them by cooking up a storm of meals, which lasted for a few months in the freezer.

'Mira wolfed it down with some pasta. Although she was wearing most of it on her face. I'm glad you were back a bit later. Gave me a chance to wash it all off.'

'And what else have you done, apart from make a yummy dinner?'

Bernie pulled back as Dougie drained the pasta.

'Well, she only cried for a few minutes after you left and then she looked at me and said, "Yog". I tell you, that baby is frighteningly clever.'

Bernie laughed. 'And somewhat manipulative. We need to watch her with you. She's already got you wrapped round her finger.'

Dougie dished up dinner and put two plates on the small table. He moved Mira's highchair to one side so they could sit next to each other.

'So you gave her some yogurt then?'

'Yes. It got messy. In fact I've spent most of the day cleaning her up. We popped round to Paul and Anna's as well. She loves Anna. I'm glad she's going to look after Mira when I go back.'

'Yes, I was so relieved she said yes.'

Anna had been an important part of Bernie's pregnancy. The vicar's wife, from Northern Ireland originally, was a calm influence on them all.

Bernie took a mouthful of food and sighed appreciatively.

'Have you not eaten all day?'

Bernie blushed.

'Oh God, let me guess, you found the chocolate and ate it all.'

'No. I mean, I found the chocolate and ate a small bit. But Matt had been to the bakers, so I had something from there, and I had a slice of cake at Greenacres Farm. And a sandwich from a garage. That's it.'

'No dessert for you then.'

'Spoilsport. Anyway, I've got a load of post to go through this evening. Apparently the new guy in the post room hadn't realised that we're together. I have one for you too.'

'OK. I'll look at it after dinner.'

After they'd finished eating and everything was cleared away, Bernie tipped the post onto the table. She handed Dougie's his and pulled out the coloured envelopes for her, leaving the boring-looking ones. She started to open them.

'God, I thought these might be baby cards. I'm going to have to apologise to people for not getting back to them. I'd better make a list.'

Bernie pulled out her phone and started to write a note with everyone's names. She gasped when she opened the last one.

'What's the matter?' Dougie asked.

She handed the card to him. It was a classic baby card with a pink teddy bear on the front. He opened it.

'God, it's from Jade. This is Zac Ambrose's mother, right?'

Bernie nodded. It was a year since she had last seen Jade Ambrose, mother of Danny, Zac and Joshua. Bernie had investigated Zac's murder the year before, not an easy task as she was also responsible for putting Danny Ambrose behind bars when she worked for Jack Thornton at the Met.

'I'd never have thought she'd send us a card,' Dougie said. 'Oh well, stranger things have happened. Right, what have I got here? Court? I didn't think I was needed for anything.'

Bernie turned back to the rest of the post – the boring ones. There was one from a school, asking if she could go in for careers day. She'd done it before when her wrist was broken. When she checked the date, she saw that it had been and gone. Another apology to add to the list. She continued through the pile and opened up a few more before she realised that Dougie was quiet.

'What's wrong?'

Dougie rubbed his forehead. 'I thought I'd got out of this.

I'm really sorry. I told the prosecution I couldn't appear because I'd be on parental leave. It's taken ages for them to get back to me. It's not a good enough excuse. I have to go to London on Friday.'

'London? But all our trials are...' Bernie paused and picked up Jade's baby card. 'You're going to the Old Bailey, aren't you? For Jack Thornton's trial? I hadn't realised it was happening yet. No one said anything. You didn't say.'

'Bernie, I'm sorry. I didn't want to bring it all up for you. We thought it better that you didn't know the trial was happening.'

A face appeared in Bernie's mind. Jack Thornton. Sandy hair and dazzling blue eyes. A detective inspector Bernie had thought she could trust with her life. Instead, he'd gambled with it.

'What do you mean, we? This is the super, right? Honestly, I'm fine.'

Dougie gave her a concerned look and she knew she wasn't fine. Beads of sweat were forming on her forehead. It wouldn't be long before her scar on the left-hand side of her abdomen would start to itch. Dougie took the card away and held her hand.

'I'll ask Anna to look after Mira. I'll only be gone for the day and I'll tell the prosecution that. It'll be OK. Now, I'm going to get you some water to drink.'

As he stood up, Dougie knocked the table and the boring letters fell on the floor.

'Sorry. You stay there. I'll get them.'

Dougie scooped them up and passed them to Bernie. Trying to distract herself, she flicked through them but then stopped.

'Oh shit,' she said.

Dougie looked at her. 'OK, now it's my turn to ask.'

Bernie held up a letter that had the same court stamp.

'Surely not,' said Dougie.

She ripped open the envelope, dreading what might be inside. She scanned the contents of the letter, scarcely believing what she was seeing.

'Bernie? Have you been called too?'

Bernie's hand went to her left-hand side as she looked up.

'Yes. But not for the prosecution. I've been called for the defence.'

CHAPTER 11

Tuesday

'I'm not doing it. I'm not going.'

DCS Wilson sighed. 'Bernie, as a serving police officer, you can't be in contempt of court. You'll be suspended and that's probably what Jack Thornton wants. Don't play into his trap.'

'But I can't defend him.'

'Don't. Just reply with short answers. Do the bare minimum. I agree that it makes no sense for you to be a witness for the defence. You'll probably be treated as a hostile witness if you don't play ball but the prosecution will love you for that.'

'Couldn't you put in a word for me? I'm investigating a possible double murder and I've got Mira to think about. It's not like it's at the local courts. I have to go to London.'

Bernie rubbed her forehead. A headache was brewing.

'I'm sorry, Bernie. This is a very important case. Even if you're being asked to be a witness for the defence, we can't afford any ripples. Reporting restrictions are already in place. Other than those in the courtroom, no one else will know the trial is happening until afterwards.' Wilson leaned forward. 'Look, I'll talk to the chief constable but honestly, it won't make any difference. Just tell the truth.'

Bernie looked away. It was telling the truth she was worried about.

MCIT was busy when she arrived a little after eight. The whole team was there, including Leigh who beamed at her. She seemed more confident. So different from the awkward young woman who had joined them a year before.

'Good morning, everyone. Sorry I'm a bit late. Needed a quick chat with the super.' Bernie did her best to sound normal even though she was still reeling from the prospect of giving evidence. 'Right, has anything come in overnight?'

Matt picked up his notepad. 'Yes. Some of the local officers at Marlborough have had reports of cars racing late at night. Ties in with the timings for our crash. They're going to see if there's any footage and then maybe we can work out where they came from.'

'Great. The sooner we can find the primary crime scene and some missing limbs, the better. Kerry?'

'Nothing overnight but that's not really surprising. Leigh and I are heading to the crash site for another walk through and then I'll get onto forensics. We're playing the waiting game really.'

'We are indeed.'

Bernie looked round the Incident room and the new layout of desks. She still wasn't sure how Matt had managed it but he'd created space for all of them.

'Thanks for sorting the room out, Matt,' she said. 'It's good to be back in here. Well, we all have jobs to do and Alice and I have another trip to see the good doctor, so we'd better get on with it. Let's check in at thirteen hundred hours.'

Bernie dozed lightly as Alice drove to Salisbury. She'd had a restless night knowing she had to go to court and then Mira had ended up in bed with them, her hot hands clamped to Bernie's arm.

'Ma'am, we're here.'

Bernie blinked her eyes open. 'Sorry. Must have dropped off.'

'No problem.'

'Maybe but I shouldn't fall asleep on duty. You didn't do that.'

Alice smiled. 'I didn't come back after nine months. My little one was super clingy at that age. Much better at a year.'

Bernie undid her seat belt and reached for the door handle. 'That would explain the limpet attached to my arm for most of the night.' She took a deep breath. Two post-mortems in two days were more than she was used to. 'Right, let's do this.'

The body of the young man was already in place, with Dr Nick White at his side.

'Good morning, DI Noel and DC Hart. Lovely to have the pleasure of your company again. Shall we begin?'

Nick White showed the same dignity to the driver as to the victim found in the boot of the car, even though the driver might have been the murderer. Bernie knew she had to keep an open mind but he must have been involved somehow.

Bernie, from the viewing platform, could see bruising to his body which appeared consistent with the crash.

Dr White felt underneath the driver's head. 'I'll know more when I open him up but he definitely took a whack to the back of his head with the impact.'

'Traffic officers think he was driving at around seventy miles per hour,' Bernie said.

White nodded. 'That would make sense. Thrown forward on

impact and then back hard onto the head rest. Even with the airbag deployed, he'd have gone back with some force.'

White continued his visual inspection of the front of the young man. Nothing else stood out to him.

'Right, let's turn him over.'

His morgue technician helped. Bernie saw the lividity marks on his buttocks. White caught her eye.

'Yes, he was in that seat long enough for lividity to settle in the bottom area, heading down into the back of the thighs. This all fits in with time of death being middle of the night.' White paused. 'Can you get me a magnifying glass?' he asked the technician.

'What can you see?'

White pushed at the pink skin, low down on the young man's back, while looking closely. 'Could you pull the skin taut, please?' he asked and the technician obliged.

'Hmm. You know how dogs and cats have either microchips or a tag on their collars to show their identity? Our chap here has something similar with a tattoo. Might need a bit of light on this.'

Bernie looked at Alice as a bright light was placed near the body. She tapped her fingers together, impatiently waiting for Dr White to say something.

'I'm not a hundred per cent but it looks like "Lewis" and "TW5". A postcode perhaps. Any ideas, DI Noel?'

Bernie looked at Alice again. 'Judging where the car was stolen from, we're probably looking at Hounslow.'

CHAPTER 12

'It's the Cranford and Heston area,' Mick said.

Everyone was back in MCIT for the one o'clock catch-up.

'I don't know the borough very well,' said Bernie. 'How close is that to where the car was stolen in Hounslow West?'

'Pretty close,' Mick replied. 'But far enough away to not be pissing in your own backyard.'

Bernie tutted. 'Honestly, Mick. Such a way with words. So, next question – is "Lewis" from TW5 known to the police?'

Matt moved his monitor screen so everyone could see. 'Yep. Here he is. Or was. Lewis Brown, twenty-two years old. In and out of trouble since the age of twelve. A few short spells in prison. Car theft does appear to be a speciality of his.'

'So, this car may have been stolen to order?'

'Perhaps. But it doesn't explain why a dead body was in the boot.'

'It could be a gang thing,' said Mick. 'HOLMES has thrown up an old case from London where a gang member was mutilated in a similar fashion. That one was solved so maybe a copycat.'

'What about the other guy?' Leigh asked. 'Do you have a name for him? Sorry, I'm just trying to get up to speed here.'

'No,' said Bernie. 'Due to his injuries, facial recognition and identification through dental records and fingerprints are out. But we're hoping DNA will give us something.'

Leigh gave her a quizzical look. 'No. Not the victim. The other guy. I watched the doorbell footage from Hounslow. Two men stole the vehicle. We only have one of them. Where's the other?'

Bernie resisted the urge to let out a long sigh. Shit. In only a few hours being on the team, Leigh had picked up on what they'd lost sight of.

'You're right. Mick and Matt, have you seen anything in the footage that suggests the other man was dropped off somewhere? I don't think he was in the car when it crashed.'

'I agree,' Kerry said. 'Having spent all day at the crash site yesterday, I saw no indication that anyone else was in the car other than the driver and victim in the boot.'

'What makes you think that?' Alice asked.

'Passenger front door was shut. If you get out of a car after an accident, you don't always think about shutting the door. You want to get away as fast as you can in case it goes up in flames. There were no footprints, no fabric traces on nearby bushes, no flattened grass in the field, no blood outside the car at all.'

Leigh looked thoughtful. 'What if – and I'm just throwing ideas out here – what if the other car stopped and went back and took him? We both saw the skid marks around the corner. Perhaps they didn't just slow down but stopped. And maybe this other guy wasn't bleeding. What's the cause of death for the driver, ma'am?'

Bernie looked at Leigh. 'Internal bleeding. He also whacked the back of his head. Dr White thinks it was probably enough to knock him out so at least he wasn't conscious when he died. You're right, Leigh. We've got to find this other man. Can you help Matt and Mick go through all the footage again? Has any more CCTV come in?'

Matt nodded. 'Yes. Mick and I picked some up this morning and the Met have more doorbell footage that they've sent. What do you want to do about Lewis Brown's next of kin? It's listed as his mother.'

Bernie sighed. The 'death knock' was always the worst part of the job. No matter what Lewis Brown had done, he was still someone's son. 'It's too far for one of us to go today. And she'll have to officially identify him anyway. Let's ask the Met to visit, see if she knows where her son is before informing her. I'm guessing he's not been reported missing.'

'No. Do you want me to call them?'

'Yes please, Matt.'

Bernie turned away. The last thing she wanted to do right now was to have contact with anyone from the Metropolitan Police force. She caught Kerry's eye. 'Just popping to the bathroom.'

Kerry joined her a few minutes later. Bernie had made sure all the cubicles were empty.

'What's up?' Kerry asked. 'Are you upset about the other guy that we'd all forgotten about, not just you?'

Bernie shook her head as she gripped the sink.

'Whoa, Bernie, what's going on?'

Bernie looked up and saw herself in the mirror. Her face was awash with anxiety. Acid rose up from her stomach. Kerry gently rubbed her back.

'Talk to me, Bernie. It isn't just this case, is it? I noticed you asked Matt to contact the Met. You'd normally do that. Is it something to do with Jack Thornton?'

Bernie nodded, not trusting herself to speak without vomiting. She focused on her breathing as she'd been taught in antenatal classes. Not that she'd needed it in labour. Mira had come so fast after silent contractions, there had been no time to think, let alone breathe properly. But it was working now. When her stomach was settled enough, she spoke.

'The trial's started at the Old Bailey. Dougie's been called for the prosecution and goes on Friday. I've been called for the defence and go next week. The letters came here and weren't passed on. I can't do it but the super said I must. I'll be in contempt of court if I don't.'

Kerry continued to rub her back. 'Oh shit, Bernie. He's right. You have to do it. Do you want me to come with you?'

'No. You need to be here to run the case. Oh God, Kerry, what do I do?'

'You go and you stick to the facts. Give brief answers.'

Bernie looked at Kerry, the only person she'd told the whole truth to. The only person she trusted to keep it confidential. Not even Dougie knew everything.

'But it's my fault—'

'No, it's not. It's not your fault that Danny Ambrose stabbed you. It's not your fault that he stabbed and killed Leesa.'

'But if Jack is found guilty of corruption, all his old cases and convictions could be up for appeal. Danny could get out. How do I face Leesa's parents?'

'Let's cross that bridge if we come to it. In the meantime, I'm here for you if you need me. OK?'

'Yes.'

Kerry gave her a hug. 'It'll be all right and my offer still stands if you want me to come with you. I'm sure the super can stand in for one day. I'd better get back. See you in a minute?'

'Sure.'

Bernie splashed water over her face. She grabbed a paper towel to dry her skin. She looked in the mirror but it was another image that forced itself into her brain. Lying on a cold, tarmac netball court, life draining out of her. A teenage girl not moving. A netball rolling along, tracking blood in its wake. Telling the truth would ruin Bernie. And her old boss, Jack Thornton, knew that.

CHAPTER 13

After a few more breathing sessions to calm herself down, Bernie returned to MCIT to find the rest of the team looking at CCTV and doorbell footage. Matt glanced up as she came in.

'Ma'am, I've spoken to someone at the Met and they're sending someone to see Lewis Brown's mother,' he said.

'Thanks for that. Now, what are you all looking at? Leigh?'

'I'm looking at the footage the Met have sent the night the car was stolen. They've managed to collect quite a lot.'

'That's because there's a murder investigation. If it was just a stolen car that had crashed, they wouldn't have done as much.'

Kerry caught Bernie's eye. Slagging off the Met wasn't a good look.

'Matt? Mick?'

'We're looking at that initial route again,' said Mick. 'Looking to see if there are places that the other guy could have been dropped at.'

'Yeah,' Matt continues. 'If he's a local lad too, then you'd think he'd be dropped off fairly quickly if he was heading home.'

Bernie looked closer at the images on Matt's monitor. 'You're right. It wouldn't make sense to drop him further along the journey unless he lived there. So, assuming he was there for the whole trip, where is he now?'

Alice spoke up, 'I'm looking at the racing cars. It's not easy to see but I'm slowing it down as much as possible. I don't think there's a person in the passenger seat.'

Bernie grabbed her chair and placed it by the others. 'OK. Let's have a think about what we know and what might have happened. Lewis Brown and another white man stole a white BMW from Hounslow West and drove to Wiltshire. At the crash site, Brown was dead in the driver seat. A black man was found dead in the boot, with his hands and feet missing and his face blown to pieces. No sign of the second man. As Leigh suggested, maybe the people in the second car took the passenger. Any other ideas, anyone?'

The team look around at each other waiting to see who would venture a theory first. Mick coughed.

'I think we can disprove this one straight away but, maybe the body was already in the car when it was stolen. However, if that was the case, you wouldn't report your car missing, would you?' he said.

'You're probably right on that one, Mick, but stranger things have happened. It might be worth talking to the owners anyway and getting DNA samples from them for elimination. I don't think the Met have done that, so it might be easier if we do it and then take it straight to the lab. Are you up for doing that tomorrow, Mick, seeing you know the area?'

'Sure.'

'Anyone else?'

'Well,' Alice said, 'maybe the other guy stayed behind to clear up the scene, wherever that is. Perhaps Lewis Brown was supposed to come back for him after dumping the rest of the body. Spread the parts around. Go to a different county.'

Leigh tapped her screen. 'Ma'am, have we had forensics back on his clothes?'

'I don't think anything's come back yet. Kerry?'

DS Allen shook her head. 'No, nothing yet.'

'OK,' said Leigh. 'Looking at the doorbell footage and then at the crash scene photos, I think Lewis Brown is wearing the same clothes. Ma'am, you said earlier that he died from internal bleeding. So, there would be little blood on his clothes from his own injuries. But you'd expect there to be more blood if he'd killed our victim and then put him in the boot. He's wearing dark grey but you'd see patches. I wouldn't be surprised if our victim's DNA isn't on Lewis Brown at all. And vice versa.'

'Meaning?' Kerry asked.

'Meaning that Lewis Brown is the removals man. Our victim was already dead and was placed in the boot by someone else.'

Bernie leaned back in her chair. She remembered what Dr White had said about the cuts on the victim's torso and Dougie's and Mick's suggestion that gangs were involved.

'This might be a lot bigger than we first thought. Dr White said the cuts on the victim were recent but a few had started to heal. They could be self-inflicted but they could also be an indicator of torture and the victim being held prisoner for some time before his death. If Leigh's right about Lewis just moving the body, then someone else killed him. Maybe the other car thief.'

'But they probably didn't torture him,' said Kerry. 'Someone else did that. Why hold someone in Wiltshire but go to Hounslow to steal a car? That wouldn't make sense if you were doing both things. So what is this then?'

'It could be rival drug gangs,' said Bernie. 'God forbid but it could even be a white supremacist group hunting down black people. But it's more than just two men stealing a car.'

The team sat silently for a minute, the different possibilities sinking in.

'We're going to need more officers,' said Matt.

Bernie nodded. 'I spoke to Dougie about the case and he thought Serious Organised Crime might want a look at this.'

'As long as we still run it,' Kerry said.

'That's what I said. Are we anywhere closer to finding the murder scene?'

'Getting there. Got possible footage from Great Bedwyn near Marlborough that the local policing team has sent us. About to check that,' Matt said.

The phone rang on Bernie's desk. She jumped up to answer it.

'DI Noel.'

'Hi. It's Shona from the emergency call centre. We've just had a nine nine nine call you might be interested in. A man fishing thought he'd found an old boot. But most boots don't have a foot in them still.'

Bernie's eyes lit up. 'Skin tone?'

'He said it looked black. Do you want me to send uniform?'

'No, we'll take it. Where is it?'

'River Avon, not far from Clench, which is a bit beyond Pewsey. I'll get better details and radio them through to you.'

'Thanks.'

Bernie put the phone down and looked at her team.

'Alice and Mick, I want you to stay here and look at the area around Clench. The rest of us will go in two cars. Alice, could you also let Lucy know, please, that we might be needing her? We're getting closer. Someone's found a foot.'

CHAPTER 14

Knowing the local area best, Matt drove in the first car with Leigh, and Kerry and Bernie went second. As passenger, Bernie was free to observe the location and realised how easy it was to avoid cameras. No wonder Mick and Matt had had problems finding the route Lewis Brown had taken.

Shona had sent through the Three Words location that narrowed down where to find the fisherman. The app that anyone could use made it much easier for the emergency services to find locations.

Matt indicated and pulled up by the side of a small bridge. Kerry did the same, and Bernie got out. She decided against putting her coat on over her suit jacket. It was a dry day with a hint of warmth. Spring was doing its best to break through the patchy cloud.

She looked over the bridge, searching for the angler who had called nine nine nine. She spotted a young man with a fishing rod to the right but couldn't work out how to reach him.

'This way, ma'am,' Matt said. 'We can get down here on the left and then follow the path under the bridge.'

'Do you know much about angling, Matt?' Bernie asked.

'I know the season doesn't officially start until tomorrow.

He'll plead ignorance.'

'Well, if he's found our victim's foot, I think we can let him off. Maybe Alice's idea of spreading the body parts around was right.'

As they reached the man, Bernie held out her warrant.

'Detective Inspector Noel. Did you call the emergency services?'

The young man nodded. He reminded Bernie of Ryan Willis and was probably a similar age.

'What's your name?'

'Charlie Spencer. I know I'm not supposed to start fishing until tomorrow but we've got barely any food in the house. We need something to eat.'

'Don't worry, Charlie. We're not going to do you for that. I'm far more interested in what you found. Where is it?'

Charlie pointed behind him. 'It's there. I can't bring myself to look at it. Made me feel sick. Thought it was just a boot to begin with.' He stepped to the side, allowing Bernie to see past him.

Bernie was tempted to swear but couldn't do so with a member of the public there.

'Matt, could you take Charlie up to the car and get an initial statement please? Kerry, could you phone Lucy, please, and tell her to get here asap?'

Bernie pulled out latex gloves from her jacket and stepped closer to the boot. There was a foul smell. The water, and possibly the fish, had added to the natural decomposition but the skin colour was still recognisable as that of a black person, most likely their victim. Bernie understood Charlie's nausea. She felt the same but hers was also fuelled by revulsion for what had happened to the victim.

She turned back to Leigh.

'Could you call Alice, please, and tell her where we are? Ask her and Mick to do a Google street search of the immediate local area. I have a feeling we're close. Ask them to look for remote houses, barns, anything that might be our crime scene. Thanks.'

As Leigh got out her phone, Bernie crouched down for a closer look at the boot. The fact that it was a boot surprised her. Most young guys seemed to wear trainers. Maybe it wasn't his choice of footwear. Could he be a soldier? Or had his captor given them to him to wear? Harder to run in boots. She hoped Lucy would be able to give them an answer. And soon.

Bernie had the road closed both ways but it didn't seem to be a problem. Hardly anyone was around. Charlie gave his statement and Bernie warned him that forensics would have to take the fish he caught.

'We don't know if they've been nibbling at that foot. We have to find out for all the anglers. Might even have to push back the start of the season.'

Charlie nodded sadly. 'I understand.'

'How many in your family?' Bernie asked.

'Me, my mum and my little brother. Dad died last year. Left us in a bit of a pickle.'

'Wait a moment.'

Bernie got her bag from the other car and got out a twenty-pound note. She gave it to Charlie.

'Get some shopping or even fish and chips for tonight. If you can bear it.'

The young man's face brightened. 'Really? I could get food for a few days with this. Maybe even a week.'

'Charlie, how bad is it for your family?' Matt asked.

Charlie looked down. 'It's pretty bad. At least with spring almost here we can turn off the heating. Not that we had it on much anyway over the winter. And I can fish. I have a licence. I thought no one would notice if I started a day early.' He looked up at Bernie. 'Thanks, this is really kind of you.'

'That's fine. Thanks for doing the right thing in calling us.'

'It's serious, isn't it?'

'Yes but I'd like you to keep it quiet for now. Do you think you can do that?'

Charlie nodded.

'Good. Where do you live?'

'Pewsey. It's not far.'

'Matt, could you drop Charlie home please?'

Matt nodded and pulled his key fob out of his pocket.

'Actually, could you drop me at the shops please?' Charlie asked. 'Then I can buy some food.'

'Sure, I can do that.'

'Can I get my rod and bait please?'

Bernie shook her head. 'I can't let you go back down there but we'll get it to you later. What's your bait?'

Charlie grinned. 'Maggots.'

'Oh hell. Well, you're in charge of that one, Matt, when you get back.'

'Thanks, ma'am. Come on, Charlie.'

Bernie watched them drive away. Kerry and Leigh joined her.

'Lucy should be here in about twenty minutes,' Kerry said.

'Alice is going to call me back in a few minutes,' said Leigh. 'She's been going through known associates of Lewis Brown. There are four possibilities for our second car thief. Oh, I think she's calling now.' Leigh pulled out her phone. 'Yes, I'll put it on speakerphone. Hi, Alice.'

'Hi, Leigh. Is ma'am there?'

'Yes, Alice. You're on speaker. What have you found?'

'Well, Mick found it. There aren't many properties in the area but if you go over the bridge towards Clench, there's a turning on the left by a house. It leads down to some barns. We can't get any closer on Street View but it might be worth a look.'

Bernie looked at the other two. 'I'm wondering if we should wait for Lucy. I've already stuffed up one crime scene.'

'There are forensic suits in the back of my car,' said Kerry. 'Take Leigh with you. If you find something then we'll know to get a bigger forensics team out.'

Bernie nodded. 'Good idea. Let's do it. That OK with you, Leigh?'

'Yes. We've still got a missing car thief who might be alive and in need of help.'

'Thanks, Alice,' said Bernie. 'We might need you and Mick here but I'll let you know.'

Kerry gave Bernie her car keys and she and Leigh drove over the little bridge. It wasn't long before the left-hand turning appeared. There was a lovely house on the corner.

'If we do find something, we'll definitely need to check in there,' Bernie said.

She drove slowly down the narrow lane, praying no one else was coming the other way as there were few passing places.

'I've got us on the map,' said Leigh. 'This is a dead end.'

They continued down the lane, hedges on both sides with grass fields beyond. Soon, the barns appeared on the right. Bernie pulled over. Fortunately, there were two forensic suits with matching foot covers in the boot, along with a box of latex gloves. It had been a while since Bernie had 'suited and booted' up for a crime scene.

It was quiet at the barns. No one else seemed to be around. One of the barns was set up with animal pens but it wasn't in use. Bernie thought about Greenacres with its lamb midwifery barn.

'Don't think they have sheep on this farm,' Bernie said.

'Not sure if they have anything here. These barns look like they haven't been in use for a while,' said Leigh.

'No, it doesn't smell like a farm either,' said Bernie. 'Unless I've become accustomed to it. There's a hint of something though.'

They turned towards the second barn and both said, 'Oh,' at the same time. There was a caravan inside.

'Wait,' said Bernie. 'We don't go in without some protection.'

She went back to the car and got batons out. Handing one to Leigh, they approached the caravan slowly. As they got near, Bernie lifted her hand to tell Leigh to stop. Bernie's heart was thumping hard. Something like this hadn't bothered her before but now she was a mother, Mira was always there in the back of her mind. A shotgun had been used on the unknown victim in the boot of the car. She should call in for an armed response. But what if it was just an old caravan in a disused barn? She didn't want to look stupid. But she didn't want to be dead either.

Bernie looked at Leigh, who nodded at her. Using her extended baton, Bernie hit the caravan door.

'Police. Open up.' She hoped her voice sounded more authoritative than she felt.

Silence. Bernie knocked and called out again. Still no response. Not just from the caravan but from the whole site. She stepped forward carefully, not taking her eyes off the caravan door in case it burst open.

Slowly, Bernie reached for the handle on the door. She twisted it but it appeared stuck and she didn't have much purchase with gloves on. She needed to use both hands. After passing her baton to Leigh, she held the handle with both hands. She twisted it hard and felt it unlock. Bernie sniffed. Whatever she'd smelt before was now stronger and more familiar. She opened the door cautiously, the odour seeping out. Bernie glanced into the caravan. A young white man in dark clothes was on the floor, not moving, his staring eyes not seeing.

'I think we've found our second car thief, Leigh,' Bernie said.

CHAPTER 15

Red and blue illuminated the scene as large lights were fixed in place to ensure the forensic team could work overnight. Once the others had arrived, another outbuilding had been found, smelling of blood and bleach. Luminol would show how much blood was splattered on the floor and walls.

A specialist forensic officer was setting up equipment to take a 3D image of the scene. Bernie hoped they could get some answers from this. Three dead young men in two days was not a good look. She wondered what kind of headlines would appear. So far, they had kept the car crash under wraps from the press but it was only a matter of time before it all came out. She wasn't sure she could entirely trust Charlie Spencer to keep his mouth shut about the foot in the river.

Someone tapped on her shoulder. Kerry.

'Have you seen the time? It's gone six o'clock. You need to get home for Mira.'

Bernie sighed. She'd been so wrapped up in the investigation that she'd lost track of time.

'OK. Can I borrow your car please? I'll go home and feed Mira and then get back here asap.'

'You'll do nothing of the sort. You stay home. Leave my car at headquarters. Matt can drive me back. And take Leigh with you. We don't want her getting out of routine either.'

Bernie put her gloved hands on her hips. 'Who's in charge here?'

'When it comes to Mira, I am. I promised Dougie I'd keep you on track. Go. If I need you to come back, I'll call.'

Bernie looked at Kerry's stern face. She was right. There was the small matter of Mira. The sooner she could stop breastfeeding, the better for her career. But she loved the closeness it brought her to her daughter.

'OK. I'll find Leigh. Call me later anyway. I want an update around nine p.m. or sooner if you find anything.'

Bernie found Leigh with Dr Nick White, examining the body in the caravan.

'Well, Detective Inspector Noel, three bodies in two days. People are going to start talking,' said White. 'I'd say the shotgun blast to his chest was the likely cause of death but I can tell you more tomorrow at the morgue. Assuming it's you who comes over. I ought to get you a loyalty card.'

'Do I win points? Get a prize? Sorry, that's bad taste.'

'I think I started the bad taste. Any luck with the driver's ID?'

'Yes. We think it's a Lewis Brown. Trying to get hold of next of kin. If we find his mother, then we might be able to do a formal identification tomorrow. Kill two birds with one stone. Sorry, bad taste again. I'm tired. I need to go home to feed Mira. Leigh, I'm taking Kerry's car back to headquarters. Do you want a lift? I'm not sure how long the others will be here for.'

Leigh hesitated. Bernie could tell she was torn between her duty of staying at the scene, and her need for regular routine.

'This is probably going to be a long case, Leigh. You need to pace yourself.'

Leigh nodded. 'OK. Tim's off today and he's cooking. After all this, it might be nice to have some normality.'

They stripped off their forensic suits and put them in the refuse bag by the scene manager. Logged out, they drove back along the narrow lane. Bernie paused by the house at the end. Dusk was settling in but there were no lights on.

'We'll need to check in with the owners. Find out if they own the barns,' Bernie said. 'I'll get Alice to do that.'

'Do you want me to text her?' Leigh asked.

'Thanks. This is all getting out of hand now. I'm going to ask the super for more people.'

Once they got out of the small country lanes, the traffic became heavier as drivers headed home, oblivious of the devastating crimes committed only a few miles away.

'When we get back to the office,' Leigh said. 'I want to look at the stolen car footage again. Double-check if it is the second car thief. I was having a good look at his clothes back at the barn. It's a bit hard to tell because of the damage done to his chest, but I could see part of a logo and I think it's the Nike tick.'

'That'll be a good start in confirming if it's him. I'm hoping Lewis Brown's mother might have some idea as to who her son was hanging out with. And then there's still our victim in the boot. Nothing has come up for him yet, not even DNA. Do you know if Kerry chased that earlier?'

'Pretty sure she called and was told it was still being processed.'

Bernie sighed. 'If only the forensic results came through as quickly as they do in a TV drama.'

'Don't get me started on that,' Leigh said.

'I'm sorry, Leigh, I've not had the chance to ask you – how are you? How's Tim?'

'We're OK. Saving for the wedding. Thankfully, we both have small families so that'll keep the numbers low. Haven't set a date yet but maybe autumn next year.'

'That will be nice. And he did pretty well with the ring.'

The streetlights were catching the diamond.

'He did and I don't twist this one. In fact, I've been doing a lot less of that recently. I'm doing better.'

Bernie glanced across at Leigh. The curtain of hair that used to hide her face had been cut with a side fringe so she could be seen more easily. And Bernie hadn't seen her twist her rings in anxiety once that day.

'I still have my moments but I'm willing to take a few more risks now. I think meeting the new chief constable has spurred me on,' Leigh said.

'Really? I haven't met her yet. What's she like?'

'Oh, she's brilliant. She visited all the police stations to meet us and did special talks for the female staff. Told us about her career. From detective inspector to chief constable in ten years. Very impressive. She encouraged us all to go for it so when Kerry called yesterday, I didn't hesitate to say yes. I had to persuade my boss but he was fine with it.'

'I'm so pleased to hear that. You've already proved your worth today. You can stay on my team for as long as you want. I know it's tricky being with us because routine is important to you, and as you've seen, there's nothing routine about MCIT.'

'Ha. For sure. But I enjoy the challenge. And Kerry and I had a good morning.'

'Pleased to hear it. I know the two of you have had your ups and downs.'

Bernie followed the road that led them back to Devizes. It dawned on her that she was driving the route that the cars probably took on Sunday night.

'Leigh, a task for you tomorrow. We've probably driven the way that the cars did the other night. Can you drive it again tomorrow, please? I know Mick and Matt were looking at the CCTV but Mick will be in Hounslow and I want to keep Matt at the scene. Are you happy to do that?'

'Yeah, that's fine. I'll see what I can spot.'

A few minutes later, Bernie pulled into headquarters. It was six forty and she was already running late to get home. But she wanted to check in with Alice and Mick first.

They were bent over their desks, their eyes fixed on their monitor screens when she and Leigh walked in.

'Just a quick check-in with you both as I need to head home,' Bernie said. 'What have you got for me? Alice?'

Alice lifted her head and rubbed her eyes. 'Sorry, I've been focused on this.' She pointed to Google maps. 'I've been gathering some intel on the properties in the local area. The house on the corner of the lane has been owned by the same family for almost twenty years – the Pinners. I can't get hold of them. Not sure yet if the barns belong to them or someone else. It's a hamlet so there are very few houses in the area and they're quite spread out.'

'Yes, it did seem quiet. We'll organise door-to-door tomorrow. People are hesitant to open the door in the dark. Mick?'

Mick twisted round in his chair. 'I checked the car racing footage from Marlborough. Wrong make of cars so nothing to do with this case. I've also been looking into Lewis Brown and his family. The Met haven't spoken to next of kin yet. His mother works as a cleaner at West Middlesex hospital in Isleworth so I'm going to start there first in the morning. I'll leave early. Is Lewis ready for identification?'

Bernie nodded. 'Yep. And I'm there again tomorrow for our third victim's autopsy. So, if you're able to bring her, it'll give us a chance to chat with her too. Maybe she could give us a name for her son's friend. Right, I'll see you all in the morning, except you, Mick.'

Bernie drove back as quickly as the speed limit allowed. Only now that her mind was freed from the crime scene, did she realise that her body was gearing up to feed her baby.

Mira didn't allow her to go upstairs, crying and pulling at Bernie. She sank onto the sofa with Mira in her arms.

'Tough day?' Dougie asked.

Bernie nodded wearily. 'Just a bit.'

'Ah. You're not going to like what I'm about to tell you then.'

CHAPTER 16

'What do you mean Anna can't look after Mira when you go to court?'

Bernie's voice rose, causing Mira to startle and cry.

'Ssh, it's OK. You keep feeding.' Bernie stroked her cheek to settle her. She kept her voice low when she spoke again.

'So, what's going to happen? I can't take her to work. And Mum and Gary are away.'

Dougie sat next to her. 'I know. I've sorted it. I'm going to take her to London with me and your granny's looking after her.'

A mental image of a small, scowling woman in the school playground, surrounded by smiling, happy mothers, came to Bernie. Her precious paintings displayed on the fridge for one day and in the bin the next. Who did that to a six-year-old? Granny.

'What? My granny who doesn't have a maternal bone in her body, who didn't do a great job of raising my mum and an even worse job of raising me, who's only seen Mira about three times – you want her to look after our daughter?'

Dougie grimaced. 'I know. But there's a big funeral Paul and Anna are doing that day for an old lady and it seems like everyone round here is going. I asked Lesley next door but she's attending it. It was your mum who suggested your granny. And one of her neighbours has a baby, so she'll take Mira there. It's only for a few hours. Mira will be fine. She loves it when old ladies fuss over her. You should have seen her at the supermarket today. I swear it took me an extra half hour to get round, so many old ladies were stopping to say hello to her.'

'Sure they weren't stopping to say hello to you?' Bernie gave a wry smile.

Dougie straightened his jumper. 'Maybe a bit of both.' He grinned and leaned forward to give Bernie a kiss. 'I'm sorry. This court case is proving to be a bit shitty. You didn't sleep well last night, did you?'

Bernie sighed. 'No. I'm worried that I'll be so sleep deprived by then that I won't even be able to say my name properly, let alone answer any other questions.'

Dougie put his arm around her. 'Look, if Mira wakes up, I'll try sleeping with her in the spare bed in her room. Although, I think it's you she wants.'

Bernie looked down at Mira, nearly asleep. Juggling work and motherhood was harder than she thought it would be. A single tear ran down her cheek, others threatening to follow.

'Oh Bernie, it's OK,' Dougie said, wiping away her tear. 'You're doing a great job.'

'Doesn't feel like it. I've had to leave a major crime scene to come home. We think we've found the initial scene, along with another body. I should be there but I had to come back for Mira. And I don't want to give up feeding her yet. It feels like I can't do both properly.'

'That's what a team is for. Let me guess, Kerry stayed at the scene. And who's best at scenes and searches? Kerry. Leaving her in charge was the right thing to do.'

'She said that she promised you to keep me on track.'

Dougie laughed gently. 'I've worked too many cases with you now. I know what you're like and how late you'll keep working. Remember when wee Molly Reynolds went missing and we worked at your flat, and I fell asleep on your sofa.'

'I do. And you brought me a cup of coffee in bed the next morning.'

'I was a gentleman.'

'You were.'

'But the tension was already there.'

'It was. But I'm glad we waited.'

'Me too. She's asleep, you know.'

'I know. How long until dinner?'

'It's a stew in the slow cooker, so it'll be fine for a while. We've got some time. I'll put her to bed and then I'll come and find you.'

'Is that a promise?'

Dougie kissed her deeply. 'Promise.'

Bernie's phone buzzed as Dougie left the room with Mira. She was tempted to ignore it, didn't want to spoil the mood she was now in. But she'd told Kerry and the others that they could message her. She pulled out her phone and saw a message from Leigh.

Hi Ma'am. Two things. CCTV footage shows second suspect was wearing a Nike top on Sunday night. Also, a call came in from the lab about the body in the boot of the car. There's a match on the database but access denied. I saw the super and he said he'll speak to you tomorrow. Going home now. See you in the morning. Leigh

Bernie frowned as she tapped a quick thank you back to Leigh. Access denied. Who was this man?

CHAPTER 17

Wednesday

Detective Chief Superintendent Wilson was normally a calm man but even he appeared rattled. Bernie watched as he clicked his pen on and off almost continuously for what seemed like ages but probably only a minute. He glanced at his watch.

'I don't know what's keeping the chief constable. She's normally very punctual. Have you met her yet, Bernie?'

Bernie shook her head. Was it the new chief constable, Hannah Drake, that was making the super so nervous? Despite Leigh's glowing admiration, Drake's reputation as a formidable officer hadn't escaped Bernie's attention. Nor the fact she had once served in the Met. That made Bernie uncomfortable.

The rap on the door was loud and quick. The super barely answered as the door opened and Hannah Drake strode in. Dark hair, streaked with grey, was tied back in a tight bun. Her uniform was immaculate. She wore little make-up. She moved quickly and with purpose.

'Sorry to keep you. Had an important phone call to make. I take it you're Detective Inspector Bernadette Noel.'

A hand was thrust in front of Bernie. She stood to shake it.

'Yes. Honour to meet you, ma'am.'

Hannah Drake flicked her hand, dismissing the courtesy.

'Let's not bother with pleasantries. We've got a job to do. Fair to say, we're in the shit here.' Hannah took the chair next to Bernie's. 'I know you've been on maternity leave, Bernadette – congratulations by the way. I was brought in after the former chief constable retired to tackle some big problems in Wiltshire Police, including, violence against women, gangs and drug problems, and the integrity of this force. As are most of the police forces in this country. Transparency is important to me.'

Bernie swallowed. Did Hannah Drake know about her past at the Met? It would be easy for her to find out.

'So, this case of yours, it seems that you've stumbled into something else, which I had no idea about. And still know little after a telephone call. Someone else has not been transparent and I'm very angry about it.'

Bernie gave a small sigh of relief. The problem wasn't with her.

'Do you have any idea what's going on, ma'am?' the super asked.

'No but I intend to find out. If I had to hazard a guess, I'd say you've walked into an undercover operation.'

Bernie looked between the two senior officers. 'So what do we do in the meantime? I'm supposed to be attending the post-mortem for the man we found yesterday and then speaking to the driver's mother if DC Parris can find her. We've got forensics down at the site. Officers due to go door-to-door in the surrounding area. Not to mention possibly trawling the River Avon for body parts. Fishing season opens today. Do we ask them to hold off for the moment?'

Hannah Drake rested her head on her hand, her eyes closing briefly. Bernie looked at the super who shrugged. Hannah's eyes sprang open.

'Sod it. This is my county and I won't have anyone run undercover ops without my knowledge. Carry on with your investigation into the deaths of the car thieves. Our mystery man will have to remain an enigma for now. But I'll keep digging, don't you worry about that.'

Hannah Drake bounded out of her chair and turned to leave. 'Update at six o'clock please, Bernadette.' And with that, she was gone.

Bernie stared at the super. 'Is she always like that?'

'Yes. I can't decide if she's a breath of fresh air or a gale force wind. She's making positive changes, though, and she's not afraid to stir things up.'

'That's pretty obvious, sir. Before I see the team, what's happening with press coverage?'

'Jane has released details about the car crash but not the body in the boot. Thankfully, last night's scene is in a quiet area but I don't think we can keep it under wraps for much longer, especially with going door-to-door.'

'Do you think we shouldn't? We could miss vital evidence.'

The super took a deep breath. 'I think you should do what the chief constable has asked you to do. Carry on with the investigation. But come to me immediately with any breakthroughs. We need to keep this case as tight as possible.'

Everyone, except Mick, was at the morning briefing. Bernie wondered how much she should say to her team. She decided to follow the chief constable's lead and be transparent.

'We have a problem and that problem stays with us. No talking about it outside this team.'

The others looked slightly worried.

'What's going on?' Kerry asked.

'Not sure yet but we may have stumbled into an undercover operation. There's a match for the victim in the boot on the DNA database but access to his name is denied.'

Matt looked puzzled. 'Who's running it?'

Bernie shrugged. 'Don't know but the chief constable is determined to find out. She has said that we can continue with looking at the deaths of our car thieves but to leave the other man for the moment.'

'But surely his death is linked with the other two,' said Alice. 'How can we take him out of the equation?'

'Quite easily,' said Leigh. 'If we find out who killed the thieves, then we stand a good chance of finding out who killed Mr X. It really is like an equation. Lewis plus Mr Y equals Mr X. I think the chief constable is being very clever here.'

Bernie nodded. 'You're right, Leigh. She is. So, jobs for today. Kerry, I want you at last night's scene. Matt, door-to-door on the very few houses in the area. I want to pause the start to the fishing season but that's straying into Mr X territory which I'm not supposed to do.'

'But Charlie Spencer might say something if he sees others fishing today,' Matt said. 'I don't think he'll actually mention the foot but he might try to dissuade other anglers.'

'OK. I'll ask the super. I'm sure Jane can come up with a good reason why it needs to be postponed. Not sure if we dare mention pollution though. Leigh, you have your task already to look at possible routes the cars took, and Alice, if you can stomach it, we have another date with Dr White.'

'Oh goody. Three post-mortems in three days. Do I get

a prize?'

'Nick White told me he's going to get me a loyalty card so maybe.'

Bernie's phone buzzed in her pocket. She took it out and saw it was Mick.

'Hi, Mick. Have you left yet for London?'

'I left before six. I'm already here and I've found Lewis Brown's mother. She's very upset but wants to see Lewis today.'

'No problem, she can do that.'

'She also wants to talk to you. Said she's been trying to talk to local police for the last few months but they've not listened to her.'

Bernie bristled at the thought of this mother being ignored.

'Tell her I'll listen. I want to know everything.'

CHAPTER 18

'I really hope this is the last body, DI Noel, because I'm running out of "we meet again" jokes.'

Bernie half-smiled. She'd never considered Dr White as a joker.

'I hope so too. People will talk if I spend any more time with you.'

Nick White groaned. 'You nabbed my one-liner. Right, let's get on with this.'

He looked at his technician who pressed record on the audio device. Bernie wondered if they would ever swap to proper visual recordings of autopsies, in case of any issues. Not that they could be shown to a jury in court. That would be a step too far.

'Body is of a young white man, possible age range of eighteen to thirty,' said White. 'Appears well-nourished and muscular. The most obvious injury is a gunshot wound to the chest. There's also bruising on the right cheek of his face. No signs of needle tracks on arms or legs but will have a closer look later. Let's turn over and see if there's an exit wound on the back.'

The technician stepped forward and helped roll the body over.

'Yes,' said White. 'There's a clear exit wound. Do you know if any bullets have been retrieved from the scene, detective inspector?'

'None so far. Forensics are still looking.'

'Hmm. Someone knew what they were doing. Hang on, this guy has a tattoo as well, same as the driver. Well, almost. Would you like a first name?'

'Yes please.'

'Aaron. And he's from TW5 as well.'

Something Mick had said on Monday clicked in her brain. She looked at Alice.

'TW5 isn't about where they live. It's the name of their gang. And I think Kerry's right about tattoos being on the boot victim and that's why his hands and feet were cut off.'

By the time Nick White had finished the post-mortem, Mick had arrived with Lewis Brown's mother. While they waited for Lewis to be prepared for viewing, Bernie asked her a few gentle questions.

'I'm so sorry that you've had to come all this way, Ms Brown.'

'Helen, please call me Helen.'

Helen Brown was a slight woman. Her eyes were red and puffy from crying. Loose strands of brown hair hung around her face, the rest tied back in a ponytail. She was still in her hospital uniform.

'DNA has confirmed that we have Lewis but a personal identification is also needed and I'm sure you'd like to see your son. Are you up for a few questions first?'

Helen gave a slight nod.

'When did you last see Lewis?'

Helen drew in a deep breath, her shoulders shaking with the effort.

'Friday evening. Fish and chip night. Lewis doesn't live with me any more but he's always back home for fish Friday.' Helen swallowed. 'If I'd known...' She picked at her fingers around the nails.

Bernie's heart went out to Helen. She'd heard that phrase so many times as a police officer.

'What did Lewis do for a living?'

'He was at a supermarket. Stacking shelves. He was lucky to get it with his criminal record.' Helen shook her head. 'I knew something was wrong when he didn't reply to my text message on Monday night. But he often lost his phone so it wasn't that unusual.'

'Local police tried to visit you yesterday but you weren't home.'

'No. I was with a friend. She's not well. I stayed the night with her. I forgot the charger for my mobile so it was dead. Your nice officer here let me charge it in the car. I found two voicemails from Hounslow police. Just said they needed to talk to me about Lewis. If your officer hadn't told me, I'd have thought he'd been arrested.'

'Does the name "Aaron" mean anything to you? And "TW5"?'

Helen sighed. 'Yes. Aaron Swan. I'm not surprised. Aaron follows Lewis everywhere. Wait.' Helen looked Bernie straight in the eye. 'Aaron's dead too, isn't he? Of course he is. They have their name and postcode on their backs. I saw them last summer when they both had their shirts off. TW5 is a stupid gang they're in. I tried telling our local community police officers but they didn't seem that bothered.'

'I'm bothered,' said Bernie, leaning forward.

'TW5 was nothing much to begin with. Just Lewis being stupid with some of his friends. They were all at school together and formed this gang. They sold weed to their classmates. Got caught. Judge decided to make an example of him. Went to Feltham Young

Offenders for two months. He met Aaron there. Aaron was in care. He had no one. I became like a surrogate mum for him but I wasn't allowed to officially foster him. When he turned sixteen, he left the care home and came to live with Lewis and me. Joined Lewis's gang. They both did car mechanics at college, which in hindsight, was a mistake. I suppose it did give them a career but not the one I was hoping for. Aaron met a dodgy guy and he and Lewis started stealing cars for this man.'

'They stole to order?' Bernie asked.

'Yes. Caught again so back to Feltham. Twice more in fact. Last time, I told them enough was enough. If they were going to keep doing this, they had to leave my home. So they did. But then they tried to turn things around. Both got jobs. I honestly thought they'd gone straight until your officer found me this morning. He told me Lewis had died in a car crash and I knew then it would be stolen. Stupid boy.'

Helen clasped her hand over her mouth, tears flowing down her cheeks. 'Why did he have to do it?'

Bernie gave Helen the time she needed to recover. She passed her a tissue from the ever-present tissue box in the family room at the morgue. After a few minutes, Helen dried her tears.

'I'm guessing that Aaron was in the car with Lewis,' Helen said.

Bernie looked at Alice and Mick. Alice had been taking notes of Helen's answers. Bernie knew she had to phrase her reply the right way.

'No, they weren't together. Lewis was in the car but we found Aaron at another location. I'm sorry but I can't say more than that.'

'Is that because Aaron's not my son? I wasn't made his legal guardian but I am listed as his next of kin. You can check that on his criminal record.'

'It's not that. This is a complicated investigation and we're still trying to work out exactly what's happened. What you've told us is very useful and it would be good if you could give us a formal statement. I'm particularly interested in the man they stole the cars for. But we can do that later. Are you ready to see Lewis?'

Helen nodded. 'And can I see Aaron too, please? You can check about the next of kin.'

'We'll need to. And I'll have to check if he's ready to be seen. But Lewis has been prepared for you to see. I'll ask you to formally identify him. You can nod if that's easier than speaking. OK?'

Helen looked at Bernie, her eyes red. 'Yes.'

The room was quiet, the light not too bright. With a slight nod of Bernie's head, the technician folded down the sheet to reveal Lewis's face. There was a sharp intake of breath from Helen.

'Is this your son, Lewis?' Bernie asked.

Helen gasped out, 'Yes.' She covered her eyes and sobbed.

Bernie gently placed her arm around Helen's shoulders. 'You can stay for as long as you want. We can get you a chair. You're allowed to touch his face but that's all for now. Once we've had confirmation about being next of kin for Aaron, you'll be allowed to see him. Mick's going to stay with you and bring you to headquarters afterwards. He and Alice will take a formal statement from you. I'm afraid I have to go now but I want you to know that I'm going to do everything in my power to find out what happened to Lewis and Aaron.'

Mick took Bernie's place as she left Helen. Outside the room, Bernie asked Alice to check if Helen was telling the truth about being Aaron's next of kin. She herself slipped away to the morgue room where the bodies were kept. She found Nick White there.

'Aaron's surname is Swan,' Bernie said. 'Just checking next of kin now but Lewis's mother claims it's her. If so, she can view and identify him. She's confirmed it's Lewis.'

'Right. Poor woman. Identifying one person is hard enough. Any news on our body in the boot?'

Bernie hesitated. She wasn't really allowed to say anything. 'Still working on that. Hope to give you a name soon.'

'Good. I hate it when we don't know who they are.'

So do I, thought Bernie. Especially when others do know and won't tell us.

CHAPTER 19

'Penny for them, ma'am,' said Alice.

The Wiltshire countryside was rushing past them as Alice drove back to headquarters.

'Sorry. I was thinking that we're missing something here. According to Helen, Lewis and Aaron were low-key criminals. Their "gang" started as a group of kids, not serious organised crime. But somehow, they ended up in an undercover operation.' Bernie looked at Alice. 'I don't get it.'

'Maybe it has something to do with the guy they were stealing cars for. They might be further down the food chain but perhaps he isn't. Maybe he's quite a powerful player who was asked to steal a car.'

'But he made the wrong choice in getting Lewis and Aaron to do it,' said Bernie. 'It feels like a major stuff up. Those young men had no idea what they were walking into.'

'A blood bath, judging by the photos I've seen,' said Alice.

Images came into Bernie's mind of the other outbuilding by the barns. Only a small amount of blood was found initially, until the forensic team sprayed it with luminol. Then the UV light showed a range of blue patterns across the stone walls, floor and ceiling, like an elaborate abstract art installation. It was horrific.

When they got back to MCIT, no one else was back yet. Alice prepared for the interview with Helen Brown while Bernie went to find the super. Before she got to his office, though, she was accosted by Jane Clackett.

'Bernie, can I have a word in my office, please?'

'Will there be chocolate?'

'Always.' Jane smiled. Bernie still wasn't used to it.

Jane pulled open a drawer in her desk. 'Plain or milk?'

'Milk. Dark chocolate does something to my breast milk and Mira doesn't like it. Mind you, I probably need to stop feeding her. That would be one way of doing it.'

'Why do you have to stop feeding her?'

'Because I can't stay here late.'

'Surely, that's a good thing.' Jane broke off a chunk of chocolate and passed it to Bernie.

'Not with this case. I really need to put the time in.'

'I'd heard you'd been told to back off a little.'

'Is there anything you don't know?'

Jane laughed. 'Not really. I know that Dougie struggled staying late. He wanted to be home with you and Mira.'

Bernie knew what Jane was getting at. 'Hmm.'

'She won't be small forever.'

'I know, I know. It's just frustrating to pick up such a big case the first week back, and then I have to go to the Old Bailey next week—' Bernie stopped. She probably shouldn't tell Jane about it. Or anyone else for that matter. Kerry was enough.

'I think I know why,' Jane said. 'I won't ask any more though. Right, let's deal with the matter at hand. My biggest problem right now is telling the fishing clubs that they can't fish in the River

Avon. The super asked me to look into it. I spoke to the council, hoping someone there would take responsibility but as it's a police issue, I have to deal with it. So, what do I say? I need to put out a statement.'

Bernie smiled. 'I'll swap you the statement if you catch our killers.' She bit into the chocolate.

'Come on, Bernie. I know the anglers look like they're quiet, deep thinkers but some of them are full of repressed rage.'

'I think those are the ones you dated. And the rage came afterwards.'

'Bernie, I'm serious. Until you find the other foot and the hands of your victim, we can't allow fishing. And people will want to know why.'

Bernie swallowed. 'OK. Pen and paper ready?'

Jane grabbed a pen and pad. 'Ready.'

'Due to an ongoing police investigation, we have to postpone the start of the fishing season on the River Avon. We hope this will not be for too long and we appreciate your cooperation. There. Easy. You didn't really need me for that, did you?'

Jane finished writing on her pad before looking up. 'No. I could have drafted that in my sleep.' She put down her pen. 'I may have overheard something.'

'Have you been listening at doors again?' Bernie asked.

Two spots of pink appeared on Jane's pale cheeks. 'Maybe. I was waiting to speak to the chief constable – I was in her PA's office. The PA was out and the chief constable was on a phone call. She's quite loud, even through a closed door. I could only hear her side of the conversation but it sounded intense. Especially when your name was mentioned.'

Bernie leaned forward. 'Who was she talking to?'

'I don't know. But you'll be pleased to know that the chief constable defended you.'

'She barely knows me and why would she have to defend me anyway?'

Jane shrugged. 'I heard her say, and I'm paraphrasing, that you're a really good detective who never gives up. Then she put the phone down.'

'And you have no idea who it was?'

'No. But she seemed pretty cross still when I went in. I just wanted to warn you. And see you. I've missed you not being around.'

'Ah, thanks, Jane. On both counts.' Bernie picked up the chocolate and broke some more off.

'I haven't missed you stealing my chocolate though.'

CHAPTER 20

The super was in a meeting so Bernie returned to MCIT to find Leigh and Matt were back. Leigh was tucking into a pasta salad she'd brought from home. Bernie's stomach rumbled. She'd missed lunch.

Leigh smiled. 'I've got lots here if you want some, ma'am.'

Bernie wrinkled her nose. Cold pasta was not her favourite. 'No thanks. I'll have to go out and buy something. Get Alice some food too.'

'No need,' said Matt, 'I was at the bakery so I picked up some extra sandwiches and cakes.' He pushed a white paper bag towards her.

'Oh Matt, you star.' Bernie took out a BLT sandwich. 'I've really missed the bacon butties from the bakery in the mornings. I eat muesli now. Apparently, it's better for me.' She groaned.

'I got lemon drizzle cake slices as well. Hope that's OK.'

'More than OK, Matt. Wait a minute. Are you buttering me up because you got nothing from the door-to-door, or are we celebrating a break in the case?'

Matt flushed. 'Bit of both and neither at the same time.'

'That makes no sense.' Bernie bit into her sandwich.

'Clench is a hamlet and all the houses are really spaced out,' said Matt. 'But people still know one another. The Pinners who own the house on the corner are away in Australia, visiting family. According to a neighbour, the Pinners own the barns and some of the land. They've been away for a month and due to be away for another.'

'So, it's unlikely they know anything about people using their barns then,' Bernie said.

'I think so. One neighbour thought she heard a gunshot in the middle of the night – Sunday going into Monday – but she also heard a car, so thought it had backfired.'

'Hmm. I suspect that was the gunshot that killed Aaron Swan.'

'Who's Aaron Swan?' asked Leigh. 'Is he our second car thief?'

'Think so. He lived with Lewis Brown and his mother, Helen, for a while. She's offered to identify him so we should know for certain soon,' Bernie said. 'Did no one else hear anything? Any more guns or screaming?'

Matt shook his head. 'Nothing else. No one goes down that lane apart from the Pinners.'

'But someone did and found the perfect spot for torture and murder.'

'They probably looked at Google maps, like us, and found it that way,' said Leigh.

'Sounds very likely, Leigh. Did you find anything?' Bernie asked.

'No. I tried a few routes, looking out for any CCTV or doorbell footage. There were a few houses I tried but people weren't in. I'm going to write a letter and go back and put them through the letterboxes. It shouldn't take me long to do. I have all the addresses.'

Bernie glanced at her watch. It was coming up to three p.m. 'Maybe Matt can help you do that. I have to update the chief constable at six o'clock tonight so if you're able to get any info before then, that would be good. We have little to go on at the moment.'

Bernie's phone buzzed. It was a call from Mick.

'Hi, Mick.'

'Hi, ma'am. I just stopped at a garage to buy some food for Helen Brown. She's identified Aaron Swan but we can double-check with his DNA. We must have his profile on the database. Should be back by four, maybe earlier. Depends on the school traffic.'

'OK. Alice is prepping Helen's interview.'

'We'll need to take it easy, I think, ma'am. She's very upset.'

'Of course. I trust you and Alice to handle it well. Take her to the family room. You know the procedure – tea, biscuits, tissues. Ask her if we can do a visual recording too. Tell her it's important for the case.'

'You want to check her body language, don't you?'

'Yes. I think it's very unlikely she's involved but I want to see if she's lying about anything. Now we have visual identification of Lewis and Aaron, we can ask for bank details, phone records. I'll put a request in. And if there's anything Helen's hiding, I'll ask for hers too.'

Bernie was alone in MCIT. Matt and Leigh had gone out on their letter drop and Alice was preparing the family room for Helen's interview. She realised that she hadn't heard from Kerry so sent a text asking for an update. A few minutes later, Bernie's phone rang and she answered without looking at the screen.

'Kerry, please tell me you have some good news.'

'Oh, I'm not Kerry,' said a slightly clipped, female voice. 'Is this Detective Inspector Bernadette Noel?'

'Yes, sorry. I was expecting my sergeant to call me. I didn't check my phone. Who am I talking to?'

'I'm Bella Fontaine. I'm on the defence team for Jack Thornton.'

'I see.' Bernie checked the time. It was after four thirty p.m. The court session must have finished.

'We sent you a letter calling you to be a witness for the defence. We hadn't heard back so this is a courtesy call to make sure you're coming on Monday.'

Bernie rubbed her forehead. Any hope of not turning up was slipping away, unless she could find a way out of it.

'I only got the letter a couple of days ago. I've been on maternity leave. In fact, it's not that easy for me to attend court next week. I'm in the middle of a live case and I need to be home by a certain time to feed my daughter.'

'You're very welcome to bring her along, with a family member or friend to help.'

'Thank you but no. Courts are no places for babies to be. Even in the Witness Room.'

'We'll do our best to make sure we finish on time so you can get home then. I'm sure you have someone else who can run your team for the day. If you could be here for nine thirty, please, and we'll have a little chat about what to expect in court.'

Bernie was annoyed. She knew what to expect. 'I've been a police officer for fifteen years. I know how the system works.'

'But have you ever been a defence witness? It's a little different, detective inspector.'

'I know. Most defence witnesses offer to give evidence.

I've done no such thing.'

There was a pause on the phone and Bernie wondered if Bella was still there.

'Well, I look forward to seeing you on Monday morning. New building. Court thirteen.'

'Lucky for some,' said Bernie.

'Indeed. Goodbye.' Bella Fontaine hung up before Bernie could reply.

Damn. Bernie knew she could have handled that better. By being difficult on the phone, she'd given away how she'd behave as a defence witness – a hostile one. And now, Jack Thornton's defence team would be ready for her.

CHAPTER 21

Bernie switched off the playback of Helen's interview. She'd given a lot more detail but hadn't contradicted herself from her earlier conversation with Bernie. Nothing in her body language indicated she was lying. Helen appeared a reliable witness but there was a nagging doubt that Bernie couldn't shift.

'Let's check Helen's bank records anyway. It's always possible money was being fed into her account without her knowing.'

'How would she not know?' asked Alice. 'She doesn't earn much as a cleaner. She must have a tight budget.'

'Could be money from Lewis, "helping" mum out,' said Mick, 'but in reality, it's coming from another source. I'll put the request in, ma'am. Phone records too?'

'Wouldn't hurt,' Bernie answered. 'Especially as no phones were found either at the scene or in the car. If Lewis or Aaron had contacted Helen, it might show up, particularly if they'd used burner phones.'

'Maybe they didn't have phones with them,' Alice said.

'I find that hard to believe. Two London lads able to navigate country roads avoiding traffic cameras.' Bernie shook her head. 'No, they had Satnav on their phones directing them. But where was the final destination meant to be? I doubt it was a few miles outside of Devizes and headquarters.'

Bernie checked the time. Just after five thirty p.m. 'What's happening with Helen now?'

'She's ringing her sister in Reading,' said Mick. 'I'll take her there after the briefing. Can't miss the chief constable joining us.'

Bernie shuddered. It had seemed a good idea at the time to ask Hannah Drake to come to the briefing rather than give a separate update, and the chief constable agreed.

'I rarely get invited to join these things any more,' she'd said. 'It'll be good to meet the team.'

Bernie hoped the rest of the team agreed. And that they turned up on time. Matt, Leigh and Kerry were on their way back but were cutting it fine.

'We'll need a few more chairs in here. I think the super is coming too and I have a feeling that Jane Clackett might pop in. With the fishing season postponed, questions will be asked by the local press. I know Clive Bishop will be probing away. Mind you, he has his uses sometimes. But I doubt even he'd know the name of our mystery victim.'

Half an hour later, everyone was back, along with the chief constable, the super and Jane. Bernie hadn't held a briefing like this since before she'd had Mira. Could she remember how to do it?

'Thank you all for coming. I think it's fair to say that we're not massively further forward in this case but that's not entirely our fault, and certainly nothing to do with the dedication of this team.

'However, we can now name our two car thieves – Lewis Brown and Aaron Swan. Lewis's mother has identified both of them. Swan lived with the Browns for a while and Helen was like a foster mother to him. Lewis and Aaron have been friends for a long time after meeting in Feltham Young Offenders. It was Aaron who got Lewis into stealing cars to order. Helen doesn't know much about the man who gave the orders but the boys would jump to it when the message came in. I've asked for phone and bank records for Lewis, Aaron and Helen.'

The chief constable frowned. 'You think the mother's involved?'

'Not knowingly. But I wonder if Lewis has paid money into her account. It's one way of hiding dodgy cash. Kerry, do you have any news from the crime scene or forensics?'

Kerry stood up. 'Forensics have almost finished at the scene. Hopefully, some results will start to come in from tomorrow, but what I can say, it's likely that more than one person was killed in the shed where the blood was found. So, it's possible that our unknown victim and Aaron Swan were both murdered there. The unknown victim was transferred to the car and Aaron was put in the caravan. A lot of evidence has been taken to the lab for testing. There's going to be multiple DNA profiles that need to be looked at.'

Bernie got the gist of what Kerry was saying – this was going to be expensive.

'Thanks, Kerry. Matt, you've been on door-to-door today. What have you found out?' Bernie asked.

Matt stood up next to Kerry, towering over her. 'Not a huge amount but the owners of the barns live in the house on the corner of the lane. They're currently in Australia visiting family and have been there for a month already. So it's hard to believe that they're involved but can't rule it out completely. I'll keep looking into them.'

'Thanks, Matt.'

Bernie turned her attention to Leigh. She wasn't sure how Leigh would be in front of the chief constable. 'Leigh, do you have anything?'

Leigh twisted her rings but stood up anyway. 'I drove along some of the possible routes the cars might have taken. I identified a few houses and businesses that have some kind of CCTV. Most people were out or there was no footage available. Matt and I put letters through the doors. We had a response on our way back here. Someone had both cars on their CCTV. It's being emailed to me.'

'Have you checked it yet?' asked Hannah Drake, briskly.

'No, the briefing was just starting.'

'Well, let's hook your laptop up to the whiteboard and get it up there for us all to see.'

Leigh gave Bernie a startled look.

'That would be a good idea,' said Bernie. 'Matt, could you give Leigh a hand with that, please? While we wait, is there anything else to add or any questions?'

'I have something,' Jane said. 'The fishing clubs are playing ball for now with the postponement of the start of the season but one of the clubs had heard a rumour of a body part being found in the river. I suspect the person who phoned it in hasn't been as discreet as you'd hoped. The club chairman took great delight in telling me that Clive Bishop is a member.'

The super groaned and covered his face with his hand.

'I'm at a disadvantage here,' said Hannah. 'Who is Clive Bishop?'

'He's a local journalist,' said Jane. 'If he gets a sniff of this, then we're in trouble. We've kept this quiet so far.'

'Ah, I see,' said Hannah. 'If we didn't have the added complication of our boot victim, then we could be freer with the press.'

'If there wasn't a boot victim,' said Bernie, 'I'm pretty sure Lewis and Aaron would still be alive.'

Bernie stared at the chief constable. After what Jane had told her, she was sure Hannah Drake knew more than she was letting on. Or maybe that was Bernie's general mistrust of senior officers.

'I'm aware of that,' said Hannah. 'I'm doing everything I can to find out more. And you'll be the first to know once I do. Right, is this footage ready?'

Bernie recognised the diversion tactic. She couldn't work out how she felt about Hannah Drake.

'Yes, ma'am,' said Leigh. 'The person who sent it installed proper CCTV after being burgled. So hopefully, it'll be good quality and a continuous clip of the cars.' Leigh pressed play.

The white BMW, driven by Lewis Brown, came into shot first. An outdoor light increased the quality as the camera wasn't in night vision. Thirty seconds later, the black Mercedes appeared. The car wasn't far from the house and the occupants could be seen.

'There are two people in the Mercedes,' said Bernie. 'I think this is the best footage so far. Mick, Matt, what do you think?'

'Absolutely,' said Mick. 'It wasn't possible to see who was in the car before but there's definitely someone in the front passenger seat.'

'Leigh, could you send that to Tom please? Hopefully, he can go through it frame by frame and see if we can get a clearer image,' Bernie said. She looked across to the chief constable and the super. 'What do you think, ma'am, sir?'

The super nodded. 'It's certainly a good start.'

Bernie turned to the chief constable, who had paled.

Hannah Drake coughed. 'Yes, I agree with Detective Chief

Superintendent Wilson, it's a good start. Let's see where you go from here. Thank you for the briefing. I'll speak to you again tomorrow, Detective Inspector Noel.'

Hannah stood up and left.

'Well done to all of you. Keep it up,' said the super, as he left too.

Jane sidled over to Bernie. 'What just happened there?' she whispered.

Bernie looked at the image on the whiteboard again before whispering back.

'I'm not sure how but I think the chief constable recognised someone in that footage.'

CHAPTER 22

Thursday

With the morning routine with Mira improving, Bernie had time to pick up bacon butties and a vegetarian sausage roll for Kerry.

'Here you go, everyone,' Bernie said as she gave them out. Leigh passed on hers but Bernie expected that. Mick or Matt would have room for one more. 'We need some energy today. I'm hoping we're going to get some forensic results back and that Tom will make progress with the footage.'

Bernie thought again about Hannah Drake's response to the image. If Jane hadn't mentioned it too, then she might have assumed she'd imagined it. Something wasn't right there.

Bernie's desk phone began to ring. She was so used to people contacting her by mobile she was thrown for the moment.

'Hello, DI Noel speaking.'

'Hi, it's Sally at reception. I have Clive Bishop here for you. Were you expecting him?'

Bernie closed her eyes. She was expecting him to turn up at some point but had hoped not just yet.

'No, he doesn't have an appointment with me but I'll see him. I'll be with you in a few minutes.'

Bernie put the phone down and sighed. 'Sorry guys. Our friendly local reporter has turned up. Just carry on with what you've been doing and I'll be back soon.'

She looked at her bacon butty. It wouldn't be particularly professional to eat it in front of Bishop but it would be cold when she returned. Then she remembered the spare one. Perhaps being hospitable to Clive Bishop was the best way forward.

She took Clive into the family room where Helen had been the day before.

'Cup of tea, Clive?'

'Oh, yes please. Thanks.'

'Got your sweeteners?'

Bishop smiled. 'I have. Surprised you remember.'

Bernie switched the kettle on. 'Well, you turning up at my flat during the Molly Reynolds case was quite memorable. Got a bacon butty too if you'd like it.'

Clive gave her a sceptical look. 'You're being very nice to me, DI Noel.'

'I'm always nice to you, Clive. Jane on the other hand...'

Clive laughed. 'Yes, the Wicked Witch of the West. And there's a reason I've come to you rather than her.'

The kettle clicked off and Bernie made the tea. Placing it in front of Clive, along with the bacon butty, she said, 'So why have you come to see me?' She took a bite of her own bacon roll.

Clive sipped his tea. 'Good cuppa that. Well, since you're being so nice to me, I'll repay the compliment. I know something's going on that you're keeping from the press. I had a phone call from a young man who said he'd found a body part.'

Bernie's heart sank. She'd thought Charlie Spencer was going to keep quiet.

'Go on.'

'Well, I told him he should call the police but he wasn't too keen on that. He told me where to find it and I've been there now.'

Bernie leaned forward. This couldn't be the foot Charlie Spencer had found.

'And?'

'I'm no forensic expert but it looks like a real hand to me.'

Bernie swallowed her mouthful before she choked on it.

'Where?'

'Canal. Not far from here.'

'Why didn't you stay with it and call nine nine nine?'

Clive took a big mouthful of tea before answering. 'You don't know who's going to turn up when you do that. I knew I had to come to you, not least because there's a rumour going round that you've already found a foot.'

Lucy bagged the hand.

'Unless there's a maniac going around chopping off hands, this should fit the DNA profile of our boot victim,' she said. 'I'll ask the lab for priority on this. See if we can get fingerprints too.'

Bernie exhaled noisily. 'Won't make much difference if we can't access his name. Shit.'

They were by the canal, a bridge just above them with a road.

Bernie looked up. 'Reckon they threw it in from there. I thought it was Lewis doing the dumping but now I'm not so sure. There isn't any CCTV footage of the white BMW in Devizes town centre.'

'Someone else then,' said Lucy. 'Probably the person who killed our mystery victim.'

'Or persons,' said Bernie, as she remembered there were two

people in the black Mercedes.

Bernie crouched down and looked at the canal. Was it hiding anything else in there? Or another river somewhere? Were the killers just careless or was there purpose in disposing of the limbs this way?

Kerry joined them. 'I've looked further up the canal but nothing obvious. This phone call Clive Bishop got – did he get a name?'

'No. Clive was told to come here.'

'So the guy who called, could be the one who put it here in the first place.'

Bernie slowly nodded. 'It could. We need to get a trace on that phone call. Someone's playing games with us and I don't like it one little bit.'

Bernie was pushing her luck but it was worth a try. She breezed into the chief constable's PA's office.

'Is the chief constable in?' she asked with a smile.

'No. I'm afraid she's out all day at a conference. Won't be back in until tomorrow. If it's a real emergency, I could get her on the phone.'

'No. It's fine. It can wait until tomorrow.'

Bernie left quickly and headed to the next office where she might get answers. She knocked and waited. She knew how much this person hated people barging in.

'Come in.'

Bernie went in and found Jane typing, her hands flying across the keyboard.

'Have you got even faster than before?' Bernie asked.

'Yep.' Jane didn't take her eyes off her monitor as her fingers typed. 'Wait a sec.'

'Sure.' Bernie sat down and waited for Jane to finish.

'Sorry about that. A report that's due in today. What can I do for you?'

'A hand's been found in the canal in Devizes. We need to test but I suspect it'll belong to our unnamed dead man.'

'Ooh. That's interesting.' Jane leaned forward. 'Who found it?'

Bernie wrinkled her nose. Jane wasn't going to like the answer. 'Clive Bishop got a tip-off. Went to investigate and spotted it.'

'Is that why he was here earlier?'

'How did you know?'

Jane raised an eyebrow in reply.

'Of course, you know everything.'

'I don't know why Hannah Drake went as pale as me last night. That one is a mystery.'

'I've just been to her office,' Bernie said. 'She's not in. Typical. We're being mucked about here. Kerry suggested that the man who called Clive might be the man who put it there. But why call Clive Bishop?'

Jane leaned back and laughed. 'Why would anyone call Clive Bishop? Seriously, though, there's been no publicity on this case. People have heard that a young man died in a car crash but that's all. If I was the killer, I'd be a bit frustrated that there wasn't more on the news about it. I'd want to send out some signals to the public and the police.'

'Or the more reason to keep it quiet then. I'm not willing to pander to someone who chops off hands and feet and hurls them into local waterways.' Bernie leaned her head on her hand. 'Sorry. I'm tired.'

'Bad night with Mira?'

'One day, I'm hoping someone's going to ask me a personal

question that doesn't involve Mira.'

Jane opened a drawer and pulled out a bar of chocolate. 'I see. Have some.'

Bernie sighed and broke off a row. 'Don't get me wrong. I love her to bits and I enjoyed my maternity leave. But Dougie often got home late and there were days on end when I didn't speak to another adult. I was looking forward to grown-up conversations coming back here. Not ones that revolved around Mira's feeding and sleeping habits. I wanted a case that I could get my teeth into, and I've got it, but I'm frustrated that we're not getting the answers we need. The name of our boot boy is crucial to all of this, I know it. If we find out who he is, then we'll find the killers.'

CHAPTER 23

Tom was waiting for Bernie when she got back to MCIT.

'Hi, Tom. Please tell me you have good news.'

Tom waved his hand from side to side. 'Sort of. I can't get a clear image of faces. But I can tell you that the person in the passenger seat in the Mercedes has very light hair. Maybe even white. And I have a partial number plate – RX2. Nothing else. I'll run it through the database, see if we get any hits. And the phone call to Clive Bishop came from a pay-as-you-go phone.'

'So, potentially a burner. Little chance of tracing that then. Thanks anyway, Tom.'

'I also have mobile phone data for Lewis and Aaron.'

'Wow, that was fast. Mind you, I did mention double homicide in my request. What do we have?'

'Text messages mostly between the two of them. Do you want me to hook it up to the whiteboard so we can all see?'

Leigh, Mick and Alice were in the office but Kerry and Matt were still at the canal.

'Sure.'

A minute later, Tom had the messages up on the screen. 'The first message is from Aaron.'

Bernie read them out.

Yo bro. Got a job for Sun night.

I'm not interested. Promised Mum.

Last one. Honest. 5k each. Car already spotted. Easy peasy.

Last one?

For sure. I love your mum too. I wouldn't hurt her.

Why so much? It's normally 2k.

Have to deliver to Wiltshire.

Wiltshire? How are we supposed to get there?

On M4.

Can't drive on M4! Cameras! Shit for brains!

They'll give us a GPS with route to follow. I'm not that stupid!

How do we get home then?

Get dropped by a train station. Take first train back.

How do we get paid?

Usual. Cash on delivery.

Can't pay that much into Mum's account. She's already suspicious. Told her it's from my wages.

It is. Come on. Last one. Won't ever have to do this again.

Sure?

Sure.

Bernie sighed. 'Aaron was right. It was their last job. Do we know how this man got in contact with Aaron?'

Tom shook his head. 'Not yet. Can't see anything on his phone but he might have had a burner. Has his place been searched yet?'

'No,' said Bernie. 'Nor Lewis's. We could ask the Met but it would be a lot easier if we did it ourselves. We'll need to get warrants though. I'll talk to the super.' Bernie pointed at the board.

'Aaron said they'd be given a GPS but nothing was found in the car or at the barns. And the route taken didn't rule out all the cameras.'

'It's virtually impossible to drive anywhere without a camera picking you up, said Mick. 'They avoided most of them, especially when they got to Wiltshire. And if it hadn't been for the young lad finding the foot, we might not have found the barns. Wouldn't have known until the owners got back.'

'About the owners, I've found out something interesting,' said Alice. 'The husband – Dennis Pinner – has a criminal record.'

'That is interesting. Do you have it?' Bernie said.

Alice went back to her desk and pulled up the record on screen. 'A lot of petty crime when he was young but then it escalates.'

Bernie saw ABH, GBH, possession of a weapon as Alice scrolled down.

'But this is where it really gets interesting,' Alice said.

She clicked on page two. There were dates but all the details were blacked out.

'They've been redacted,' said Bernie. 'Why?'

'Maybe the cases are sensitive,' Leigh said.

'I bet they are,' said Bernie. 'I think Dennis Pinner's an informant.'

'Convenient that he's out of the country when two men are brutally murdered on his property then,' said Mick.

'Isn't it?' said Bernie. 'I'm thinking some serious guys wanted payback on Dennis and this was one way of doing it. Either he agreed to them using his place – maybe even to store the stolen car or cars – or they knew he was away and used the barns to throw shade onto Dennis. You can order a hit, even if you're out of the country.'

'That's if it was planned,' said Alice. 'Maybe it all went horribly wrong when they dropped off the car. Perhaps they weren't paid enough.'

'That would work if there wasn't another dead man in the boot. Or even a man with all his limbs intact. Cutting off the hands and feet took time. I'm pretty sure his body was like that when Lewis and Aaron turned up. And I also think our mystery man had been there for a few days at least. The scars on his torso were recent and Kerry said there was food in the caravan. But I can't see what ties him to Lewis and Aaron. If we just had his name.'

Frustration was building in Bernie. She was sure the chief constable knew something. Could an undercover operation really happen under Hannah Drake's nose without her knowing?

CHAPTER 24

Bernie spent the morning chasing up forensic reports. She knew the service was stretched but they did seem to be taking longer than normal. Had they been told to go slow on this case? Getting the warrants for Lewis's and Aaron's homes had been easier and Mick was preparing to go with Alice.

'Are you sure you're OK to go again, Mick? You were only there yesterday,' Bernie said.

'It's fine, ma'am. Plus, I sort of stuffed up yesterday. I forgot to get the DNA samples from the BMW owners. Sorry. I was so pleased to have found Helen that I just came straight back. I remembered last night.'

Bernie sighed. There was no point in getting cross with Mick. His actions weren't deliberate. At least she hoped not.

'Make sure you get them today, Mick. Forensic evidence is key in this case. We can't afford any more delays.'

'Yes, ma'am. We'll be in touch if we find anything at the searches. I've given the local police a courtesy call too.'

'Yes. I suppose it's best to do that. See you later, or maybe even tomorrow.'

Bernie's phone buzzed. She looked at the screen before

answering, making sure she knew who the caller was this time. It was Kerry.

'Hi, Kerry. How's it going?'

'Think we're done now. Lucy's finished. Matt's wondering if we need to postpone fishing on all waterways in Wiltshire.'

'That'll cause a stir. Think the decision needs to come from higher up. Chief constable is out so might need to talk to the super.'

'OK. It's nearly lunchtime. Do you fancy meeting me at the bakery for something to eat?'

'Two visits in one day? Don't tell Dougie. Meet you there in twenty minutes.'

Unsurprisingly, the bakery was packed and there was nowhere to sit. A weak spring sun provided light but not much warmth as Bernie and Kerry sat huddled together on a bench by the duck pond on the green.

'We could go back to the office,' said Bernie.

'Better to have the fresh air,' replied Kerry. 'And no prying eyes.'

'What do you mean? I think we can trust Leigh now, Kerry.'

'I don't mean her.'

'Who then?'

'Not sure exactly.'

Bernie frowned. 'What's going on? Have you been tapping into your police grapevine again?'

'Maybe.'

'Kerry. If you know something, you need to tell me.'

Kerry sighed. 'It's nothing definite. I had a little look at the chief constable.'

'Our chief constable? Hannah Drake? That's a bit risky.'

'I know. I was discreet.'

'But why do it?'

'She'd know if there was an undercover op going on in Wiltshire. And she went as white as a sheet when she saw that car footage at the briefing. So, I made a few calls when I got home last night. Don't worry. I didn't mention the case. It was more of a "how can I impress the new boss" type of thing.'

Bernie looked down. She'd asked Kerry before to find out things but never with such a senior officer. This could be dangerous for both of them.

'What did you find out?'

'Hannah Drake was a DI in the Trident Operational Command Unit. She knew Jack Thornton.'

Bernie's head snapped up. 'What?'

'You didn't know?'

'No. Our op was a branch off of Trident and I was put undercover so quickly there wasn't time to get to know anyone other than the immediate team. Do you think she knows who I am?'

Kerry shrugged. 'No idea. She might have been there before your time but I thought it best you should know.'

'Jane said she heard Hannah Drake defending me to someone on the phone. Said I was a good officer. I did wonder why she'd think that when she's only just met me. Perhaps she knew of me back then. Oh God. Will I ever be free of this man?'

'You will. Next week.'

'Dougie's going tomorrow. Taking Mira with him. Apparently my grandmother is babysitting which is hilarious. She hated looking after me.'

'Do you want me to see if Debs can have her? She's got a day off but she is feeling a bit delicate at the moment.'

'Oh, is she ill? She won't want to look after a baby.'

'I don't know. Might be good practice.' Kerry grinned.

'No! You never said. That's great news. So happy for you both.' Bernie hugged her.

'It's early days. She's nine weeks and feeling pretty sick. We were going to wait until the scan before saying anything. We've been at this stage before and it's gone wrong. Please don't say anything.'

'Of course not. And she must rest. No babysitting duties. Granny will be fine. She does seem quite fond of Mira.'

'Of course she is. Your daughter's a delight.'

'I know. But I am enjoying being back at work.' Bernie crumbled her sandwich bag into a ball and threw it into the bin.

'Good shot,' said Kerry. 'School basketball team?'

'No.' The sound of a bouncing ball echoed in her head. 'Netball.'

CHAPTER 25

'Postpone fishing on all the waterways in Wiltshire? I'm not sure, Bernie,' said the super. 'Where do we draw the line? Do we have to contact Cotswolds Water Park too? I know they're in Gloucestershire but they're only just over the border.'

Don't I know it, thought Bernie, as she remembered her last major case. One of the victims had been found in a lake at the water park.

'We've been lucky to keep a lid on this so far, Bernie. A ban like this will raise questions.'

'The questions are already being asked, sir. Are we really going to allow another member of the public to find a hand or foot while they fish?'

'Was the person this morning fishing?'

Bernie paused. Clive Bishop had given a statement but there was little to go on in regard to who gave the tip-off.

'I don't know, sir. But I'm sure people driving over the little bridge noticed our presence. People are probably already speculating on neighbourhood websites.'

'That's a good point. Ask Jane to check them. I think we'll have to wait until the chief constable is back in tomorrow. Hopefully, it's just a twenty-four-hour bug.'

Wilson rubbed his forehead. He didn't look great himself. Hope it's not catching, Bernie thought.

'She's sick? She did look pale last night.'

'Yes. I thought so too. If she's not back in the morning, I'll call her. But I think we need to hold fire for now.'

Bernie knew there was no point fighting the super over this and she left to see Jane.

'He wants me to do what?' asked Jane.

'Scan the neighbourhood sites for any gossip about the river finds. Don't worry, I'll ask Leigh to do it. But I have some gossip for you.'

'Ooh. I'm all ears.'

'I was told by Hannah Drake's PA that she was at a conference. But the super got a message from her saying she was sick. He'd noticed she looked pale last night, as did Kerry. So maybe she was ill?'

'Hmm. Doesn't make sense for the PA to say she's at a conference if she's unwell. Unless she wants to look like Superwoman who's never ill.'

'Or,' Bernie said, leaning forward, 'she knows something about the passenger in the Mercedes and she's gone to investigate it.'

'We've got some forensic reports from Therese,' said Kerry as Bernie walked back into MCIT.

'Thank God. Let's hope they give us some answers.' Bernie pulled her chair over to Kerry's desk. 'What do we have?'

Kerry tapped on her keyboard to open the results. 'They're all interim at the moment. So, more to follow. Let's have a look at the white BMW first. Ah.'

Bernie read it aloud so Leigh could hear. 'Multiple fingerprints and multiple DNA inside the car itself. If it was a family car then that's not unusual. Blood droplets only found in the boot and belongs to victim. Same with the smudge on the back of the car. Require DNA samples from the owners to narrow down search. Well, Mick will get those today. I've told Alice to remind him. What's the next report, Kerry?'

'Aaron Swan's clothes. I'll read it out. Blood is his and there's gunshot residue on his top. Nothing much there. Let's check Lewis Brown's clothes.' Kerry clicked on another report. 'Only a small amount of blood on his sweatshirt at the back of the neck.'

'Probably from where he hit his head,' Bernie said.

'Yes.' Kerry read on. 'No other blood or DNA or gun residue on his clothing. I'm trying to work this out.'

'I have a theory,' said Leigh.

'Come and tell us then,' Bernie said.

Leigh left her desk and perched on another next to Kerry's. 'Really I need four people to demonstrate this but let's imagine someone else is here. Kerry, you're Lewis, and ma'am, you're Aaron. I'm the unknown shooter.'

'Are we actually going to act this out?' asked Kerry.

'Sort of. I just thought a visual representation might help. Well, it will help me.'

'Carry on, Leigh,' Bernie said.

'So, I'm already at the barn with my accomplice plus a dead, mutilated man. The two of you turn up in the car. While I talk to you and give you the money – probably less than what was agreed – my accomplice puts the body in the boot of the BMW. There's an argument and for some reason, Lewis leaves the barn. Either he does so in anger or Aaron tells him to.'

'Do I have to leave the room?' Kerry asked, with a bemused look on her face.

'Not quite. Just go to the door for now.'

Kerry shook her head a little but did as Leigh asked.

'Now, I'm arguing with Aaron and he's really pissing me off. So, I pick up the gun I used on the body and shoot Aaron in the chest. Sorry, ma'am.'

Leigh made a pretend shotgun with her arm and fired at Bernie. She slumped in her seat.

'You die instantly. Lewis hears the shot.' Leigh turned her head towards Kerry. 'What are you going to do?'

'Get the fuck out of there,' said Kerry. She smiled. 'He jumped back in the car and drove, not knowing about the cargo in the boot. He drove to save his life, not knowing where he was going. They followed and caused him to crash. Even if Lewis survived, he'd have to explain why there was a dead person in the back of the car. Am I right?'

'Yes,' said Leigh, nodding enthusiastically. 'Exactly that.'

Bernie sat up. 'It's definitely plausible. Although, where is the shooter's accomplice? Why doesn't he stop Lewis? I can imagine him putting the body in the back of the car, shutting the boot – and that's probably when he made the smear – but where is he when Lewis comes running out?'

Leigh shrugged. 'I haven't got it all worked out.'

'Of course not and that's fine. Maybe the accomplice had gone to the caravan or somewhere else and wasn't quick enough to reach Lewis. Or maybe at the sound of the shot, he ran towards the barn as Lewis ran away. Whatever happened, it's fair to say that Lewis was terrified. His poor mother. No one wants their child to die in fear.'

'Pretty sure our unknown man died in fear,' Leigh said.

Bernie thought about the scars on the young man's torso. If they hadn't been self-inflicted, then he'd been tortured for a while. How would they explain that to his mother?

'Think you're right on that one. Kerry, is there anything on the crime scene itself? The outbuilding with all the blood?'

Kerry returned to her desk and looked at the reports. 'No. And that's one we definitely need. If Aaron had been shot in there, then he would have bled out while the culprits chased Lewis.'

Bernie put her elbows on Kerry's desk and rested her head in her hands. 'So who deposited the limbs? I thought it was Lewis at first but now I'm not so sure. It all happened in the middle of the night. There was time for a clean-up and for the culprits to throw the limbs away, and in doing so, throw suspicion onto Lewis. But they were stupid putting one so close.'

'Maybe they didn't,' said Leigh. 'Perhaps it was put in further upstream and it floated down.'

'Yeah, that's possible,' said Bernie. 'I wish the super would agree to closing all the waterways. Not that we have enough people to search them all.'

'No,' said Leigh. 'But we can carry on searching CCTV for more sightings of the Mercedes after the time of the crash. Now we have a partial number plate, we might have more success in tracking it down. And we could see if it went anywhere near rivers and streams. I'll get onto it.'

'Good idea, Leigh. I can always rely on you to think outside the box.'

Bernie's mobile buzzed. She looked at the screen. It was Mick.

'Hi, Mick. Are you there already?'

'Not quite. Just coming up to the Cranford junction. Going to see the car owner first. But he's warned me that he has three kids and up until a couple of weeks ago, he worked as an Uber driver. So a lot of people have been in there.'

'We know. Forensics have found that already. Get the samples anyway. Might be useful at some point. Thanks, Mick. Give me a call once you've searched the properties. Bye.'

Bernie put her phone away. She tapped her fingers on Kerry's desk. She hated admitting it but they were stuck. Whoever had killed the young men had been professional enough to leave little trace at the scene. But a little trace was all she needed.

CHAPTER 26

It was almost five thirty when Mick rang back. Matt had returned from the canal and was helping Leigh with the Mercedes search. Kerry and Bernie were piecing a detailed timeline together, including all the CCTV footage of the cars. As Leigh and Matt found something, Kerry added it in.

Bernie answered her phone.

'Hi, Mick. Please tell me you have something.'

'I have a few things. Do you want to put me on speaker?'

'Sure. I'll ask Kerry to take notes.'

She beckoned the others over and put her phone on her desk. Kerry had a pen and pad.

'OK. All ready here. Go ahead, Mick.'

'Right. Samples from the car owner and his family are done and double-bagged. So there shouldn't be any crossover from them. I searched Aaron's room and Alice has done Lewis's. They were only a couple of roads apart. Both in houses of multiple occupancy. Aaron's one is a bit rough. All probationers. They weren't going to let me in until I explained that Aaron had been murdered. Then they were happy to help. Said that Aaron was friendly, a cheeky chap who pushed his luck a bit but never violent.'

'Did they know about the stolen cars?' Bernie asked.

'They didn't mention that. I spoke to a couple of them. Anyway, the landlord came and opened Aaron's room. Yeah, that was interesting. A complete mess and pretty smelly. Landlord wasn't impressed. But I found a few things. Six pairs of designer trainers in pristine condition still in their boxes. A fake Rolex. Eight thousand pounds roughly in cash. Kept finding bundles under various piles of stuff so will need to do a proper tot up. Small amount of cannabis, probably for personal use judging by the smell of his room. But crucially, no laptop, no phone. No digital devices at all.'

'Any kind of paperwork?'

'Letters from the probation service. He had a meeting last week with his officer. Might be worth checking in with her. Not much else. Can't see any bank statements. Landlord said rent was paid by housing benefit but Aaron paid bills in cash. He never asked where it came from.'

'That kind of landlord then,' Matt said.

'Exactly. Those are the highlights from Aaron's room.'

'No weapons then?' Kerry asked.

'No. Which was surprising. Considering the people he was dealing with, you'd have thought he'd have something.'

'Maybe it had been on him,' Leigh said, 'but the killers took that too.'

'Perhaps. I've bagged and boxed up what I think is relevant. I have the key so we can check again if we need to. I'm going to drive round to Alice now.'

A video call icon flashed up on Bernie's phone.

'Oh, Alice is calling me now. Speak to you later, Mick.'

Bernie pressed the icon and the screen changed to a video call.

'Hi, ma'am.'

Bernie could see Lewis's room behind Alice.

'Hi, Alice. I hope Lewis's room was in a better state than Aaron's. Mick's just been telling us about it.'

'Oh, yeah. He sent me photos. Gross. Lewis was much tidier. Clothes in drawers and wardrobes. Nothing under his bed except dust. Found a phone charger but no mobile. However, we do have a laptop so I'm hoping Tom can do some magic. I'm going to turn the camera round so you can see.'

The image flipped and a neat bedroom came into view. Alice slowly scanned round the room.

'God, even the bed's made,' said Bernie.

'Yeah,' said Alice. 'After speaking to Helen yesterday, I really got the impression that Lewis was trying to turn his life around. Look, he even has a photo of him and his mum on his chest of drawers.'

Alice moved and focused on the photo. Helen and Lewis were smiling. They were in a countryside setting with a brilliant blue sky above. Bernie spotted something behind them.

'What's that in the background? I can see stones. Is that Stonehenge?'

Alice picked up the photo. 'You know what. I think it might be.'

'So, Lewis has been to Wiltshire before. Are there any other photos anywhere?'

'Not that I've seen.'

'Have you checked on top of the wardrobe?' Matt asked.

'As best I could. I'm not as tall as you, Matt. Oh wait, I think Mick's here. I can hear him calling. Hang on.'

The view changed to the ceiling while Alice let Mick in.

'OK, I can check for you,' Mick was heard saying. 'Is there a chair?'

'No, you'll have to get one from the kitchen.'

The phone was picked up.

'Sorry, ma'am. Be with you in a minute.'

Mick came into shot, carrying a wooden chair. He climbed up.

'I can see something up here. Wait a minute. It's right at the back. I'll put some gloves on first.'

Bernie and the others waited as Mick donned some latex gloves.

'Right.'

Crowded round Bernie's phone, they all watched as Mick reached up. He pulled out what looked like a photo album.

'That what I think it is?' Bernie asked.

Mick opened it and turned a few pages. 'Yes. Lewis looks younger so probably from a few years ago. Hang on, this is Wiltshire.'

Mick got off the chair and placed the album on top of the chest of drawers. He turned over each page while Alice kept the phone still so the others could see. There were more photos of Stonehenge.

'I wonder who took these photos,' Bernie said. 'Oh look, that's the standing stones at Avebury. Keep turning, Mick.'

More landmarks came into view including a chalk white horse.

'Anyone know which one is that? Matt?'

'I think it's Pewsey but I'd need to check.'

Bernie looked at Matt. 'Pewsey? That's getting a bit—'

There was a loud gasp from the phone.

'Ma'am. Look,' said Alice.

Bernie turned back and focused on the photo being shown. A lovely looking country cottage on the corner of a road, with Lewis, Helen and another woman standing outside the door, smiling for the camera. Helen and the other woman looked strikingly alike.

'So, Sunday night wasn't the first time Lewis had been to this place,' said Bernie, 'and more than that, he knew Mr and Mrs Pinner and the lane that leads down to our crime scene.

'Mick and Alice, I know you're tired but see if you can find Helen Brown. She has some questions to answer.'

CHAPTER 27

Dougie wasn't thrilled about Bernie heading back to work after feeding Mira.

'You have other officers who can talk to this woman, you know,' he said as he passed her a plate of tuna pasta bake.

'I know. We tried that already. She managed to pull the wool over their eyes.'

'And she won't do that with you?'

'Not now we have photographic evidence.' Bernie took a mouthful of food. 'Mmm, this is delicious.'

'Thanks. Mira thought so too. Another meal we can add to her repertoire. I've got some to take with me tomorrow.'

Bernie swallowed her food uncomfortably. 'Ah, yes. I almost forgot about that. What time are you leaving?'

'After rush hour. I need to drop Mira off at your granny's in Clapham. I'm going to leave the car there and take public transport to the Old Bailey. They want me for one thirty. I explained to the prosecution team about Mira so they moved me to the afternoon session.'

'Does that mean the defence will know too? That you're bringing Mira to London?' Worry pulsed through Bernie.

Dougie placed his hand on hers. 'No. They just said to the judge that I have a few issues getting there. Don't worry. I haven't put Mira at risk. And I've spoken to your granny again. The neighbour that has a baby the same age as Mira, her husband works from home so both will be there. I'm sure your granny will cope with all that help.'

Bernie nodded but was still uneasy. She ate more of her dinner but then pushed it away.

'Sorry, I think I ought to head back. Maybe I can eat this later.'

'I'll put it in a tub and you can take it with you. You can reheat it.'

Bernie laughed. 'Oh my God. You've really turned into Mr Domesticity and in less than a week.'

'OK. I'll be honest – I'm a bit bored. So, when she's asleep, I cook. I even made tiramisu for dessert.'

'You didn't give her that.'

'No. Far too much booze and caffeine for a little baby. I'll spoon some out for me and you can take the rest in to share with whoever else is there.' Dougie kissed her. 'Don't stay too long. I miss you.'

Bernie raised her eyebrows.

'I know, I know,' said Dougie. 'I was doing the same. I get it now. Let me sort this food out.'

Kerry was waiting for Bernie in MCIT.

Bernie lifted up the tub with the dessert in it.

'I come bearing gifts. Dougie's made his mother's tiramisu recipe. It can be our treat after we've chatted to Helen Brown. Where is she?'

'Interview room one. Thought we'd take a step up from the family room. I've got copies of the relevant photos. Matt's logging the album and the other evidence. Mick's dropping off the DNA samples from the car owner and his family. Alice and Leigh have gone home. I've written a list of questions to ask.'

Kerry handed Bernie her notepad.

'Did you go home to eat like I suggested?' Bernie asked.

'Er, no. But I've eaten lots of biscuits. That'll tide me over until it's tiramisu time. What do you think of the questions?'

Bernie nodded. 'They're good. You take the lead.'

Helen Brown stared at Bernie and Kerry as they walked in.

'Is this how you treat a bereaved mother?' she snapped.

'No,' replied Bernie, as she sat down across the table from Helen. 'You had that yesterday. Today, we need to question you. You're not under arrest but I am going to caution you.'

Helen's eyes widened. 'Why would I need to be cautioned?'

'Because of the nature of our questions. We'll also be recording.'

Bernie nodded at Kerry. She pressed record on the audio equipment. Bernie stated their names, time and date, before cautioning Helen.

'Do you understand the caution?' Bernie asked.

Helen nodded.

'For the recording, Helen Brown has nodded her head. Kerry, if you'd like to start.'

Bernie leaned back in her chair to watch Helen as Kerry asked her questions, mundane ones to begin with about Lewis's room. Helen seemed steady but her fingers were worrying the cuffs on her jumper.

'So, you went to stay with your sister in Reading last night?' Kerry asked.

'That's right.'

'Is she your only sister?'

Helen paused. 'Yes.'

'Has she lived in Reading for long?'

'I don't see what this has to do with Lewis.'

Kerry kept a steady gaze on Helen.

'No. She used to live in Wiltshire. Until she got divorced. She moved to Reading about eighteen months ago.'

'And her ex-husband?'

'Lying bastard kept the house and married his bit-on-the-side.'

'Was it this house?'

Kerry pushed a copy of the photo of the house towards Helen.

Her hand went straight up to her mouth. 'Where did you get this?'

'It was found in Lewis's room, along with more photos.'

Helen bit her fingernail. 'I didn't know he still had them. Dennis – my sister's ex – was really into photography. We stayed with them a few summers ago, before the split obviously. They took us out to Stonehenge and Salisbury. We even went to Bath. Dennis took loads of photos and he printed the best ones and made an album for Lewis. Where did you find it?'

'On top of his wardrobe.'

Helen shook her head. 'Can't believe he kept it after what Dennis did. Lewis was very angry about it. He looked on Dennis as a father figure. His own dad left years ago.' Helen took her hand away from her mouth and touched the paper copy of the photo. 'It was the Christmas after this that it all came out. We were with them. Caz was devastated. She lived with us for a bit until Dennis coughed up some cash. Bastard.'

Kerry looked at Bernie and pointed to a question further down the pad.

'Did you ever go down to the barns at the end of the lane that belonged to Dennis?' Bernie asked.

'No. He just used them for storage. They came with the property, along with some of the land. He leases the land to another farmer. But Lewis went down there. Dennis taught him to drive on the lane. Why are you asking?'

'I told you yesterday that Lewis died in a car crash but Aaron died somewhere else. The "somewhere else" was near the barns that Dennis owns.'

Helen gulped. 'I think I'm going to be sick.'

CHAPTER 28

Matt offered to drive Helen to her sister's in Reading. Bernie was more inclined to have her dropped at the train station but she was a grieving mother. It wouldn't look good if Helen made a complaint.

'Thank you for answering our questions, Helen,' said Bernie, as she walked Lewis's mother out to Matt's car. 'I'm afraid we'll probably need to ask more.'

'I understand. Would it help if my sister came too? She'll know about Dennis's "dealings" and now she's not married to him, I'm sure she'll spill his secrets.'

Bernie thought about the redacted parts of Dennis Pinner's criminal record. If she could discover what those related to, then maybe she had a chance of solving this case.

'That would be very helpful, thank you. Would you be able to come tomorrow?'

'I'll ask her and see. She works so might have to be the weekend.' Helen held out her hand to Bernie. 'Thank you, DI Noel. I know you'll find out who's responsible.'

Bernie took the offered hand and shook it. 'I will do my best for Lewis and Aaron. I'm sorry we went hard on you in there.'

'No, I get it. You found evidence that linked Lewis to the place where Aaron died. And you weren't that hard. You're not the first police officer I've ever talked to. I guess you might be one of the last though.' Helen dropped her head and walked over to Matt's car.

Kerry spooned a large mouthful of tiramisu into her mouth as Bernie came back into MCIT.

'Started without me, I see.'

Kerry swallowed. 'Sorry. I couldn't resist it any longer. I got you a bowl ready.'

Bernie sat down at her desk to eat Dougie's dessert. 'Mmm. This is so delicious.'

'He could open a restaurant when he retires,' Kerry said.

'Not sure he'd want that pressure. And he's got years to go yet. Anyway, what are your thoughts on Helen?'

Kerry had another mouthful of food before answering. 'She seemed genuine enough but there are lots of unanswered questions.'

'Such as?'

'Well, if Aaron lived with them for a bit, why didn't he go to Wiltshire with them?'

'Maybe he lived with them after the Pinners split up. Would make sense for Helen and Lewis not to mention Dennis. We need to get a clear timeline on this. But it does seem odd that Lewis and Aaron had to deliver the car to that particular place. Helen's going to ask her sister if she'd be willing to talk to us. Might find out what those black lines are covering up on her ex-husband's record.'

'That would be good. We also need to find out who's the main man behind the car-stealing business. Is it Dennis Pinner?'

'When I first spoke to Helen, she said it was someone Aaron knew. But I'm wondering now if it was Lewis who started it with Dennis, especially as his uncle taught him to drive. Maybe he was even doing it to get cash for his aunt. That would be ironic.'

Kerry laughed. 'Ingenious more like. One way to screw his uncle over. But something must have gone wrong. If those text messages are right, he didn't want to steal the car. Did he know something about Dennis's business dealings that had put him off? Or did he just want to go straight?'

Bernie sighed. 'So much we don't know – yet. And we're not stopping until we find out.'

Bernie slipped into bed just before midnight. She found a sleeping Mira next to Dougie. He woke up as Bernie pulled the duvet over her.

'Sorry,' she whispered. 'Go back to sleep.'

'It's OK.'

'What happened with Mira?'

'Teeth, I think. She was distressed. Wanted you. Gave her meds and brought her in here. She could smell you if nothing else.'

Bernie gently rubbed Mira's little hand. 'Poor baby.' She drew her daughter towards her. Mira stirred. 'Ssh. Mama's here.' Mira snuggled into her.

Bernie tried to go to sleep but her mind kept drifting back to Helen and Lewis. Had Helen done this with her son when he was a baby? Should Helen have done more to protect him? At what point do you let your adult children have full responsibility for their lives?

'You're never leaving home, young lady,' Bernie whispered to Mira.

CHAPTER 29

Friday

MCIT was quiet when Bernie arrived the next morning. She'd told Mick, Matt and Kerry to come in at ten a.m. after working late the night before. She'd thought about doing the same as Dougie had pulled a screaming Mira from her neck. It didn't bode well for the day ahead in London.

Bernie tried not to think about Jack Thornton's trial but her stomach was cramping at the thought of Dougie being there and her own appearance on Monday.

'Morning ma'am,' Alice said. 'How did it go with Helen? She was very quiet in the car.'

'She wasn't too impressed about being interviewed until we showed her a copy of the photo of Dennis Pinner's house. He's her ex-brother-in-law. She claimed not to know that Lewis and Aaron were probably stealing cars for Pinner. She's going to talk to her sister and see if she can persuade her to do the dirty on her ex-husband. There's a good chance she could fill in the blanks on his record,' Bernie said.

'That would help a lot,' Leigh said. 'Would you like me to check if Mr Pinner really is in Australia? He might have just told a neighbour that. He could be anywhere.'

'Good point. Yes, do a passport check, please. If there was a stopover, he might have got out there. The others will be in for ten so I'll do the briefing then. In the meantime, Alice, can you keep looking into Dennis Pinner, please? Known associates and all that.'

'No problem.'

Bernie's desk phone rang.

'MCIT, DI Noel speaking.'

'Good morning, Bernie.'

She recognised the super's voice.

'Good morning, sir. How can I help you?'

'Hannah Drake has asked for a meeting with both of us at ten a.m. in her office. I assume you can make that.'

Bernie knew she had no option but to be there. 'Yes, sir, I can be there.'

'Bring your logbook and make sure it's up to date.'

She inwardly groaned. The logbook was the bane of her life and she hadn't missed it during maternity leave.

'Yes, sir. See you then.'

Bernie put the phone down and slumped into her chair.

'That good, eh, ma'am?' Alice asked.

'Meeting at ten with the chief constable and an up-to-date logbook. I've been rushing out in the evenings to get home for Mira so it's not quite as detailed as it should be.' Bernie sat up straighter in her chair. 'I'd better get on with it.'

'Give us a shout if you need a hand.'

'Thanks, Alice.'

Just before ten o'clock, Bernie was outside the chief constable's door with logbook in hand. She could hear Hannah Drake talking to someone and assumed it was the super. The outside door to the office opened and Detective Chief Superintendent Wilson walked in.

Smiling at Drake's PA, he said, 'Hello. Is she ready for us?'

Bernie frowned. If the super was here, who was Hannah Drake talking to?

'I'll just check.' The PA lifted a phone.

The super sat down next to Bernie.

'Good. You have the logbook. I expect she wants a full update.'

'Not sure how much we have. Until we find out who this other young man is, our hands are tied.'

'You can go in,' said the PA.

Bernie got up to follow the super but paused. Who was Hannah Drake talking to? She didn't really want to talk about the case in front of someone else. Maybe it was Jane. Having a strategy in place for the press would be a good idea. As she walked into the office, she realised it wasn't Jane but a man she didn't recognise. Or did she? There was something about him she couldn't quite place. He stood up as they came in.

'Ah, DCS Wilson and DI Noel. Thank you for coming. I'd like to introduce you to DS Colin Ferguson,' said the chief constable.

The super held out his hand and the two men shook. Ferguson then turned to Bernie. She looked at him clearly. He was dressed in a smart suit, although not as good as any of Dougie's suits. His face suggested he was in his forties but his hair didn't. His white hair brought an image to mind for Bernie. Now, she understood why he was familiar. She might be wrong but he looked like the passenger in the black Mercedes.

'Please, take a seat,' said Hannah Drake.

Bernie pulled her eyes away from Ferguson as she sat next to the super.

'Right, let's get straight to business,' said Drake. 'As you are all aware, a car crashed in the early hours of Monday morning. The driver died at the scene and DI Noel found a second dead body in the boot.'

Bernie glanced at Ferguson. All aware? What did he know? Was he in the Mercedes?

'On Tuesday,' Drake continued, 'the body of another young man was found by DI Noel in a farm building. We have the names for the driver and the third young man. You'll be pleased to know that DS Ferguson is able to tell us about the second young man, found in the boot of the car.'

Ferguson gave a nervous cough. 'Yes, although in order to explain fully, I need to tell you which department I work with. I'm with Witness Protection.'

Bernie startled. She'd expected him to say he was on an undercover operation.

'The young man in question was due to give evidence in a court case. We had to move him quite a few times to stop his whereabouts from being discovered. He ended up in a caravan in the barn where you found Aaron Swan, DI Noel.'

How do you know his name? I don't like this, thought Bernie.

'We're still investigating how his location was discovered. It was almost in the middle of nowhere but the officer with him received a text from his wife, saying that one of their children was very ill and she'd called an ambulance. Understandably, he left his post but called in that he was doing so. Myself and another colleague agreed to take over but we were delayed in getting there.'

'Wait a minute,' Bernie interrupted. 'You allowed an officer to leave his post?'

'Yes. I know it's unprofessional but his child was sick. Do you have children?'

Bernie's stomach lurched. She nodded.

'Wouldn't you want to get there as fast as possible if your child was in hospital?'

Bernie couldn't argue with that. 'Yes. Please continue.'

'Thank you. As we were almost there, we saw a white BMW pull out from the lane, driving at great speed. We guessed something was wrong. We went straight to the caravan, expecting to find our witness injured and found Aaron Swan instead, not that we knew his name at the time.

'We realised our witness was likely to be in the BMW so we went searching and eventually caught up with the car. Unfortunately, he crashed in front of us.'

Bernie fumed. Ferguson was making it sound like a complete accident.

'Did you stop and check for signs of life?' she asked, trying to control her temper.

'Of course. There was no pulse on the driver. Lewis Brown, I believe.'

'And did you search the car for your witness?'

Ferguson gave a faint shudder. 'Yes. I hate to think how he suffered in the few hours we were away from him. Not sure I'll ever forgive myself.'

'You shouldn't.'

'Bernie,' Wilson warned.

'I'm sorry, sir, but this isn't just about the witness. Two other young men have died in all of this.'

'They weren't exactly innocent though, were they?' said Ferguson. 'It's likely they killed our witness.'

'No. They stole a car. That's all they did. Stole a car from Hounslow and delivered it to Wiltshire. They walked into something they weren't expecting. And died as a result of it. The only blood on Lewis Brown was his own. According to his autopsy, he died from internal bleeding. It wasn't instant. If you checked for a pulse fairly soon after the crash, he should have had one.'

Ferguson glared. 'There was no pulse.'

'Then I suggest you re-take your first aid course.'

'Officers, this stops now,' said the chief constable.

Bernie turned to Hannah Drake. Her stern face caused Bernie to stop talking but her anger was still building.

'I think it's fair to say,' Drake continued, 'that this has been a monumental cock-up.'

Bernie gave a slight smile at Drake's words.

'Not only was I not told about a protected witness in my county, you failed to tell me after his death who he was.' Drake's stern look was now directed at DS Ferguson. 'That is not acceptable. DI Noel has lost valuable time in her investigation because you failed to disclose. I had to go on a fact-finding hunt myself yesterday to procure some of this information.' Drake's voice rose in anger. 'I will not have the Met thinking that my county is available for them to do what they like with. You will now tell us everything you know so DI Noel and her team can find the killers responsible.'

Ferguson looked nervous. 'We've already started our own investigation—'

'Like hell you have. DI Noel has been to three post-mortems this week. She's spoken to Lewis Brown's mother. And unlike you, she stayed at the scenes when she found three dead bodies and called them in. Wiltshire Police will investigate and the Met Commissioner knows this. I had a face-to-face meeting with him yesterday. So, you will cooperate. Let's start with our mystery man. Name please.'

Ferguson looked at Drake and then at Bernie. 'Ma'am, it might be better if we do this in private—'

'Name.'

Ferguson gave a slight nod. 'Of course. I think it's one DI Noel already knows. Carlton Jones.'

CHAPTER 30

Stabbing pains attacked Bernie's left side. Clutching her scar, her muscle memory processed the information quicker than her brain. She tasted bile in her throat and gagged. A waste bin was thrust in front of her but she managed to not vomit. Now she understood why DS Colin Ferguson hadn't wanted to say the name in front of her.

Carlton Jones. The man arrested for the bus sexual assaults the summer before. The man who had grabbed Leigh Roberts. The man who had grown up in Peckham and had been part of Danny Ambrose's gang, who had watched when Bernie was stabbed.

The bin was removed and a glass of water was placed in her hand. She felt as though she wasn't really there. Not quite an outer body experience but definitely a disconnect, as though her brain was trying to protect her.

A gentle touch on her arm brought her back a little.

'Bernie,' said the super. 'It's OK. Take your time.'

She sipped some of the water. It was cold and helped to trigger her brain back into action. She was relieved to see she was still upright in her chair.

'I didn't faint,' she said.

'No, which is progress. I suspect not being pregnant helped this time.'

Bernie drank more, washing away the acidic taste in her throat.

'I'm so sorry,' said DS Ferguson. 'I had no idea it would affect you this way. I can continue this conversation with the chief constable without you if you prefer.'

'No way,' said Bernie. 'I have questions. Lots of them. Just give me a minute.'

She closed her eyes. Images of the three young men filled her head. Criminals but also victims. Breathing slowly in and out, she calmed down. She needed to step carefully with DS Colin Ferguson.

Opening her eyes, Bernie put the glass down next to her chair. She looked directly at Hannah Drake.

'Ma'am, I'd like permission to formally interview DS Colin Ferguson.'

Drake looked between them both.

'Permission granted.'

While waiting for the police federation rep to turn up for Ferguson, Bernie filled her team in on the latest development. As she had thought, Leigh was seriously unimpressed.

'Why was Carlton Jones out of prison?' she demanded. 'He was meant to be on remand until his trial. He abducted me. He was classed as a danger to women and a flight risk. Why did they let him out?'

Bernie placed her arm around Leigh's shoulders and gave her a tight squeeze. The chances of Leigh slipping into a meltdown were high. The squeeze would help with releasing tension.

'I'm going to do my best to find out why this happened.

If you want to go home—'

'No, I'll be worse at home. Here, I can do things. Keep occupied.'

'OK. But if you want to leave at any point, then you're free to do so. Just let Kerry know if I'm not around.'

Bernie focused on the rest of the team. 'We have an hour or so before DS Ferguson's rep turns up. The super and I will interview him. At some point, we'll have to speak to the other officer in the car as well. But what I need from you right now is everything we have on the Mercedes movements, plus a fairly clear timeline of both cars in regard to CCTV footage. Obviously, we know that times on cameras can be out a bit but let's get the best idea that we can.

'Our three victims were convicted criminals. Some would say good riddance. But I can't look Helen Brown in the eye and say that. No matter what our personal opinions are, we owe it to the families to find out what happened and find the people responsible. So, Matt and Mick – take the BMW. Alice and Leigh – focus on the Mercedes. Kerry, could you put the timeline together for me, please? I'm going to write my interview questions. Thank you all.'

As the others busied themselves at their desks, Kerry caught Bernie's arm.

'Are you OK?' she asked.

Bernie gave a slight nod. 'Just. Had a wobbly moment in the chief constable's office but didn't black out so that's good.'

'If you need me to step in for you on the interview then I can do so.'

'And let the super ask all the questions – no chance. I'll be OK. Thanks for asking though.'

Bernie sat down at her desk and got a pen and pad out. The last police officer she'd questioned was DCI Jack Thornton. She didn't relish doing it again.

CHAPTER 31

Bernie pressed record on the audio equipment. She cautioned Colin Ferguson before diving into her questions.

'Can you tell us what happened in the early hours of Monday morning, please, with as much detail as possible?' she asked.

The super, next to her, picked up his pen. It was strange having him scribe for her. But since she had a better grasp of the operation, they'd agreed it made more sense for her to ask the questions.

Ferguson coughed a little and sipped some water. Was this a delaying tactic? He'd had a good hour to get his story right while waiting for his police rep to appear. Longer really. Since Monday.

'I got a call just after midnight on Monday from my colleague who was with Carlton Jones. If you don't mind, I'd rather not name who that is in a formal interview for classified reasons.'

It wasn't ideal but Bernie nodded.

'One of his kids was sick and had to go to hospital. He wanted to go and we all understood that. I sustained an injury playing football a few weeks ago so I'm not driving at the moment. I got a train and a taxi here today. I had to wait for another colleague to pick me up in the early hours of Monday morning. All of this took some time, plus we don't live locally. I suppose it was coming up to two fifteen, two twenty in the morning when we reached Clench. The turning for the barns was coming up on our right and I saw a white BMW come haring out of the lane. As the senior officer, I took the decision to go to the barns first. We went straight to the caravan, expecting to find Carlton Jones. He wasn't there but another young man was and he was clearly dead. I know now that his name was Aaron Swan.

'My next thought was that Carlton was in the white BMW. We raced back and started to look for it. It took a while but we managed to spot it. We didn't use our sirens but we did put our blue lights on and flashed our headlights so the driver knew we were police. Instead of stopping, he sped up. I don't know the roads round here particularly well but this other driver seemed to know them. He led us a right dance so we got behind a bit sometimes before catching up again.

'I knew we'd gone past the outskirts of Devizes and were heading south. I think we drove past a farm and then as we approached a bend in the road, we heard the crash. We narrowly avoided the white BMW as we braked. He'd hit a tree. I got out and went to check the car. I expected Carlton to be in there. I saw the driver was white. I automatically reached for gloves before opening the door and checking for a pulse. I couldn't feel one. I looked in the rest of the car for Carlton but he wasn't there. Then I checked the boot.'

Ferguson paled. 'I had to use my phone torch to see by. I don't ever want to see that again. It's just as well there's no next of kin to identify him. Sorry, I just need a moment.'

He picked up the cup of water again. Stalling again? Bernie wasn't sure. And no next of kin for Carlton. Bernie could never condone his crimes but she was sad he had no family left.

'It wasn't possible to identify Carlton but I was fairly sure it was him. I went back to our car. My colleague had stayed in there. I called my boss and we were told to stand down. This was shortly after two forty-five a.m.'

Ferguson took another sip of water.

Bernie looked at the super who gave a little nod. Time to begin ripping the statement apart.

'How long had Carlton Jones been living in the caravan?' she asked.

'Since the Friday. We'd moved him from a previous address due to safety concerns.'

'And where was that?'

Ferguson shook his head. 'Can't tell you. It's classified.'

'But you'd met him before?'

'Yes. I'd had a few shifts with him.'

'How long had he been out of prison?'

Another shake of the head.

'I think we need to stick with the events of the night in question,' said the police rep.

'For now, maybe,' replied Bernie. 'What did you do after the car crash? Where did you go?'

'We went home.'

'So you left the scene of an accident?'

Ferguson hung his head. 'Yes. Although it wasn't our fault.'

'Wasn't it? You were chasing Lewis Brown. You'd used your lights to let him know you were there. He didn't slow and you pursued.'

Ferguson looked up. 'Yeah, well, that's stupid young men for you.'

'Scared young men too.' Bernie held his gaze until he looked away. 'So, you didn't go back to the barns then? Have a look around?'

'No.'

'No? Weren't you curious as to what had happened? Your protected witness was dead, the driver of the car was dead and there was another dead man back at the caravan. Three young men. Are you even a police officer?'

Ferguson huffed and folded his arms. 'I called it in.'

'You know, you thought Carlton looked bad in the middle of the night; you should have tried seeing him in early morning sunshine. The whole full effect. Naked. Face destroyed by gunshot wounds. Hands and feet missing. Any ideas about that one?'

Ferguson tilted his head so he couldn't see Bernie. 'Probably identification purposes. Plus he had an ankle tracker.'

Ah, thought Bernie. That's why one foot was amputated higher.

'Any other identifying marks?' Bernie already knew Carlton Jones had a tattoo on his wrist from his Peckham days. She wanted to see if DS Ferguson knew too.

'Yes, a tattoo on his wrist.'

'And what about the marks on his torso?'

Ferguson twisted his head back. 'His torso?'

'Yes.' Bernie decided not to enlighten him further.

'I... I don't know about any marks. What kind of marks are we talking about?'

Bernie hesitated. She didn't want to give too much away. 'Cuts.'

'Oh. I don't know. Maybe whoever killed him did that to him.'

'They weren't fresh according to the pathologist.'

'Oh, well, there you go. Probably happened in prison—'

'But they were recent and likely done in the week before his murder. So, I'm going to ask you again – when was Carlton Jones released from prison and where was he living before Friday?'

Ferguson picked up the cup and took another sip of water. 'I can't tell you that.'

'Can't or won't?'

'Both.'

Bernie resisted the urge to sigh. Ferguson was winding her up and he knew it. She was certain what his next answer would be but decided to ask the question anyway.

'Why was Carlton Jones a protected witness?'

Ferguson put the cup down and leaned forward on the desk. He looked directly into Bernie's eyes.

'I'd have thought that was obvious, wouldn't you?'

CHAPTER 32

Bernie put the lid down on the toilet and flushed it. She hadn't been able to hold it together in the interview room as the bile hit her throat. She heard the door to the toilets open. Great. She didn't need anyone else in here to witness her weakness.

'Bernie? It's Kerry. You in here?'

Rising slowly to her feet, Bernie unlocked the cubicle door and came out. Kerry was probably the only person she was willing to see.

'Oh Bernie. Have you been sick? The super told me what happened.'

Bernie washed her hands and then splashed water onto her face.

'I'm so embarrassed,' she said. 'I was trying to keep it all in check during the interview and then...' She shook her head. 'If he'd been more cooperative, not given all the "that's classified" shit, then maybe I'd have handled it better. It's the way he looked at me too. Straight in my eyes, almost as if he was delivering a message.' Bernie gasped. 'Oh God, that's it. Dougie.'

Kerry touched Bernie's arm. 'I don't know what you mean. You're going to have to back up here. The super just said you gagged and ran out of the room. What did this DS say?'

'I asked why Carlton Jones was a protected witness. Ferguson leaned forward, looked me straight in the eye and said, "I'd have thought that was obvious, wouldn't you?" Carlton Jones grew up in Peckham. He was in Danny Ambrose's gang. I think he was supposed to be a prosecution witness against Jack Thornton. That's why he was being protected.

'I know Dougie wasn't there when Carlton Jones was arrested but he led the team. And he's in court this afternoon and Mira's with my grandmother. If Jack Thornton can get to a protected witness, what might he order for Dougie or Mira?'

'He'd be bloody stupid to try that,' Kerry replied. 'Look, you need to take all this to the super and probably the chief constable too. It sounds as though Thornton still has people loyal to him in the force. Do you think this Ferguson guy's involved?'

'I'm not sure. He's being really difficult but some of it is confidential. But I can't get past the fact that he left all the crime scenes. That he was apparently told to leave by his boss, so that we'd have to deal with it. *I'd* have to deal with it.'

Kerry gripped both of Bernie's arms. 'I don't know about Ferguson but we're not going to let Thornton win. You're saying about Dougie but we need to think about you too. I'm coming to court with you on Monday. Anyone tries anything, I'll flip them over my shoulder.'

'Ah, Kerry. What would I do without my little ninja?'

'Not so much of the little, thanks. Go to the chief constable, now. I'll carry on with the timeline. We have the Mercedes registration so we're looking for their route into Clench to check the times Ferguson gave. I'll find a way to unravel him.'

Hannah Drake listened intently as Bernie told her what they had discovered from Ferguson and who she thought might be behind it.

Drake didn't respond straight away. She stood up and opened the door to her PA's office.

'Claire, you can go to lunch now.'

'I was going to go later—'

'Now's good.'

'But I have an optician's appointment booked for one p.m.'

'No problem. Come back after that.'

Hannah Drake waited for the PA to leave before returning to her desk.

'Sorry about that. You don't always know which walls have ears.' Drake leaned back in her chair. 'Thank you for telling me all of that. You're probably wondering if you can trust me. I'd think that too if I were in your position. If it helps, I once was in your position. About ten years ago, I had concerns about another officer. We were both detective inspectors in a large homicide team in London. He had an impressive clear-up rate. Evidence against some suspects appeared circumstantial at best, and set up at worst. A lot confessed far too easily for my liking.

'And then, there was how he handled his team. There were very few women and quite often, they transferred to my team within a matter of months, citing sexist comments and inappropriate touching. Nothing serious like sexual assault but a hand on a lower back, stroking an arm and in one incident, pushing her hair away from her face, caressing her cheek at the same time. Enough to make a female officer feel uncomfortable.

'I thought it was my duty to speak up. So I did. Two things happened. I was offered a Chief Inspector role in uniform – so, a promotion. He was moved sideways to a task force, which in my opinion, was a mistake. Because' – Drake held out her arms – 'here we are today.'

'You worked with Jack Thornton,' Bernie said.

'Yes. As did DS Colin Ferguson, although he was an impressionable DC back then. He still had that white hair though. I recognised him from the CCTV footage but I think you might have guessed that anyway.'

'I knew something wasn't right.'

'I spent most of yesterday with the Met Commissioner. He's as keen as me to rid the police of corrupt officers. I was given full access to Carlton Jones's file and Dennis Pinner's. I've asked the same for your team. I can't be sure that Colin Ferguson's involved but I believe someone from the witness protection service is. If your team finds evidence against anyone from the WPS, then we'll hand it over to Internal Affairs. In the meantime, you will go home.'

Bernie stood up. 'What? No. Why is this being done to me again? It's like you all think I can't handle it.'

'Bernie, please sit down. I have two priorities right now – find out who killed these young men and keep Dougie and Mira safe today. If you give me your grandmother's address, I'll ask for a patrol to go past, maybe even a car in her road on surveillance. We can get a message to Dougie and arrange for someone to take him straight to your grandmother's house afterwards. No going on public transport.'

Bernie's stomach lurched as she thought of the two people she loved most in the world. She would willingly trade herself for their safety.

'But let's not forget that the defence has also called you, thinking that you can be intimidated into saying good things about

Thornton. I know you will speak the truth. You will be better than I was ten years ago. If I'd pressed it more, you might never have met Jack Thornton. Please trust me. I will lead the case in your absence. That will send a signal back to Thornton. I'm not here to play any more. Go get the bastard, Bernie.'

CHAPTER 33

Bernie paced her little cottage. Her first instinct had been to jump in her car and drive to London but Hannah Drake had warned her against that.

'Go straight home and stay there. Don't go outside your village this weekend. I'll make sure someone drives you to London on Monday and brings you back afterwards. Tell the truth and we'll finally see Jack Thornton put away.'

As much as she was concerned for her family's safety, it was also the 'telling the truth' part that was worrying Bernie. So many memories from that time were flooding her brain – good as well as bad. She had to be careful and Jack knew that. No wonder she'd been chosen to be a defence witness. She had her own reputation to hide and protect.

As the memories continued to play like a TV show in her head, she decided to write some of them down. No doubt she'd be asked about her undercover role in Peckham. Like Ferguson earlier, she would have to be careful about how much to reveal.

As she wrote, things came back to her that had seemed unimportant at the time but with hindsight, became significant. How she was chosen for the role, the inadequate training she received and how, despite being of dual heritage, being raised in a white household meant she was not prepared to become part of a black community. It was like she was set up to fail.

It was dark outside when she heard Dougie's car pull up. Bernie raced out the front door.

'Are you OK?' she asked as he opened the car door.

'Yes, we're fine. Mira nodded off about thirty minutes ago but I'm sure she'll wake up soon. She's already in her sleepsuit for bed.'

As Dougie got out, Bernie threw her arms around him.

'Whoa. I don't normally get this greeting. What's going on?'

'I'm just glad you're safe. You got driven back to Granny's from court, right?'

'Yes. Another officer offered me a lift.' Dougie frowned. 'It was a bit chaotic when I got to court at lunchtime. There should have been another witness this morning but he didn't turn up. And now you're concerned about my safety. Bernie, what's going on?'

Bernie lowered her voice. 'They were right to be worried about the missing witness.'

A grizzling noise came from inside the car.

'I'll feed her and then we can talk over dinner.'

Bernie opened the passenger door next to Mira.

'Hey, little one. Mummy's here.'

Bernie took Mira out of her car seat.

'Mama.'

They clung to each other.

No one will hurt my baby, Bernie thought. No one.

'Shit,' said Dougie. 'The missing witness was your dead man in the boot of the BMW. And that was Carlton Jones, the guy we arrested last summer. That is a massive screw-up.'

Bernie picked up hers and Dougie's empty plates. 'You're telling me. I left my team looking at endless hours of CCTV, trying to spot any holes in the story that Ferguson has given us.'

'Do you think the chief constable will let you back in on the case?'

Bernie shrugged. 'If she does, it won't be until after I've given evidence on Monday.'

'How are you getting there now? You can't get the train. I'll drive if you want me to.'

'No, you must stay here with Mira. Kerry's coming with me.'

Bernie put the plates next to the sink before turning on the hot tap.

'God, I never thought I'd be this torn. I want to protect you both.' Concern flashed across Dougie's face.

'How was it? I know you can't give details.'

'It was OK. I treated it like any other court appearance. I was there to give evidence against the defendant. The fact that he was a police officer was irrelevant as far as I was concerned. The defence barrister gave up with me in the end.' Dougie took Bernie's hand. 'Just tell the truth and stand your ground. And then Thornton will be out of our lives.'

Tell the truth. Bernie thought about the memories that she'd written down, the ones she could share in court. The others would stay locked up in her brain forever. She'd never be free of Jack Thornton.

CHAPTER 34

Monday

Bernie's phone buzzed. She picked it up to turn off the alarm but then realised that it was Kerry calling her.

'Kerry?'

'Bernie, I'm so sorry to call you this early. I have a huge problem. Debs started bleeding last night so we're at the hospital. I can't leave her which means I can't drive you. Matt can take you but he can't stay. We'll arrange for someone to bring you home though. OK? We won't leave you on your own.'

'Oh Kerry, don't worry about me. How are you and Debs?'

'Debs is pretty distraught.' There was a catch in Kerry's voice as she tried to hold back tears. 'I'm trying to be strong for both of us. I know you sort of believe in the big man upstairs so, send up a prayer for us, please.'

Bernie's heart ached. Kerry had never asked her to do that before. If she was honest, the faith she had been brought up with was hanging in tatters but she couldn't say no to Kerry.

'Of course. And I'll text Paul and Anna. They're the ones with a hotline to God. Go and focus on Debs and give her my love. Bye.'

'Bye, Bernie.'

'Who was that?' said a sleepy Dougie.

'Kerry. Debs is in hospital. She can't come to London with me. Matt's going to take me and they'll find someone to bring me home.'

'Hmm. OK.' Dougie turned over and fell back to sleep.

Bernie rubbed her stomach as an anxious knot formed inside her. It wasn't the car journeys where she'd miss Kerry. It was the Old Bailey, knowing that Kerry wasn't in the waiting room for her. She was going to go against the defence barrister and she really needed an ally to help her with that.

'Perhaps you could pray about that too,' said a familiar voice in her head.

'Pops,' Bernie whispered.

'Bernadette Susan Noel, you know what you need to do. You give this day to the Lord and you give him Debs and Kerry too. An ally will come.'

Tears rolled down Bernie's cheeks. She hadn't thought about her deceased grandfather for a while. He'd been at her bedside in ICU after she'd been stabbed and then in court when she gave evidence. If nothing else, she'd have the memory of him with her today.

The journey to London had been surprisingly uneventful for a Monday morning. Bernie had to guide Matt round London. She hoped he'd find his way back out again.

She sipped the coffee she'd bought from the cafeteria at the Old Bailey. It was hot and wet but not much taste. Even the custody suite coffee was better than this. She'd like to have brought in her own but that wasn't allowed. Sneaking out for lunch would probably be impossible and definitely unwise. So, she had more cafeteria food and drink to look forward to.

A woman in a black gown and a white wig swept into the witness room and beamed at her.

'Bernadette? I'm Bella Fontaine. We spoke on the phone. Thank you for coming. I'm the second barrister for the defence team. Roger Howe-Turner is the main defence barrister and he'll be asking you questions this morning. We might make it to cross-examination before lunch but if not, definitely after lunch. Hopefully it'll all be wrapped up by the end of today's session and you can get home in time for your baby. Any questions?'

Do you ever breathe? Bernie thought.

'I do have one. Although, it's more of a request. I'd like a screen up please, around the witness box.'

Bella Fontaine jolted back. 'Really? Why? If you were a prosecution witness then I'd understand but you're here for the defence. It would look bad for our client if you had a screen.'

'It's got nothing to do with your client and everything to do with me being a serving police officer. I won't give evidence without a screen. I don't know who's going to be in the courtroom.'

'It's a closed court. Only people relevant to the case are allowed in and some journalists but they're not allowed to report until after the verdict. You'd be quite safe.'

Bernie remembered what Dougie said – stand your ground.

'No screen, no witness.'

Bella Fontaine huffed. 'Very well. I'll ask the judge but he won't be happy with such a late request.'

'He probably wouldn't be happy that I've only had one week's notice for this court appearance either.'

Bella Fontaine folded her hands together. 'Let's get through this, shall we? Then after today, it will all be over.'

Bernie gave a tight smile. Oh Bella, how little you know, she thought. Until we get the evidence to prove that Thornton is behind three recent deaths, it's very much not over.

Bernie stood in the witness box, a red curtain screening her from the main part of the court. All she could see was the judge, the jury and the barristers. But she could sense Jack Thornton, in the way a gazelle might sense a predator. Her hand was on the Bible.

'I swear by Almighty God that the evidence I shall give shall be the truth, the whole truth, and nothing but the truth.'

After removing her hand from the Bible, she gripped the sides of the box. She'd tell the truth. But maybe not all of it.

PART TWO

CHAPTER 35

Then – Six years before

PC Bernie Noel flipped her warrant card at the man on the hotel reception desk.

'Noise complaint?' she said.

'Room twenty.' He gestured with his head to the stairs. 'Third floor. Lift's out of action.'

That didn't surprise Bernie. It wasn't her first time here and the place was very run down. In fact, the word 'hotel' was a bit of a stretch in describing it. The walls might have been white once but now they were a dirty grey, the carpet threadbare and all the surfaces felt greasy to touch. Bernie avoided opening the door to the stairs with her hand and used her hip instead to push it. Despite the 'No Smoking' signs, the stairwell smelt of cigarettes.

It didn't take Bernie long to find room twenty. The corridor was silent and her knock echoed as she rapped her knuckles on the door.

A man in his mid-forties swung the door open. He was good-looking with salt-and-pepper hair. He was wearing a towel around his waist and nothing else.

'Can I help you?' he asked.

'There's been a noise complaint, sir.'

'Has there? It's all quiet here. Although, I think that might change in a minute.' He reached out and grabbed Bernie's arm and pulled her into the room. His breath was hot on her face. 'Mind you, if I remember correctly, it's usually you who makes all the noise, PC Noel.'

Bernie kicked the sheet off her. It was a hot day in June and there was no air-con in the hotel room. She'd been coming here most weeks since the beginning of the year. It was the Christmas party that had set everything off. Having an affair with Inspector Gareth Ashby had never been part of her plan. Each time she climbed the stairs (the lift had never worked), she'd tell herself it would be the last time. He was married. It had to end. But he'd sweet-talk her round, tell her his marriage was over, they slept in separate rooms, he was staying for the children's sake but they were almost adults. He'd leave his wife next year.

Bernie turned on her side to face him. He'd been away for a couple of weeks in Spain with his family and was tanned almost all over. She traced her finger down his chest.

'Missed you while you were away,' she said.

'Missed you too.'

Bernie doubted that. He'd looked pretty happy in the holiday photos on Facebook. For a police officer's wife, his partner had very little privacy settings on her account, especially photographs. Bernie wasn't sure if that was naivety or a deliberate ploy to show the world how happy her husband was in her company. To show Bernie. Or any other woman.

'Bernie, I have something to tell you.'

Oh God, she knows, Bernie thought.

'I'll announce it properly this evening when we start shift—'

'You're leaving?'

Gareth paused. 'No. You are. You passed your DC exams and a placement has opened for you. But it means leaving. Joining a completely different team.'

Bernie couldn't quite believe what she was hearing. She'd been trying for a couple of years to pass her detective exams but kept missing by a few marks. And now she'd done it. But did she really have to move police stations? She propped herself up so she could see his face.

'Isn't there a space on CID at our nick? Why do I have to move?'

'Bernie, a great opportunity has come up for you. You'll be working with a prestigious team.'

'Where? Who with?'

Gareth didn't make eye contact with her as he spoke. 'You'll be working in Peckham on a task force with DI Jack Thornton. I can't tell you much more about it at the moment.'

'What about us?'

He sighed. 'We won't be able to meet any more. We've had a great time, Bernie, but all good things must come to an end.'

'That's a load of crap and you know it. Your wife's found out, hasn't she?'

'Bernie—'

'Hasn't she?'

'Yes.'

'So, you're sending me to the other side of London so you don't have to look at me any more. Never mind the fact that I have lots of mates at the station and it'll be harder to see them. Fuck you.'

Bernie got out of the bed, gathered up her clothes and went to the bathroom. The water pressure for the shower was woefully inadequate but she managed to wash herself clean.

She came out, dressed, to find him still in bed, looking at his phone.

'Did you ever care about me?' she asked.

He put his phone down. 'Yes. Of course. I care about you a lot. I care enough to let you go and move to a team that's going to transform your career. Once you've served with DI Jack Thornton, life will never be the same again for you. You can trust me on that one.'

Bernie shook her head. 'If you really cared about me, you'd find a way to see me.'

The room was packed. The hot June day had turned into a hot June night and Bernie already felt damp in her uniform. She could barely bring herself to look at Inspector Ashby as he read out the pairings for patrol that night.

'Finally, I have some good news that's also a bit sad,' said the inspector. 'Our amazing Bernie has passed her detective exams and is now a detective constable.'

There was a round of applause and a loud cheer. A few people clapped Bernie on the back.

'That's the good news,' he continued. 'The sad part is that she'll be moving to pastures new next week and this is her last shift.'

Bernie flicked her eyes up. He hadn't told her that part. Just how quickly did he want her out of his life?

'So, those of you who feel up to it in the morning, we'll have a farewell breakfast. Right, stay safe everyone.'

'Yes, boss,' the night shift chorused as they got out of their seats. Penny, an older colleague who'd been Bernie's partner when she first started on the beat, came over to her.

'Congratulations, Bernie. I knew you'd do it. You're going to make a fabulous detective. Where are you going?'

'Peckham. Not sure what I'm doing but I'll be with DI Jack Thornton.'

Another officer, Larry, leaned over. 'Did you say DI Jack Thornton? Bloody hell, Bernie, who did you sleep with to get that gig?'

Bernie's cheeks burned. She hoped it wasn't obvious to the other two.

'Larry! That's a terrible thing to say,' Penny said.

'Yeah, sorry, Bernie. Well done. Thornton did a great job at Project Trident so I'm sure whatever he's doing now will be excellent. Good on ya. See you at breakfast.'

Penny and Larry left and Bernie saw the new recruit waiting for her by the door. He'd only been with her for a few weeks.

'So, you're abandoning me,' he said, as she approached.

'Sorry. It's all happened so fast. I only knew myself today.'

'It's all right. I'm sure you'll be great at your new job.'

'Thanks.'

I hope so too, Bernie thought. Especially as I don't actually know what it is.

CHAPTER 36

Then

A week later, Bernie found herself in a packed briefing room. A middle-aged man with sandy coloured hair, dazzling blue eyes and a healed broken nose, stood at the front waiting for the noise to quieten down.

'OK. I think everyone has arrived now so we can start,' he said. The room became silent. 'My name is DI Jack Thornton. Most of you have been working with me for a while but we have a few new people that I'll introduce later. Welcome to Operation Willow. We're a task force that has come out of Project Trident, focusing on drugs and gangs in the Peckham area.'

Thornton clicked on his laptop and a slide appeared on the interactive whiteboard. 'We're looking into this gang to begin with. SE15, named after their postcode, and previously known as the Peckham Panthers. Apparently, postcodes are now cooler names.'

Thornton clicked again. A young black man was shown. 'Danny Ambrose is the leader of SE15. We have intel that shows he's dealing a large amount of drugs in the area. Unsurprisingly, his mother's flat, where he still lives with her and his two brothers, is always clean when we raid it.

'We've been building a case against Ambrose for quite some time but hard evidence is proving difficult to come by. So, it's time for a new tactic. We're going in. We already have an informant in the gang itself but we've noticed that Danny Ambrose appears to have a hold over some of the teenage girls in the area. We believe he's using them to hide drug supplies and possibly weapons too. We need to get a female officer close to them, gain their trust, find the intel and then pass it back to us.'

Bernie looked around the room and her heart started to beat faster. There were a few ethnic minority male officers but no females, except her. Surely Thornton wasn't talking about her?

'So, to that end, I'd like to welcome DC Bernadette Noel to the team.'

All eyes were on Bernie as murmurs of 'hello' rippled around the room. She gave a faint smile but was struggling to process what Thornton was saying. He hadn't said it directly to her but if he was saying what she thought, then she would be going undercover. She wasn't trained for that.

'And I'll introduce the two other new members of the team – DC Ben Harper, who'll be working on surveillance, and Lisa Gower, who'll be joining the HOLMES team. We'll need all that new intelligence collated as quickly as possible.'

Another click. A photo of a tattoo of a black panther.

'This is why they were called the Peckham Panthers to begin with. All the males in the gang have this tattoo somewhere. Most have it on the inside of their arm, by their wrist. Some have it on their ankle. Danny Ambrose has a large one on his back. It's rarely seen as he doesn't often remove his shirt in public, even on hot days like this. So, if a teenage girl says that she's seen it, it's likely he's had sexual relations with her and therefore, likely she has some of his stash. So, that's something for you to listen out for, DC Noel.'

Bernie thought her heart was going to explode. This wasn't what she signed up for. Heck, she hadn't signed up for any of it. It was her inspector who had sent her packing to Jack Thornton, so she could be 'out of sight, out of mind'. Bernie appreciated what Thornton was trying to do in Peckham but she couldn't be involved. No way.

She waited for the briefing to end before approaching her new detective inspector.

'Hi, sir, I'm DC Noel. Could I have a word with you in private please?'

Thornton smiled at her. 'Of course, Bernadette.'

'I prefer Bernie.'

'So I've heard.'

Bernie faltered. What else had he heard?

'Shall we go to my office?'

Bernie followed Thornton down the corridor to his office. He had the build of a rugby player and she wondered if that's where he got his broken nose.

There were piles of paperwork on Thornton's desk.

'Apologies for the state of the place. I've changed offices and need another filing cabinet. It's a wonder we still have so much paperwork when most of it is online. Anyway, what can I do for you, Bernie?'

Thornton gestured to her to sit down while he leaned against his desk. She was immediately at a height disadvantage.

Bernie twisted her hands. 'I'm very honoured to be asked onto your team, especially as I've only just qualified, and I think that's where the problem lies.'

'What problem?'

'Forgive me if I'm wrong, sir, but from what you just described in the briefing, it sounds as though you want me to go undercover.'

'Yes.'

'But I'm not trained for that. It takes months normally to prepare for this role and I've just come straight off the beat—'

Thornton raised his hand.

'Let me stop you there, Bernie. The fact that you've just come off the beat is a good thing. You got to know your local area, how to speak to the people who lived there, how to interact with them. From what I've heard about you, you were well-loved. People trusted you. There were times when people gave you valuable information about crimes and quite often, that came from black members of your community, even people who were normally antagonistic to the police. Yes, officers often take months to prepare but they don't have what you have – a natural way with the public.

'Now, the other thing at play here, is that we're time pressured. Intel suggests that Ambrose will be making a move over the summer holidays to shift a lot of gear. We need you in place for that. We'll develop this more but the basic premise of your legend is that you're a summer youth worker, brought in to engage with the local teenagers at a youth outreach centre. You will have six weeks maximum to find that information.'

'And what if I don't find anything?'

'You will, Bernie. I have faith in you. Not least, because from tomorrow, you'll start an intensive three-week course on undercover work and surveillance. Ben Harper's going on it too.'

'He doesn't have experience either?' Bernie couldn't believe what she was hearing.

'He has some but more training is always useful. Now, I hope

I've allayed your fears. If you don't mind, I've got lots to get on with and you've got a team to meet. I'll see you later on.'

Bernie was ushered out and the door closed behind her. As she walked back along the corridor, she felt as though her fears weren't allayed at all. If anything, they were greater. What kind of DI ran an operation like this?

CHAPTER 37

Then

'You know why you got this job, right?' DC Ben Harper asked Bernie.

They were into their second week of training and Bernie thought her head would explode with all the extra information being loaded into her brain.

'No. Not a clue,' she lied. She wasn't about to tell Ben about her affair.

'There aren't many black female officers, are there? That's why. You're the only one who fits the bill. Well, almost. I'm guessing you're mixed race. So, you're probably the only one who knows how to talk to these kids.'

'So, being "mixed race" means I know how to walk onto a council estate in Peckham and immediately be able to engage with the kids there.' Bernie shook her head. 'I was brought up in a white household, with my white mum and my white grandparents. I never knew my father or his family. Most of my friends are white. I don't know what it is to be black other than trying to deal with my curly hair. If the DI thinks he's found a winning ticket in me, then he's very much mistaken.'

Ben tilted his head. He was a bit older than Bernie and had more experience in covert operations than her. 'That's what you use then.'

'I have no idea what you're talking about.'

'Going back to your roots. You want to know what it's like to be black. To know who you truly are. The girls will lap it up. They might tease you but there'll be some who want to help. What kind of food did you eat growing up?'

'Pretty traditional British food. Roasts, shepherd's pie, fish and chips, sausages and mash. Granny eventually branched out and included pasta. But no Afro-Caribbean food if that's what you mean.'

'Yeah, it is what I mean. That's what will get you into their homes. The mums will want to cook for you and you can have a little sniff around the houses at the same time.'

Bernie shuddered. She hated this. Hated the deception. Was it too late to back out? She hadn't told her family what her new role was about, just that she'd become a detective constable. Her mother had been thrilled. Granny had given her usual muted response, not that Bernie had expected any praise. Only Pops had looked at her as though he could see straight into her soul and see her turmoil.

Out of earshot from her mother and grandmother, he'd said, 'Bernie, I'm very proud of you. But I get the feeling that you're worried about this next step.'

'You're going to say that God's with me, aren't you?'

Pops had chuckled. 'Of course. But I'm with you too. I know you have a team that's meant to look after you but if you ever need me, call me, and I'll get in my car and I will come to you, wherever you are.'

'Oh Pops.'

Bernie had thrown her arms around him and squeezed tight.

'I'm going to be away for a while with this job, Pops, and I don't know if I'll be allowed to contact you.'

Pops had pulled back from her. 'So, we'll have a secret message that you can send me. How about, "can you buy me an iced bun for tea"? I know how much you love iced buns, all pastries in fact.'

Bernie had laughed. 'True.'

'I mean it, Bernie. I'll come and get you if you're in trouble.'

As much as Bernie loved the idea of Pops being there for her, she couldn't ask him for help. She'd be reliant on Ben and the rest of the team for support.

'Earth to Bernie.'

She snapped back to Ben.

'Does that sound like a good idea? Get a dinner invitation and then you can snoop?'

Bernie gave a slight nod.

'Great. I'll add that to the plan. Were you good at sport at school? Play in any teams?'

'Netball.'

'Excellent. You can start a netball team.'

'What do you mean? I haven't played for years.'

'Bernie, you have to engage with these girls. They're not going to sit and spill their guts with you. Team sports are a great way to build respect and trust.'

'And what are you going to be doing while I try to build trust and get these girls to talk?'

'Watching and listening. So I'll know if you deviate from the plan or screw up your legend. You'll wear a very small wire. Remember to take it off at night. Otherwise I'll hear you snoring while you sleep. And don't worry, I won't listen when you go to the loo. I'm not that voyeuristic.'

Bernie wasn't so sure about that. 'Where will I live?'

'There's a small flat attached to the youth centre. You'll be there.'

'And you?'

'Will be somewhere else. But not far.'

'And if I need to talk to DI Thornton?'

Ben looked up. 'Ideally, you don't. Everything you say on the wire will go to him.'

'But if he needs to tell me something—'

'Then we'll get a message to you. And don't try to work out who the informant in the gang is. You'll put his life in danger if you do. Right, tell me your legend again.'

Bernie sighed. She kept making mistakes when she did this and she knew she had to keep practising until she got it right.

'My name's Libby Smith. I'm twenty-four. I've been doing some shitty jobs—'

'Don't say shitty.'

'I'm keeping it real for the kids. OK. I've had some boring jobs – worked at McDonald's, Tesco and in offices as a cleaner. Fed up with my life going nowhere so I'm looking for a more worthwhile job. I'm trying youth work to see if I like it. Might even do a social work degree. Grew up with my mum in South West London. She's white. Never knew my dad. My favourite food is any cake or pastry from a bakery. I can't cook – and no, I didn't learn at McDonald's. I cleared the tables and cleaned the toilets. That's all I was trusted with. At school, I liked Art and playing netball, and that was about it.'

Bernie shrugged at Ben. 'I think that's it.'

Ben shook his head. 'Favourite film, book, colour?'

'I'll just keep my own for those.'

'So?'

'*Inception, Bridget Jones's Diary* and blue.'

'Really? Inception I get – it's a cool movie. But *Bridget Jones's Diary?*'

'What do you want me to say? *Jude the Obscure?* God, Ben. It's for six weeks with teenage girls. I'm not pretending to be an English teacher.'

'Maybe not. But if you stuff up, those girls will tell Danny Ambrose. And if that happens, you better hope we can get you out in time.'

CHAPTER 38

Now

'Detective Inspector Noel, can you please explain how you know the defendant?'

With a curtain next to her, shielding her from Thornton, Bernie was a bit more confident. She looked at the jury as she answered.

'I worked with Jack Thornton for a short period of time.'

'How short is short?'

'Around ten weeks.'

Bernie looked back at the defence barrister, Roger Howe-Turner. Did he have any idea how ridiculous this would all sound to the jury?

'And why was it for this time period?'

'It was for a specific operation.'

Bernie was determined to keep her answers short and frustrate the barrister. It was already beginning to have an effect.

'Could you elaborate a little further perhaps?'

'I'm not sure how much I'm allowed to divulge about the operation.'

The judge coughed. 'Detective inspector, I appreciate that some things may need to remain confidential but perhaps you could tell us when you worked with the defendant and where, and the ranks that both of you held at the time.'

Bernie inclined her head to the judge. She wasn't about to piss him off.

'Of course. I worked with the defendant six years ago, from the middle of June until the end of August. The operation was based in Peckham. I was a detective constable and Jack Thornton was a detective inspector.'

'And at that time, what were your thoughts on Jack Thornton?' asked Howe-Turner.

Bernie picked up on the wording used – 'at that time'. Cunning, she thought.

'At that time, I thought, workwise, that he was determined, passionate about his job and concerned for his team. As an individual,' Bernie began, then paused. Memories bombarded her. His smile, twinkly eyes and his charm. 'He was quite brilliant. Charismatic. No matter what doubts you had, he'd find a way of turning them around.'

Bernie's eyes dropped. She couldn't quite believe the words coming out of her mouth but they were true. At the time, that was how she felt. But not any more. Not now that she'd had time to think it all through.

'But with hindsight—'

'Thank you, detective inspector. You've answered my question,' said Roger Howe-Turner.

Bernie looked at the defence desk. Bella Fontaine was glaring at her. Bernie wanted to laugh. *If you think I'm bad now, just wait until the prosecution starts. I'll sing like a bird.*

'The operation you spoke about,' said Howe-Turner, 'it was covert and you played an important role in that. Could you tell us more about that role, please?'

Bernie looked at the judge. 'Do I have to answer that?'

'State the relevance, please,' said the judge.

'Of course, your honour. The witness has already suggested that this operation was sensitive. The role she played demonstrates the importance of her relationship with the defendant.'

'I'll allow.'

Bernie looked carefully at the jury before she answered. Seven women and five men. Of the women, one was Asian and one was black. Of the men, two were Asian, the rest were white. It wasn't a very diverse jury and the lack of black men concerned her.

'Detective inspector?'

Bernie brought her gaze back to the defence barrister.

'The judge has ruled that you should answer the question.'

Bernie breathed in slowly. After giving evidence against Danny Ambrose, she'd hoped she'd never have to tell this story again.

'I was placed, covertly, as a summer youth worker on a council housing estate in Peckham. My role was to gather information about a local gang.'

'You were to befriend the gang members?'

'No. The girls who hung around them.'

A face appeared in Bernie's mind. A dazzling smile that was there at the beginning of the summer holidays but gone forever before the end. Leesa. Bernie gripped the stand. She couldn't allow a panic attack to hit now. Screw Thornton. She wouldn't give evidence for him. She'd give it for Leesa.

Bernie released her grip.

'Jack Thornton believed the girls were hiding drugs and weapons for the gang. My job was to find out which girls so that raids could be planned. As a covert officer, I had to trust that Jack was right about this. One false move and I could be dead.'

'So, you had faith in Jack Thornton as your senior officer? That he had your back?'

Roger Howe-Turner was putting words into her mouth and she didn't like it. Two can play at that game.

'At that time, yes.'

CHAPTER 39

Then

First day of the holidays and it was pouring with rain. Bernie watched it stream down the windows in the youth centre. She couldn't see all of the Fourways Estate but she could see the twenty-storey tower dominating the skyline. The rest of the buildings were only three storeys and the ground-floor flats even had little gardens, with splashes of colour. The graffiti that appeared to daub nearly all the shop shutters in Rye Lane was restricted to one wall of the youth centre on the estate. The dedicated space allowed for creativity in return for keeping the other buildings clear. It was mostly respected. Bernie had only spotted a handful of tags when she wandered around a few days before. The multi-use games area had been installed the year before, giving a much-needed outlet for the kids to expel their energy. But not today. Only a handful of younger children were in, playing a board game. There had been an Xbox but it had been stolen. No one nicked the board games.

'Crap weather, eh?' said a voice next to Bernie. It was Tanya, the leader of the youth centre. She was black, in her forties but looked younger in her bright fuchsia T-shirt and black cycling shorts.

She seemed unaware of Bernie's real reason for being there but presumably someone high up in the council knew.

'Yeah. Is it always this quiet?'

'No. Weather isn't helping but most of the teens will still be in bed. They'll be in after lunch.'

'Do you get a good mix of boys and girls?'

Tanya shook her head. 'Nah. Mostly the girls but we'll have Joshua. He has Down's syndrome. You'll love him. He's a gorgeous boy. Same can't be said for his brothers though.'

'What are they like, then?'

'They're older. Think they're "it". Especially Danny.'

Bernie's ears pricked up. Was this Danny Ambrose?

'How many brothers does Joshua have?'

'Two. Danny and Zac. But they don't want to look after Joshua while their mother's at work. He'll be here soon enough.' Tanya sighed. 'If the weather stays like this, then I don't think you'll be playing netball this afternoon.'

'Hmm. You're probably right. Any other suggestions I could do with any girls that turn up?'

'I would say nails but quite a few of them have signed up for netball. Not sure they'll all come but there's sixteen on the list. But they won't want to break their nails.'

Bernie thought back to her teenage years and the clothes designs she used to spend hours on.

'Maybe we could design some clothes or make jewellery,' Bernie suggested. 'I saw a bead kit in the storeroom.'

Tanya tapped Bernie on the arm. 'That's not such a bad idea. We've got a sewing machine.'

'Oh, I'm not so good at the sewing part.'

'You don't need to be. We've got Leesa for that.'

'Leesa?'

'She's a lovely girl. Pastor's daughter. Just done her GCSEs and she took Textiles. That girl's a whizz on the sewing machine. I know she'll be in because she promised to help with Joshua. You might be onto a winner there. Maybe you could organise a fashion show. We've got some old clothes. You can do whatever you want with them.'

Bernie thought for a moment. It had been a while since she'd done any drawing, let alone designing, but maybe she could leave that to the girls.

'OK. We can give it a go.'

A few hours later, eight teenage girls and one boy were chattering away as they designed clothes or jewellery.

'Are we really going to make these?' one girl asked.

'Possibly,' Bernie replied. 'Have a look at the clothes we have over there and material. See what you can come up with. Jewellery might be harder. Don't think we've got any gold or jewels stashed away.'

'My brother has,' said the boy.

'Ssh, Joshua,' said one of the girls.

'But he has. He's got gold chains he buys for my mum.'

Bernie stayed quiet. She didn't want to say anything that might lead Joshua on. Plus she knew that evidence from a Down's syndrome child might not be considered reliable. But one of the girls might say something.

'Libby, what do you think of this?' said Joshua.

A piece of paper was thrust in Bernie's face. She still wasn't used to her new name. She looked at the drawing. It was definitely an animal and black in colour but that's all she could work out.

'That's great, Joshua. Tell me more about it.'

'It's a panther. My brothers have them on their bodies. But I want one on a T-shirt. Can we make it?'

'We can try. Although, I'm not sure the best way to do it.'

'I know,' said a voice behind Bernie.

'Leesa!'

Joshua threw his arms around the teenage girl. She was tall with beautiful long braids held back in a ponytail. She gave Bernie a dazzling smile.

'You must be Libby. I'm Leesa. Tanya was just telling me about the clothes show you want to do.'

'I think it's more the clothes show that Tanya wants. I'm here to teach netball really.'

'I'm sure we could do both. So, Joshua, you want a black panther on a T-shirt. We could either cut one out of black material and sew it on, or we could make a stencil and use fabric paint. What would you prefer?'

'What's quickest?'

Leesa laughed. 'You don't like waiting, do you? Well, if there's a white T-shirt and fabric paint, then that'll be fastest. Have a look through the bag of clothes and see.'

'I can draw the stencil,' said Bernie.

'I bet Leesa can draw it better,' said one of the girls. 'She's probably seen Danny's in the flesh.'

'I have not,' Leesa replied, indignantly.

'Zac's then.'

'Zac's tattoo is on his wrist. Same as Carlton Jones. Everyone at school has seen them.'

Bernie started drawing the panther but listened to the conversation, hoping that Ben could hear it too.

'I've seen Danny's,' said another girl, quietly.

'Shit, no,' said another. 'You fucked Danny?'

Bernie raised her head slightly so she could see who the girl was. She was pretty and looked younger than Leesa. Was she underage for sex?

'Shut up. I don't want everyone to know.'

'Was it good?'

There was silence. Bernie wondered if her presence at the table was stopping the conversation. But she really needed to know what this girl was going to say. And she needed her name.

Leesa moved round the table to the girl.

'Hey, Goldie,' she said, 'it's OK. You don't have to tell us anything.'

Goldie whispered back but Bernie just heard her. 'It hurt. I didn't know it would hurt so much.'

'You don't have to do it again.'

'He doesn't want me anyway. Said I was shit at it.'

'It was your first time. It won't always be that bad. Try to wait for someone who really cares about you. Now, what do you want to make?'

Bernie took a mental note of Goldie's name but it didn't sound promising. If Danny didn't like her sexually, then she thought it unlikely he would hide drugs at Goldie's home. But Leesa was someone who clearly knew things and was the person Bernie needed to keep close.

CHAPTER 40

Then

Bernie blew her whistle. Fourteen girls collapsed, laughing, onto the hard netball court.

'That was so much fun,' said one girl.

'I'm so unfit,' said another.

'That's because you ain't done PE for months.'

Bernie smiled. It was the third training session she'd done with the girls and they were really getting into it. She was still surprised that so many had turned up but she'd heard Leesa had spread the word about the 'new, cool youth worker'. It saddened her to think that if the girls knew who she really was, they'd never be in the same room as her, let alone enjoying her company.

'You all did really well today. Same time tomorrow?' Bernie said.

'Can we do the fashion stuff tomorrow? My muscles ache already,' said the unfit girl.

Bernie laughed. 'Let's see how we're all feeling tomorrow.'

'Oi! What you ladies doing lying on your backs? You waiting for me?' said a male voice.

The girls sat up quickly and Bernie noticed the playful mood disappear. She turned and looked at the young man behind her. No one had to tell her who it was. She recognised him from the photo at the briefing – Danny Ambrose. Two younger men stood behind him, and then further back, Bernie spotted Joshua.

'Hi, Joshua,' Bernie said. 'Do you want to come and play catch with us?'

'He can't fuckin' do that,' said Danny. 'I'm happy to play catch with you though.' He gave her an appraising look, starting at her feet and working his way up.

Bernie was in two minds whether to scowl at him but she didn't want to antagonise him, not least because he might have a weapon.

'If you want to play, then it'll be netball.'

Danny looked at the other boys.

'Zac, Carlton – wanna play netball?' They nodded and he turned back to Bernie. 'We're up for that.'

'Know how to play?'

'Sure.'

'You'll need four girls on your team. Then you need to sort out your positions.'

'Positions?'

'Yes. Centre, goal attack, goal defence, goal shooter—'

'Yeah, yeah, yeah, we know.'

As the boys swaggered onto the court, it was clear to Bernie they didn't know what they were doing and they weren't listening to the girls. Within seconds of starting play, she blew her whistle.

'What?' asked Danny.

'This isn't basketball. You can't run and bounce the ball. You must be standing still when you throw it and you have three seconds to pass to another player. You're allowed one bounce to a fellow player. And you must stay in your designated areas.'

'What the fuck are those?'

'I thought you knew how to play netball.'

'I do!'

'If you're not sure, ask one of the girls. And you'll play better if you pull your jeans up. They'll end up around your ankles otherwise.'

Bernie knew she was pushing it when she saw Danny's middle finger out of the corner of her eye. But that's what was going to work with him. Banter.

She blew her whistle and play continued. Bernie smiled as the girls outplayed the boys to begin with. Slowly, though, the boys picked up the rules and one of them scored a goal.

'Go, Zac!' Joshua cried from the sidelines.

Bernie got lost in refereeing the match. It didn't feel as though she was there with a gang leader and his drug-dealing buddies. Instead, they were a bunch of young people, having fun playing netball on a sunny day in July.

Having already played a match before, the girls were drooping so Bernie called time after the first fifteen minutes. The score was one all.

'That weren't bad,' Danny said to Bernie. 'Are we allowed to play again?'

'That would be up to the girls.'

'Bit sexist. Girls can play football.'

'It's more that it's time for them. To have a chance to hang out together in a safe space.'

Danny leaned in closer. 'They'd be safe with me. You too.' He gave her another lingering look.

'I'm too old for you.'

'I like a woman with experience. These girls are good, right, but sometimes they bounce around like I'm a bouncy castle, you know what I'm saying?'

Bernie looked Danny directly in the eye. 'I'm a youth worker and it would be inappropriate for me to engage in any kind of relationship, other than professional friendship, with anyone attending the youth centre.'

Danny grinned. 'I ain't attending the youth centre.'

'But you're here now.'

'Yeah. Joshua told me about you. Had to check out who's looking after my little bro.'

Bernie kept her breathing even but her heart was beating overtime. Her job was to engage the girls, not Danny.

'You can play netball once a week if the girls agree.'

Danny nodded. 'OK. But if you want to "play" more often than that, I'm around.' He pulled back. 'Come on, Joshua. Need to get you home before mum gets back.'

Danny swaggered off, his crew tucking in behind him.

Leesa came up to Bernie. 'You OK? Danny can be a bit much.'

'I'd noticed. But I can handle him.'

'Hmm. Maybe. Anyway, I told my parents about you and they wondered if you'd like to come to church this Sunday and then lunch afterwards. You don't have to do the church bit if you don't want to.'

'No, I'll come. Thank you.'

Ben had been right – get the mothers cooking for you. She was in with Leesa.

CHAPTER 41

Then

Leesa's church was far livelier than the Baptist one Bernie had grown up in. It was easy to get swept up with the powerful gospel singing. Bernie hoped Ben was enjoying listening to it. He hadn't enjoyed her conversation with Danny and she'd received a text message telling her to stick with the girls and back away from the gang leader.

The service was longer than she anticipated but she didn't really notice the time. Leesa's dad was one of those preachers whose voice went up and down in volume to get his point across and the congregation called out 'amen' if they agreed with him. It was loud, it was colourful and it was friendly. Bernie loved it.

She was disappointed to find that Sunday lunch was at the church. She thought it unlikely Leesa had anything hidden in her bedroom but it was a missed opportunity to check. But at the same time, Bernie was relieved. She didn't want to find drugs or weapons in Leesa's room, didn't want her to get into trouble.

'Libby, this is my mum, Gloria.'

A woman in bright African dress stood next to Leesa. She held her hand out.

'It's so lovely to meet you, Libby. I've heard lots about you. Leesa's always enjoyed going to the youth centre but I've never seen her this enthusiastic before.'

'Same with Joshua,' said a female voice over Bernie's shoulder.

Bernie turned round to see a woman dressed in denim shorts and a royal blue T-shirt. A heavy gold chain hung round her neck and she had big gold hoops in her ears. Her long nails matched her blue T-shirt. Her black hair was so long and smooth that Bernie suspected it might be a wig. Bernie felt Gloria tense next to her.

'Jade, it's lovely to see you at church,' Gloria said, although Bernie wasn't convinced she meant it. 'Have you met Libby?'

'No but I've heard so much about you from my boys, especially Joshua. He thinks you're wonderful. Danny seems to think you're OK too, so you must have done something right there.'

'I let the boys join in with the netball. They seemed to really enjoy it. And Joshua's making a T-shirt, aren't you?'

Bernie had spotted the quiet boy hiding behind his mother. He popped his head out and beamed at her.

'Are you staying for lunch?' Gloria asked Jade.

'No, I have to go home and sort out lunch for my boys. Can't feed one and not the other two.'

'Take some food with you. There's plenty here for everyone. Then you don't have to cook yourself. Have some time off.'

'Thank you, Gloria. I'll do that. Come on, Joshua.'

After Jade left, Gloria sucked her teeth. Bernie was shocked that a pastor's wife would do that. Gloria saw her look.

'Oh, I'm sorry. That was the wrong thing to do but that woman gets my goat. She used to be fine. We helped her a lot after her husband died and she had to raise three boys by herself. But then Danny took a wrong turn and instead of sorting it out, she turned a blind eye. That gold round her neck is from bad money. He'll end up in prison one day and it'll be her fault.'

'Mum, don't say things like that.'

'Sorry, Leesa. I know you like Zac and Joshua but Danny...' Gloria shook her head. 'You cannot trust that boy.'

Leesa took Bernie's arm. 'Come and meet my dad.'

Bernie smiled at Gloria. 'It was nice to meet you.'

'And you, Libby. Come back anytime.'

Bernie followed Leesa through the bustling congregation who were piling food onto their plates. There were a lot of colourful dishes to choose from and plenty for everyone. Other than rice and beans, she wasn't sure what the other dishes were. Maybe she could finally learn a bit more about her black heritage.

Bernie could see Leesa's father in amongst a group of people, mainly women. Sharing her father with so many people must be hard for Leesa, Bernie thought.

Leesa didn't hesitate in butting in.

'Sorry, aunties, for interrupting.'

The women around the pastor bristled.

'Dad, meet Libby. She's the new youth worker I was telling you about.'

'Ah, Libby. The way Leesa talks about you, I thought Jesus had come back as a woman.' The man roared with laughter. 'Seriously, though, we're very grateful to have someone taking interest in our children. My name is Barnabas. It's a pleasure to meet you.'

'And you. But I have to say that I couldn't do my job without Tanya.'

'Yes, she's a good and faithful woman to our community. But

no one has reached the older teenagers like you. You're a gift to us. Leesa says you're only here for the summer but I hope you stay longer than that.'

Staying longer than six weeks was the last thing Bernie wanted to do.

'My contract is only for the holidays. So, we'll see.'

Bernie felt a vibration in her bag that was over her shoulder.

'If you don't mind, I need to use the bathroom,' she said. 'It was very nice to meet you, Barnabas.'

'And you, Libby. You're welcome here and in our house, any time.'

Bernie smiled. That was the invitation she needed.

'I'll show you where the toilets are,' Leesa said.

Once inside the cubicle, Bernie got out the burner phone in her bag. There was one message.

Trafalgar Square. 4pm. 4th plinth.

Bernie read it and then deleted it. She checked the time. Just after two o'clock. During her training, Bernie had been taught different routes to take if she needed to come into London. Ones that the locals might be less likely to take. She'd need to catch a train soon from Queen's Road Peckham station to Charing Cross via Whitechapel. And make sure she wasn't followed.

Bernie excused herself after eating some of the delicious food available. It was far spicier than she was used to but she liked the tingling sensation on her tongue.

She made her way safely to Trafalgar Square. By the fourth plinth was a familiar face but not one she expected. She thought it would be Ben but instead DI Jack Thornton was waiting for her.

'Not here,' he said, as she approached. 'Follow me.'

He led her through a back way to a car park. His silver Ford Mondeo was on the top level, tucked away in a corner. Although it was sunny outside, there was little light inside and the air was cool. Bernie got in next to him. She noticed straight away that there was no police radio. This was his personal car.

'How are you doing?' Thornton asked.

'Good. Better than I thought, actually. The kids are great and they seem to like me.'

'Yes, I've heard the tapes. Everyone is singing your praises. On the one hand, that's a good thing as it means they trust you. On the other, they're going to feel very betrayed when they find out the truth. That means we'll have to get you out before that happens. You're doing well with the girls. But you need to back off Danny Ambrose. He won't hesitate to hurt you if he finds out who you really are.'

'I'm not the one making moves on Danny. He sought me out.'

'I know. But be careful of him anyway. His mother too. She's provided a few alibis for him in her time. Her kids are precious to her. There's not much she won't do for them. Make sure you're never alone with Danny because he will try it on with you and he doesn't like it when women say no to him.

'You're doing well with Leesa but you need to check out some of the other girls too. This Goldie girl. The fact he's slept with her is a good indicator that she might have some of his gear. But you're doing a good job, Bernie. Unless you hear otherwise, I'll meet you again here in a week's time. Hopefully, you'll have more for me by then. Time to go.'

Bernie was surprised by how brief the meeting was. She'd barely said anything before she was told to leave. She made her way back to Trafalgar Square and then into the National

Gallery. Standing in front of huge paintings by Monet and Seurat calmed her down. She didn't like this double life at all. The sooner she got DI Thornton the intel he needed, the better. She hated lying to people who were rapidly becoming her friends.

If Bernie thought the morning church service was long, the evening one was even longer. She was used to her grandparents being back from theirs by eight o'clock but Pastor Barnabas's congregation was still going strong at nearly ten p.m. After returning from seeing DI Thornton, Bernie had planned a night in front of the TV but a text from Leesa inviting her to the evening service had scuppered that. Bernie didn't dare turn down the chance to get to know the community better.

Bernie looked around the church. There were fewer people than the morning service. Most of the parents were home with their children. There were more teenagers and people in their twenties. Probably missed the morning so came in the evening. There was definitely a different, younger vibe and Bernie liked it. Pops would be stunned that she was enjoying a church service and two in one day.

'And now, brothers and sisters, a final prayer to send us on our way,' said Barnabas. 'May the Lord bless you and keep you; the Lord make his face shine on you and be gracious to you; the Lord turn his face toward you and give you peace. Amen!'

Amens sounded around the room and Bernie found herself doing the same thing. She could do with some peace. But she wouldn't get that until the operation was over.

The congregation spilled out onto the pavement outside. Bernie felt a tap on her shoulder. She turned and saw Leesa.

'Are you heading back to the youth centre now?' she asked.

'Yes.'

'Walking?'

'I was planning to. It's a warm night so should be a nice walk.'

Leesa shook her head. 'My dad will drop you home and walk you to the flat.'

'There's no need. It's only a ten-minute walk, if that.'

'Libby, I've heard that things are a bit on edge tonight.'

'What do you mean? What's happened?'

'I don't know for sure but Goldie texted me earlier to say she wasn't coming to church. Said there was tension on the estate. You didn't notice anything?'

Bernie thought before she spoke. 'No. I was coming back from London when you texted me so came straight here. It all seemed fine this morning.'

'Might just be that someone from outside has come in. Maybe from Brixton.'

Bernie frowned. 'Does that matter?'

Leesa almost laughed, 'God, yes. This is Danny's patch. No one comes in without his say-so. Please let Dad drive you. We live in the road next to the estate so it's not out of our way.'

Bernie relented. Any extra time with Leesa and her family was a bonus.

Barnabas parked his car as close as he could to the youth centre but it was still a few minutes' walk away.

'I'll be fine from here,' said Bernie.

'No,' Leesa replied. 'You mustn't go on your own. It's not safe.'

'Then it's not safe for you to be left in the car. Honestly, I'll be fine. Thank you for the lift, Barnabas.'

'My pleasure, Libby. Go quickly to your flat, now.'

Bernie got out of the car before Leesa could protest again. As soon as Leesa had mentioned someone out of the area had come in, Bernie had wondered if her cover was blown. Maybe someone had followed her to her meeting with Thornton. She walked briskly but avoided running. If someone was watching her from the walkways or balconies, then she wanted to look as comfortable as possible with her surroundings. No fear showing.

She walked past an area that had large rubbish bins, the stench overwhelming with the summer heat.

'You shouldn't be here,' someone hissed at her.

Bernie froze. She twisted her head round quickly to survey the area. If someone was about to challenge her, she wanted to be ready. A figure dressed in black stepped out from behind the bins.

'I mean it, you shouldn't be out here. It's not safe.'

As the figure stepped closer, she saw it was Zac.

Bernie whispered, 'What's going on?'

Zac beckoned her over to him. 'Some guys from Brixton have turned up. We don't know why. But if they cause any trouble, we're ready.'

Bernie's eyes drifted around the estate, wondering how many boys were hiding in the shadows, keeping watch on the walkways and stairwells.

'What should I do?' Bernie whispered.

'I'm not supposed to leave my post but you need to get in safely. Danny will probably kill me. Fuck it. Walk quickly and quietly. Stay close to me.'

Zac moved swiftly and Bernie followed. The safety of the youth centre was only two minutes away but it felt more like five as they dodged past streetlamps, staying in the dark as much as possible. Bernie felt for her keys in her pocket so she had them ready to get into the flat. It was hard to tell if the oppression in the air was the humidity from a hot day, or the foot soldiers waiting for orders from Danny. Bernie hoped nothing would kick off. The last thing she needed was gang warfare on her doorstep.

They turned down the side of the youth centre. They were more protected here. Zac pushed Bernie past him and she pulled out her keys. She mouthed thank you as she opened the door.

'Stay alert,' he whispered. 'The last time things kicked off, the other gang started a fire in front of the youth centre.'

Bernie's eyes widened.

'Don't worry too much. It wasn't a big fire. Keep safe.'

'You too.' Bernie was surprised to find that she meant it.

CHAPTER 42

Now

Court had never been Bernie's favourite place. The last time she'd been in the Old Bailey was to give evidence at Danny Ambrose's trial. It was one of the oldest and most senior criminal courts in England, the likes of Dennis Nilsen, the Kray twins and the Yorkshire Ripper having been brought to justice here. It was a place that often intimidated people and Bernie was feeling the pressure, especially as she didn't know what to expect as a defence witness. Normally, as a witness for the prosecution, she would have some idea of what questions she'd be asked. Roger Howe-Turner was giving nothing away in his demeanour. He took his time over the questions.

'So, you were in place on the council housing estate. You're making friends with the teenage girls, winning their trust.'

Bernie inwardly winced. She hated what she had done. Gaining trust and then betraying it.

'You had back-up if you needed it. Jack Thornton was available to meet with you weekly, more often if required. You were being supported. So what went wrong?' Howe-Turner looked at the jury as he spoke.

In that moment, Bernie knew why she was a defence witness. It wasn't about disproving Jack Thornton was a corrupt cop. It was about demonstrating she was an incompetent one. If the defence could cast doubt on one of the corruption charges, then it would affect the rest. She wasn't having that.

'I believe I was betrayed. Despite the lack of training I received, *at that time*, I did my job to the best of my ability. I'm the first to accept it wasn't enough though. That operation haunts me and I bear a literal scar from it.'

With that, Bernie felt an itch on her left side. She placed her hand on her scar and was glad the stand was in front of her, hiding what she'd just done. She didn't want the jury to see what she was doing. Her breathing was quickening. *Stay calm. Stay calm.*

Roger Howe-Turner looked surprised. 'You were betrayed? By whom?'

Bernie remembered the conversation she'd had a year before with Jade Ambrose, mother of Danny, Zac and Joshua. She'd implied it was Thornton but never actually said his name. It had been enough, though, for Bernie to change her mind about her former boss.

'I believe it was Jack Thornton.'

Bernie looked at the jury. She saw a few of them shuffle in their seats. The black woman wrote something down. One of the Asian men coughed.

'Do you have proof of that?'

Bernie paused. She couldn't mention Jade.

'No. But once—'

'Thank you, detective inspector. No further questions.'

What? Bernie screamed in her head. *You're going to leave it like that? No!*

She looked at the judge. Surely he could see this was all a farce. That she was being made a scapegoat. He gave her a brief sympathetic glance. At least the prosecution was up next. Bernie would give them everything they wanted to know to get Jack Thornton.

The Asian man coughed again but this time he didn't stop. He stood up, swaying slightly. The clerk of the court went to check on him.

'We will take an early break for lunch,' said the judge. 'If the juror is better, we will start back for the afternoon session at one thirty p.m.'

Bernie sighed in relief. She wanted to get her head together before facing the prosecution. And she wanted to check on Mira.

'Everything's fine,' Dougie said. 'We've been swimming. She's doing really well, loves it in fact. She'll be swimming in no time.'

'Seriously, you've taken her swimming? Dougie, you've got to be careful with her today.'

'I am being careful and I'm not going to let that bastard dictate what we can do. Bernie, I won't let anyone hurt our daughter. You know that.'

Bernie knew Dougie would protect Mira.

'Sorry. It's getting to me. I'll talk to you about it tonight.'

'OK. See you later. Let me know when you leave.'

'I will. Love you.'

'Love you too.'

Bernie hung up. The street outside the front of the Old Bailey was bustling. It was a risk being out of the building but the security guards were close behind and Bernie felt safer on a busy street rather than the quiet back one.

She texted Kerry, desperate for news on Debs. A reply swiftly came.

Bleeding stopped. Keeping her in for observation overnight though. Helps when you go to the hospital you work at. Staying with her. Drake knows. Call MCIT when you can. Some interesting developments. Xx

Bernie sent a quick reply before calling the office.

'MCIT, DC Matt Taylor speaking.'

'Matt, it's Bernie. What's happening? Kerry's told me there's been some developments.'

'Yes. I was about to go out. Any chance you could call me on my mobile, please?'

'Sure.'

Bernie gave Matt a couple of minutes before calling back.

'Were you really on your way out or couldn't you speak?' she asked when he answered.

'Bit of both. Heading to the bakers now to get lunch for everyone. Plus, the chief constable was in talking to the super. Thought it would be better to talk to you outside the office.'

'What's going on then?'

'We can't find Helen Brown and her sister.'

'What? Did they come in for interview on Saturday?'

'No. Helen rang and said her sister was ill. She rearranged for this morning but they've not come in. No answer on her phone. We've asked Thames Valley and the Met to go to their properties but no sign of them. Just before you called, Thames Valley officers had found a neighbour who said they'd left very early yesterday morning. She heard a car engine running and looked out of her window. Saw the two women with suitcases getting into a taxi.'

'Shit. We need their statements. Are you checking all ports?'

'Yes. Mick's doing that. Heathrow seems the obvious choice from Reading but will look everywhere. Alice is trying to find the taxi firm in case they were going to a station and are still in the UK somewhere. There's more.'

'Oh God, what?'

'Dennis Pinner and his second wife don't appear to be in Australia.'

'Where are they then?'

'Good question. Border Control has no records of Dennis and his wife leaving the UK in the last year.'

'False passports used?'

'Possibly. I hope so. The alternative doesn't bear thinking about.'

Bernie closed her eyes. She knew exactly what Matt meant. Were there two more corpses waiting for them somewhere?

'Have you gone into their house yet?' she asked.

'Not yet. We only got that information this morning. Drake's planning to go in this afternoon. Although, maybe we should wait for you to come back first. You're the one who's been discovering the bodies.'

Bernie shuddered. 'I'll leave it with you, thanks. I think three last week were enough for me. I'd better go. Nearly time to go back in. Text me later. I hope for your sake that the house is clear. See you tomorrow.'

'Bye, ma'am.'

Bernie went through security again before looking for the toilets. She kept a close eye on the people around her. It seemed unlikely anyone would try anything but a history of bad interactions at the toilets at school always made her wary.

She checked the cubicles and all were empty. Good. Bernie

went to the toilet and then washed her hands. The hand dryer was useless and left her with warm, damp hands. She looked in the mirror and straightened her shirt. She hoped the prosecution had picked up on her need to tell the truth and would allow her to do so. She was about to leave when the door opened.

'Ah, there you are.'

Bernie turned. It was Jade Ambrose.

CHAPTER 43

Then

The tension of Sunday night had evaporated by Monday morning. No one from a Brixton gang had been on the estate, just someone's relatives visiting. Bernie was glad to have the update from Leesa but wished she'd known sooner. It had been a restless night and she was tired as she got the youth centre ready.

'Libby!'

Bernie was still getting used to her covert name but she recognised Joshua's voice. He ran up to her.

'What are we doing today?' he asked.

Bernie spotted his mother behind him.

'What would you like to do? Tanya has put out some games and there's painting too. And I think we'll look at our fashion show this afternoon. Netball after that.'

'Can I practise catch?'

'Yes, of course. I'm sure one of the girls will play with you.'

'Yeah, the girls are better than my brothers. I'm going to do a painting now.'

Joshua darted off. Bernie smiled at Jade Ambrose but remembered DI Thornton's warning about her.

'Thought I'd drop Joshua in this morning. He's been so happy coming here since you arrived.'

Jade looked around the room. It was still the younger kids who were in early.

'He's all right with the younger ones, isn't he? Not a problem?' Jade asked.

'He seems fine. I don't want to be rude,' said Bernie, 'but I'm guessing his mental age is younger than his actual age. So he gets on well with the younger ones. But he also gets on with the teenagers too. He's a sweet boy.'

Jade wrinkled her nose. 'He is but he's fourteen and puberty is starting to hit and sometimes testosterone gets the better of him. You'll let me know if he does anything inappropriate?'

'Of course.' Bernie decided to fish for some information. 'I guess having older brothers must affect him.'

'In what way?' Jade's tone was sharp.

'You said about puberty and I assume your older sons are dating. He must see them with girls.'

'Is that your unsubtle way of finding out if Danny's with anyone?'

'No. I'm here as a youth worker and a friend. Nothing else.' Bernie kept her voice as smooth as possible. Lying about being a police officer was hard.

Jade slowly nodded her head. 'OK. I'm off to work now. Either Danny or Zac will pick him up. I'll just say goodbye to him.'

Bernie watched as Jade hugged her youngest son goodbye. Joshua squeezed her tight. Thornton was right. Jade would do anything for her boys.

Bernie wasn't surprised when Leesa offered to play catch with

Joshua. Although the other girls didn't mind hanging out with him, Leesa was the only one who genuinely cared.

The netball match had finished and the others had gone. Bernie was collecting up the netball bibs. Joshua was improving with Leesa's help.

'That's it, hold your arms out but only a little bit apart. Then when the ball is in your arms, pull it in for a hug. Ready?'

'Ready.'

Bernie watched as Leesa gently threw the ball to Joshua. He did as she said and pulled the ball in tight.

'I caught it.'

'You did. Let's try it again. This time, I'm going to throw it closer to your hands.'

Leesa threw the netball but Joshua didn't pull the ball in quickly enough and dropped it.

'Oh,' he said.

'That's OK. We'll try again. Practice makes perfect, Joshua.'

'That's what my teacher says.'

Leesa threw the ball again and Joshua caught it in his hands.

'Yes! Well done, Joshua.'

Joshua beamed and dropped the ball. He ran over to Leesa and gave her a hug. Then he kissed her full on the lips. Leesa squirmed and tried to push him away but he held on tight. Remembering what Jade had said, Bernie went over.

'That was good catching, Joshua. You need to let go of Leesa now. It's best to ask someone before you kiss them, OK?'

Joshua stepped back as he heard Bernie's voice.

'Oh, I didn't know that. I'm sorry, Leesa.'

Leesa had her hand to her mouth. She nodded. 'It's OK. But as Libby says, it's best to ask.'

'Danny and Zac don't ask.'

'Maybe they should,' Bernie said.

Movement caught Bernie's eye. Outside the court, she saw Danny Ambrose slide something into his pocket. Had he seen what Joshua had done? She hoped not for Joshua's sake. There would be a lot of nasty teasing. But she probably ought to tell Jade next time she saw her.

'Joshua, Danny's here to collect you,' Bernie said. 'Run in and get your painting. It should be dry now, despite all the paint you poured on.'

'OK, Libby.'

A minute later, Joshua was back with his painting. 'See you tomorrow.'

As he ran over to Danny, Bernie turned to Leesa.

'You OK?' she asked.

'Kinda. He kissed me quite hard. I think I might need something cold on it.'

'Come on. Let's get a cool pack on it.'

Bernie turned back as Leesa went ahead of her. She saw Danny and Joshua walk away. Danny put his hand into his pocket and pulled out his phone. Was that what he had in his hand before?

Leesa was in the kitchen by the fridge.

'I'll get it for you. Sit down. I'll put a tea towel round it as you don't want it too cold.'

Bernie took out the cool pack and found a tea towel. She heard a ping.

'Is that you or me?' she asked.

'Me,' Leesa replied. She turned pale as she looked at her phone.

'You OK?'

Leesa looked up and opened her mouth to say something but didn't.

'Leesa? Are you all right? Is it bad news?'

The teenage girl nodded. 'Sorry, I have to go home. Thanks for your help. I might not be in tomorrow.' She left in a hurry.

It took a moment for Bernie to twig. She had a good idea what might have appeared on Leesa's phone – a photo of Joshua kissing her, taken by Danny. He could do whatever he wanted with that picture. More importantly, he could get Leesa to do something for him. Bernie's natural instinct was to protect Leesa. She'd seen what had really happened and could back Leesa's version. But she knew what DI Jack Thornton would say – keep a close eye and let it play out. Bernie would just have to find a way to save Leesa too.

CHAPTER 44

Then

Leesa didn't appear for the rest of the week. She sent a message with one of the other girls saying she was ill. Bernie was worried about her but also worried about herself. Her next rendezvous with DI Thornton was fast approaching and she had nothing for him. She'd tried to engage Goldie in conversation but got little out of her. Apart from her earlier confession that she'd slept with Danny, there didn't appear to be anything between them.

Joshua hadn't been in either and Danny and Zac weren't hanging around the youth centre. It felt oddly quiet to Bernie. Was something happening in the background that she wasn't privy to? Or was something about to happen? She hoped Thornton had some answers.

The car was parked exactly where it was before. Bernie had taken a different route into central London this time. It was longer but she was keen to not establish a pattern of behaviour that others might pick up on. That was one thing she'd learned from covert training.

'I'm guessing you have nothing for me,' Thornton said. 'There's been little on the wire.'

Bernie shook her head. 'Goldie's a no-go. I'm worried about Leesa though. Apart from Monday, I haven't seen her all week.'

'What happened Monday?'

'She played catch with Joshua and he got a bit overenthusiastic with her. Gave her a massive hug and kissed her on the lips.'

'And you saw this?'

'Yes. You must have heard when I told him not to kiss someone without asking first.'

'I did but I didn't know it was on the lips. Did anyone else witness it?'

Bernie hesitated. It had niggled her all week. Had Danny Ambrose taken a photo and sent it to Leesa? Is that why she'd not been in?

'I think Danny might have done... and possibly taken a photo too.'

'And you didn't think this was worth following up?'

'You told me to look for girls he'd slept with.'

'Yes but think outside the box, Bernie. Blackmail is very powerful. It wouldn't look good for the pastor's daughter to be locking lips with a disabled boy who's a couple of years younger than her. It might look bad enough for Leesa to be coerced into doing a favour for Danny. Like hiding drugs for him. My informant has said that a shipment is coming in after next weekend. You'd better get in there with Leesa and find out what's going on.'

Bernie was quiet. She didn't want to say she had already thought all these things because Thornton would want to know why she didn't follow up on it.

'I don't want Leesa to get into trouble. None of this is her fault.'

Thornton sighed. 'I know. We'd have to arrest her initially but we wouldn't press charges. Especially if she cooperates.'

'And then she'd be known as a grass throughout the community. What kind of life would that be?'

Thornton turned to Bernie. 'We could look at witness protection if needed. Move the whole family.'

'But her father is the pastor of the local church. He's one of the main leaders in the community. There must be a way of catching Danny with the drugs, rather than allowing them to be moved to Leesa's house.'

'I told you already. Danny doesn't handle the drugs. It's how he's evaded capture so far. This is our only option.'

'Then you'll have to find another. I'm not screwing up Leesa's life.'

Bernie opened the car door and got out. She heard Thornton a few seconds later.

'You can't walk away from this. You need to do your job or you'll be out on your ear.'

Bernie turned round. 'I'd rather that than what you're proposing.' She stood firm and stared at her senior officer.

Thornton laughed and shook his head. 'I'd heard you're a bit of a handful. I thought it was just in bed but maybe there's more to it.'

Bernie's legs turned to jelly but she managed to stay upright. Her former colleague, Larry, had been right. Sleeping with Inspector Ashby had got her this job but not in the way suggested. He'd been getting rid of her and hadn't hesitated to tell Thornton why. Now, the DI was just as bad as Danny Ambrose – blackmailing her.

'Do your job, Bernie.'

CHAPTER 45

Then

Bernie waited a few days before going to Leesa's house. She'd been hoping that Leesa would turn up of her own accord but hadn't done so. She got the address from Tanya who was concerned about her too.

Gloria, Leesa's mother, opened the door.

'Oh, Libby. How nice to see you. Have you come to see Leesa?'

'Yes. I've been worried about her. I haven't seen her for over a week.'

'She's ill. At least, that's what she says. I think it's something else.' Gloria tapped the side of her nose. 'Mothers know these things.'

Bernie was intrigued. Had Gloria discovered something?

'Oh. What do you think it is?'

'I think it's a boy who's broken her heart. If I find out who, I'll be breaking him into little pieces.' Gloria laughed. 'I'm just kidding. But I would have strong words with him, that's for sure. Come in. See if you can find out who's broken my baby's heart. She's upstairs in her room. Barely left her bed. First door on the left.'

A delicious smell of cooking wafted past Bernie's nose as she went up the stairs. She tapped on the door.

'Leesa, it's Libby. Can I come in?'

No response. Was she asleep? Maybe she really was ill but Bernie didn't think so. And neither did her mother. She knocked again. This time she opened the door.

'Leesa? I'm worried about you. Please can I come and talk to you?'

Despite the summer sunshine outside, the room was dark but warm. Bernie could just make out Leesa in her bed.

'If you have to.'

Bernie closed the door behind her. It was then that the fug hit her. Leesa's unwashed body and lack of air.

'Right, apologies if I sound like your mother but I'm going to open a window and pull back the curtain a bit. The fresh air will do you good.'

Leesa didn't reply as Bernie let light and air into the room.

'That's better. I'm sure the heat in here isn't helping you. What's going on, Leesa?'

Bernie found a chair next to a desk and sat down. The room was medium sized and neat. There were a couple of wardrobes and a chest of drawers, plus the desk and chair. Not many places where drugs could be hidden but there was space under the bed too. Not everyone had the imagination to lift up floorboards.

Leesa was in her bed, facing the wall. She stayed silent. Bernie persevered.

'Are you sick?'

No response.

'Come on, Leesa. You're my right-hand woman down at the youth centre. Netball's going OK but I need your sewing skills for the fashion show. I can come up with designs but I can't make them.'

Leesa didn't turn over.

'Your mum thinks it's a boy.'

Leesa shuddered.

'Ah.' Bernie pulled the chair nearer the bed. 'Is it about Joshua? I saw what happened. I know it wasn't your fault. And I'm prepared to say that.'

Bernie waited for her words to sink in. She hoped offering Leesa a lifeline would work.

Slowly, Leesa turned over to face Bernie. Her face was drawn. Bernie wondered if she'd slept at all over the last week.

'Oh Leesa. Talk to me. Maybe I can help fix it.'

'He won't listen to you.'

'Who?' Bernie was tempted to say his name but didn't want to lead Leesa on.

'Danny. He doesn't listen to anyone.'

'He might. Plus, Jade had told me that morning that Joshua was being a bit inappropriate in his behaviour. She might listen to me, even if Danny doesn't.'

Leesa wiped her face. 'It's too late. He's already sent the photo to all the boys in the gang. They've sent me disgusting comments. He's not told the girls yet. Said he won't if I do something for him.'

'What does he want you to do?' Bernie leaned in, knowing the wire would pick up Leesa's words.

Leesa shook her head. 'I can't say.'

'You can tell me anything. Does he want sex?'

'No. Libby, please don't ask me any more.'

'Leesa. I want to help you. It's not fair he has this hold over you. It was Joshua who kissed you.'

'But it doesn't look like that in the photo. Don't you see? I have to do what he says. It's not just about me but my parents too. The photo is shameful.'

'Leesa, is he asking you to do something illegal?'

'Libby, please. I'm not going to the police.'

'I could go for you.'

'No.'

'Or we could use Crimestoppers. It's completely anonymous and won't be traced back to you or me.'

'But Danny would know. The SE15 gang would know. And then they'll come for me. They've done it before.'

Bernie's heart thumped hard. Just how dangerous was Danny Ambrose?

'What happened?'

'Eighteen months ago, a girl from the estate was gang raped. She never named her attackers but we all knew. So, thanks for the offer of help, Libby, but there's nothing you can do. I have to go along with it. It'll be over soon anyway.'

Bernie leaned back. 'Until the next time. People like Danny don't stop, until you stop them. If you want me to help, then I'm willing to do so. Think about it. I'll come and see you again on Friday, if I don't see you before.'

Bernie stood up to leave. She waited at the door.

'I can help you, Leesa. You just have to trust me.'

Leesa looked up, her eyes sad. 'Thanks, Libby. I'm trusting you not to say anything. Not to my parents, or Tanya or any of the girls. This is just between you and me.'

Bernie nodded slowly, knowing full well that Leesa's words were being heard and recorded by DC Ben Harper.

'OK. Between you and me.'

CHAPTER 46

Now

'I've been looking everywhere for you, Bernie,' Jade said.

It had been a year since Bernie had last seen Jade Ambrose, after the murder of her second son, Zac.

'What are you doing here?'

'Almost the same as you. I'm here for the trial but I'm not giving evidence.'

'Then we can't speak until after I've finished. Although, I will say thank you for the baby card. I only got it when I went back to work last week. Keira must have had her baby by now.'

Jade smiled. 'Yeah. He's a cutie. Looks a lot like Zac. She was going to name him after his dad but her parents persuaded her not to. He's called Eddie. Eddie Howard. I was hoping she'd use Ambrose but no.'

'Do you get to see him much?'

'Not really. Her parents thought I was beneath them. Until I reminded them I'm not the only one with a son in prison. They changed their tune then.'

'And Joshua?'

'Still in Jamaica with my family. It's better for him out there.

I miss him though.'

Jade looked at the floor. Bernie thought she looked tired, not her normal feisty self.

'You OK, Jade?'

She looked back up. 'Yeah. Just a bit hard going listening to all this stuff in court.'

'Jade, we mustn't talk—'

'With the curtain across, you can't see who's in there. Leesa's parents are here.'

Bernie reached out to a sink to steady herself. 'Don't say any more. I need to go back now. If you want to talk after I've finished giving evidence, then we can. But not before. Excuse me.'

Bernie moved past Jade and made her way back to the witness room. Bella Fontaine was there waiting for her. She looked a bit grumpy.

'Ah, DI Noel. I was about to send out a search party for you. We have a problem. The juror that was taken ill has gone home but will hopefully be better for tomorrow. So court is adjourned for the afternoon and we'll resume in the morning. Can you be here for a ten o'clock start?'

Bernie sighed. She wanted it all to be over and done with today. On the plus side, she'd be back for Mira but it meant missing another day at work.

'I suppose I don't have any choice in the matter. I'll see you in the morning.'

Bella Fontaine swished away in her black gown and wig.

Bernie pulled out her phone and texted Dougie, letting him know she'd be back early. She was about to call Hannah Drake to ask about her lift home when a security guard poked his head round the door.

'DI Noel?'

'Yes, that's me.'

'Your car's here. I've sent it round to the back entrance. There's quite a lot of press out the front for a different case so it's a bit busy.'

The guard led her through to the back door and a covert police car was outside waiting for her. She saw where the blue lights were so knew it was safe to get into. She opened the rear passenger door and climbed in the back. She was about to strap herself in when another person pushed in next to her.

'Budge up.'

It was Jade.

'What are you doing? You can't come with me. I'm going home.'

'You can drop me in Swindon then. I'll visit Keira and Eddie.'

'Jade, this is a really bad idea. You're going to compromise me as a witness.'

'No one will know we travelled together.'

Bernie pointed at the driver.

'There's a police officer right there.'

Jade shrugged. 'We won't talk about the trial. We'll talk babies. I want to hear all about your little one.'

Bernie stared at Jade. She wasn't going to leave.

'OK. We'll give you a lift into Swindon. As long as it's OK with this officer.'

'Fine with me, ma'am.'

He sounded vaguely familiar to Bernie and she wondered if she'd worked with him on a case.

The car pulled away and was soon caught in London traffic. Jade stuck to her word and she showed Bernie photos of her grandson. Bernie was hesitant to do the same but shared one of Mira.

It was a while before Bernie realised something wasn't quite right.

'Are we going the right way?' she asked.

'Diversion in place, ma'am.'

Something about his voice again. She wished Matt could have stayed the day with her but he was needed at MCIT. Maybe Hannah Drake had arranged for a Met officer to drive her. Bernie looked out the darkened window. They were crossing the River Thames.

'Why are we crossing the Thames?'

'As I said, diversion, ma'am.'

'We don't need to go south of the river to get to the M4. It was fine this morning on the way in.'

Bernie's stomach lurched as worry built, not just for herself but Jade too. Maybe this car hadn't been sent by Hannah Drake. She tried the door handle. The door was locked.

'Officer, I demand to know your name and your route.'

The driver stayed silent.

'Officer, I command you to tell me your name and your route.'

No response.

Bernie's breathing quickened as adrenaline started to pump through her body. If the driver had been sent by Hannah Drake, he'd have spoken by now.

'I don't know what's going on here,' Bernie said, 'but this woman has nothing to do with this. Please pull over and let her get out.'

The car drove on. Bernie looked at Jade, expecting to see alarm in her face. But she appeared fairly calm.

'I'm really sorry about this, Bernie. Please check your emails,' Jade said.

Bernie fumbled for her phone, wondering if she could send out an SOS alert somehow but with Jade right next to her, that seemed impossible. She clicked on the email icon and saw there was a new message. She opened it and found some photo attachments. It took a moment to load but then, there in front of her, were five photos of Granny with Mira, taken on Friday.

Bernie jerked her head up. 'What the fuck is this?' she asked Jade.

'As I said, I'm really sorry. You have to come with us.'

Bernie looked back at the driver in front of her. 'And who exactly is us?'

'I'm not surprised you don't remember me, ma'am. But I'd know your voice anywhere. I spent weeks listening to it.'

Bernie's eyes widened as she realised who was in the driver's seat.

'DC Ben Harper,' she said.

CHAPTER 47

Then

You're trying too hard with Leesa. Back off and give her some space.

Bernie read the text message. It was on her burner phone and had appeared not long after her conversation with Leesa. She thought it more likely it had come from DC Ben Harper than Jack Thornton. The DI was pushing for results, not shying away from them. She was tempted to text back but decided not to. In some ways, he was right. Bernie had given Leesa an offer of help. It was up to her whether she wanted to accept it or not.

Bernie wondered about talking to Jade Ambrose about Joshua's behaviour but that would alert Danny. It was fast becoming a mess and at the centre of it was the sweetest teenage girl. And her own ineptitude. If only she'd had more training like she'd requested.

Her flat at the youth centre was compact. The bedroom had a double bed squeezed into it and there was barely any space to turn round in the bathroom. The kitchen/diner/lounge wasn't much bigger but Bernie was grateful to have a place to escape to after spending all day with teenagers. She felt vulnerable though. Cannabis hung in the air like a permanent air freshener. The estate was never completely quiet, not even in the middle of the night.

There was always some music playing somewhere and foxes would add to the sound with their screaming. Daytime wasn't any better with traffic and construction noise. Money was being invested into Peckham but Bernie wasn't sure it was going to the right places.

She was tired, though, and got ready for bed. Putting her wire away carefully, Bernie changed into shortie PJs. There was a small TV with a built-in DVD in the lounge, and a rom com and tub of ice cream were beckoning her.

Halfway through the film, there was a knock at her front door. She had her own entrance away from the main youth centre but so far, no one had come to it. She was hesitant about opening it, especially as she was in her nightwear. There was no spy hole either. She was in two minds about opening the door when a knock came again.

'Who is it?' she called out, hoping it might be Leesa.

'It's Danny. I need to talk to you.'

Shit.

'Just a minute.' Bernie went into her bedroom and quickly put her clothes on. She didn't want to be in nightwear for Danny Ambrose. A few minutes later, she opened the door.

'How can I help you, Danny?'

He looked her up and down. Bernie was glad she'd got dressed.

'Can I come in?' He leaned on the doorframe.

'No. This is my space and I'd like you to respect that.'

'OK. You seen Leesa?'

Bernie swallowed. 'Yes. Earlier this evening. Why?'

'Cos I ain't seen her about.'

'She's not well. Some kind of virus.'

Bernie hoped her voice wasn't trembling too much.

'Right. What you talk about?'

'When I saw her? Not much. She's worn out so I didn't stay long. Why are you so interested?'

Now it was Danny's turn to be uncomfortable. He shifted away from the door. 'Joshua was asking. He misses her.'

'I'm sure your mother could call Gloria to find out herself.'

Danny snorted. 'Yeah, right, cos we're the favourites at church. They do nothing for us.' He stepped back further. 'If you see Leesa, tell her I was asking after her. Hope she gets better soon. Don't want her missing the summer. Due to be good weather this weekend. Might even go to the beach. Take a picnic. Have some sandwiches. Laters.'

Danny swaggered off, his jeans still hanging low, showing off his designer underwear. She closed the door. Bernie couldn't help but think there was a coded message for Leesa in that conversation. Hopefully Ben Harper heard it OK. Damn. Bernie tapped her chest. She hadn't put the wire back on. She quickly wrote down what Danny had said, as best she remembered. But it wouldn't work as evidence. She texted it to Ben anyway. Thornton had mentioned a shipment after the weekend but maybe it was being brought forward. She would definitely have to see Leesa on Friday.

CHAPTER 48

Then

When Leesa still hadn't shown up at the youth centre by Friday, Bernie knew she had to visit her. Gloria was relieved to see her at the door.

'Oh Libby, I don't know what to do any more. My baby girl has never been like this before. The doctor came and said it's depression. But she was fine one day and not the next. It makes no sense. I keep praying and asking God to tell me what's wrong but He's not answering either.' She threw her hands up. 'Libby, what do I do?'

'I'll speak to her again.'

Bernie knocked on Leesa's bedroom door.

'Leesa, it's Libby. I'm coming in.'

The room smelt worse than before.

'Have you showered at all in the last couple of weeks?' Bernie asked.

Leesa, under her duvet, turned over.

'That's not a nice thing to say.'

'Maybe not but you might feel better after a shower.'

Leesa didn't respond.

'Everyone misses you. They've all been texting.'

'Have they? I turned off my phone.'

'Well, that's why you didn't get their messages.' Bernie paused. She had to say the next bit carefully. 'Danny came to see me.'

Leesa poked her head out from under the duvet. Her eyes flickered with fear.

'He wondered where you were. Hoped you'd be better by the weekend so you could go to the beach for a picnic. Take some sandwiches.'

Bernie watched Leesa closely. Having checked in with Ben Harper, Bernie now knew that 'sandwiches' referred to two layers of cocaine with a layer of heroin in the middle. Serious stuff for a small-time gang leader. Danny Ambrose was going up in the world.

Leesa bit her lip. A drop of blood appeared.

'Are you going to tell me what's going on, Leesa?'

The girl shook her head.

'Leesa, I'm not stupid. I can use Google. I know what a sandwich is and I can guess what Danny has asked you to do and why. He's blackmailing you with the photo. Let me help you, please.'

Tears streamed down Leesa's face. 'No one can help me. I have to do it.'

'No, you don't. I can go to the police for you.'

'No! He made that very clear. No police.'

'Oh Leesa.'

Bernie closed her eyes. She hated lying. She wasn't cut out to be a covert officer. It was wrong to let Leesa take the rap for this. Despite what DI Jack Thornton had said, Bernie couldn't be sure the Crown Prosecution Service wouldn't press charges. She couldn't take that risk. Looking around the room, Bernie spotted a notepad and pen on Leesa's desk. She wrote something down. Putting her finger to her lips to hush Leesa, she showed the teenage girl what she'd written.

Too late. Police know. I'm sorry.

Leesa's eyes opened wide. Bernie kept her finger to her lips for a few seconds and then pointed to her chest where the wire was. It took a moment for Leesa to realise but then she grabbed the notepad and wrote something. Bernie leaned over to see.

You're police? Wearing a mic?

Bernie nodded. Leesa scribbled something else.

What's your real name?

Bernie shook her head. She'd given away too much information as it was. Leesa wrote more.

How do you know I won't grass you up to Danny?

Bernie took the pad back.

Because you're a decent human being. A lovely girl with a great future ahead of you. I can't let you take the rap for Danny. I was there when he took the photo. I know what really happened. Let me help you.

How can you help me?

Find out time and place for meet. Be late. We can swoop in for a raid before you get there. I ought to say something as there's been a long gap.

'Leesa, it's no good giving me the silent treatment. I thought we were friends.'

Leesa took back the pad.

What do I do?

Switch your phone back on. Contact Danny. Tell him you'll do it. Get as much info as you can. Screenshot it and send to me. Be late for the meet but still go. Look scared and run away. Hopefully, some of the gang members will see. If you don't turn up at all, then they'll think you've grassed.

'If you're going to be like this, then I can't help you,' said Bernie. 'If you change your mind, then text me. As I said, I'm willing to back you up.'

Bernie wrote more.

Destroy these pieces of paper after I've gone. OK?

Leesa nodded. 'I'm sorry, Libby. I can't tell you anything. Please go and leave me alone.'

'OK. I'll leave for now. But you need to get out of bed, shower and spend some time with your family. Your mother is very worried about you. OK?'

Bernie opened the door but took a last look at Leesa.

The girl nodded. 'OK. I'll do as you say.'

CHAPTER 49

Then

Bernie left her little flat early on Saturday morning and headed towards the bus stop by Peckham Library. She didn't want to use the one closest to the estate. The 381 bus to Waterloo was already at the stop, so Bernie picked up speed. The journey would take about an hour but she still had plenty of time before her meeting with DI Thornton. The number 12 bus would have been quicker and more direct but more likely to have some of the kids on board, and varying her journey was important. There was a queue of people waiting to get on and Bernie noticed a tussle going on at the front.

'Show some respect,' an older black woman said. 'Let your aunties get on the bus first, young man.'

Bernie held back. The sun was in her eyes a little but she was sure the young man was part of Danny Ambrose's gang. He was wearing a black tracksuit and had a black baseball cap pulled down low over his face. He was on his own, which struck Bernie as odd. The gang members weren't normally up this early on a Saturday morning. Nor were they normally on their own.

The young man got on the bus after the aunties and then a few more people. Bernie hesitated. Should she get on? She had no idea when the guy would get off and if he would see her. But curiosity got the better of her. Where was he going and why was he alone?

'Are you getting on, love, or what?'

Bernie blinked. The driver was talking to her. 'Oh, yes. Sorry.'

She stepped onto the bus and paid. No sign of the young man downstairs. He would have gone upstairs for sure. It would be foolish for her to follow suit. The perfect seat was waiting for her at the back in the corner. She'd have a good view of anyone getting off but they might not notice her.

Bernie settled into her seat. She was above the engine so expected some vibration. She didn't expect the heat though. The warmth wrapped itself around her bare calves. She was glad she was wearing shorts.

Despite being a Met officer, this was an area of London Bernie was unfamiliar with. Pulling out her phone, she found a map of the route. It curved its way through Bermondsey and Rotherhithe before following the River Thames west towards Waterloo station. The areas improved the closer they reached central London, old buildings giving way to gleaming new ones at Canada Water. Trees lined the roads.

Bernie checked each time the bus stopped but the young man didn't get off. The bus trundled on and soon, landmark sights like The Shard came into view. It looked as though the gang member was doing the same as her and heading into central London.

It wasn't until the final stop by County Hall that she saw him at the bottom of the stairs. Once he left, she got up and followed the last few passengers off. He was ahead of her but she kept her eyes on his black baseball cap as he moved up the road. She assumed he'd cross the river at Westminster Bridge. Despite being a Saturday morning in August, traffic was still heavy and the lights were against her as he crossed before her.

Shit, she thought. She was tempted to dart through the cars and buses but it wasn't worth the aggro. Once over, she caught sight of him further along the bridge. She ran to catch up, weaving past the tourists taking photos of the Houses of Parliament.

There were a few people in between them as they left the bridge. Bernie held back as he crossed the road on the pedestrian light, only following in the last few seconds as they counted down. She was oblivious to the splendour of the Houses of Parliament on her left-hand side, her eyes only fixed on a black baseball cap. Turning onto Whitehall, she followed and Bernie had an idea of where he might be heading. This road led to Trafalgar Square and beyond it, the car park where the DI was due to meet her at eleven o'clock. She was an hour early. Thornton was meeting his gang informant before her.

Bernie kept a steady pace, always keeping a few people between them. Once they reached Trafalgar Square, though, it was almost impossible to follow him. Tourists swallowed him up and he wasn't the only one with a black baseball cap. Undeterred, Bernie pushed against the tide of people. If he was going where she thought, then it didn't matter if she lost him for a bit.

Once she was through, Bernie headed for the car park behind the National Gallery. She stood at the entrance to the stairs and heard footsteps above her. There was a creak, followed by the bang of a door. Bernie crept up and went to the top floor where she'd met Thornton before. She opened the door slightly and listened for voices. She couldn't hear anything so assumed they were in Thornton's car.

Bernie went back down a flight of stairs and hid behind the door to the next level. There was a circular window in it. She hoped to catch a glimpse of the young man without him spotting her.

Bernie's legs ached from standing. It had been twenty minutes since she'd hidden behind the door. It wouldn't be long before it was her time to meet Thornton. Surely, the gang member would have left by then. Through the heavy door, there were muffled voices. The door swung open. Bernie risked a quick look as the young man came through. The cap was still firmly on, covering his face but he had his phone to his ear.

'Yo bro. I had to do something for my mum,' he said. 'Laters, OK?'

Trainers scuffed the steps as he went down. Bernie didn't relax, though, until she heard the door at the bottom of the stairwell open and shut. She rubbed her face. Thornton had specifically told her not to try to find out who the informant was but now she knew. She recognised his voice. It was Carlton Jones.

DI Jack Thornton looked at Bernie. She'd waited in the stairwell until it was time to meet him. She'd shown him the screenshots Leesa had sent, giving the time and place where Leesa was supposed to pick up the drugs and take them back to her house until they were needed by Danny.

'So you've told Leesa to be late so she won't get arrested,' Thornton said.

'Yes but that she must still go. Hopefully one of the gang will see her and think that she hasn't grassed them up.' Bernie hesitated, choosing her words carefully before speaking. 'Does this tally with the intel from your informant?'

Thornton nodded slowly. 'More or less. I was given a bit later for the timing, though, so that's interesting.'

'Sounds like someone pulling a fast one to me.'

'Or Danny not trusting either of them.'

Bernie paused. She hadn't thought of that. Was Danny suspicious of a grass in his group and so had deliberately given different times? Carlton Jones was playing a dangerous game.

'Shit. So, if the police turn up before Leesa, then he knows it's her. If he hears the police arrive later, then he knows it's the informant.'

'That's my concern, yes.'

'What do we do then?'

'Well, generally speaking, it's not a good idea to go rogue and reveal your true identity before speaking to your commanding officer. What were you thinking?'

Bernie had told Thornton the truth. Ben Harper had been suspicious of the gaps in her conversation with Leesa and had told the DI. 'I was thinking... I was thinking that if she knew I was an officer and that I could help her, then she'd be more willing to cooperate. And she is. She's given us all this info.'

'Assuming she hasn't told Danny the truth and this is what they've sent to each other to make it look like it's happening at that time.'

'We can put a mobile phone data request in. Get all her messages.'

'There isn't time. The deal's tomorrow morning according to this, during church, giving Leesa time to hide it at her house.'

'Would the later time the informant gave be enough for Leesa to get the drugs back to her house before her parents returned?'

'How long's the church service?'

'It was two hours when I was there, with a lunch afterwards. But I don't think that happens every week.'

Thornton rubbed his face and sighed. 'No, there won't be enough time. Leesa's information is more likely to be correct. But she'll be in danger.'

'Where do you want me? I can be ready to intercept her.'

'You'll be at church.'

'What?'

'You can't be anywhere near the raid. Your cover might be blown with Leesa but it isn't with anyone else. You're still in place.'

'But I thought I'd be finished once the raid was done?'

'You thought wrong. If Danny isn't there when we go in, your job isn't over. If you want to protect Leesa, then you need to stay there and do as I say. No more going rogue. Understood?'

Bernie nodded her head. She felt like a naughty child being told off but Thornton was right. She'd endangered Leesa but at least she'd discovered the right time for the meet. Thornton's informant was mucking him about.

CHAPTER 50

Now

Bernie's natural instinct had been to fight against Jade when she had taken her phone and watch away and then produced a pillowcase.

'Put it over your head,' she had said. 'Think about the photos on your phone.'

Bernie couldn't let anything happen to her daughter so she'd complied. She'd attempted to keep track of the turns they were taking but there were too many. She wondered if Ben Harper was deliberately driving in circles to confuse her. She'd lost contact with him after the Danny Ambrose trial; both had moved to different teams.

The car started to slow down. Bernie listened out for sounds that might be familiar. There were less cars but she heard the heavy thud of trucks. An industrial area perhaps? There was machinery too, a continuous noise followed by something that sounded like heavy rain. She couldn't place it. The car stopped and Bernie heard a metal shutter open. The car edged forward and the little lightshe did have through the pillowcase disappeared. Bernie was sure she was in a warehouse somewhere but no idea of its location in London. Even if she could escape, she wouldn't know where to go. The engine cut off and a car door opened. The driver's door. Bernie felt a slight breeze against her legs and with it, a hint of dust in the air. The heavy rain sound came back to her. She knew what it was – an aggregate plant. The sound was the stones falling. Shit. What kind of plant was it? Did it have a crusher or was it a sorting and washing plant? Bernie hoped it was the latter. She didn't want to think about what a crusher could do to the human body.

The weight of the car changed as Harper got out and his door slammed shut. Jade hissed next to her, 'Trust me.'

Bernie wasn't sure she could do that but she thought Jade was being forced into this. It was in her best interest for Thornton to be found guilty as Danny could then appeal his conviction. None of this made sense.

Her door opened with a swoosh.

'Unplug your seatbelt and get out,' said Ben Harper.

'Bit hard to find the button with this on my head,' Bernie replied.

'Feel for it. That's what most people do.'

Bernie rummaged around with her left hand to find it but Jade got there first and released it for her. She stroked Bernie's hand. Another sign to trust Jade. But could she?

A hand grabbed her arm and pulled her out of the car.

'Careful. I nearly fell over then,' she said.

'Seriously, you want me to go easy on you?' Harper snapped.

'You don't want me looking bruised in court tomorrow.'

'*If* you're in court tomorrow.'

Bernie swallowed slowly, relieved the pillowcase was still over her face. She didn't want Ben Harper to see how scared she was. She was very aware that Carlton Jones hadn't made it to court. For

Mira's sake, she had to cooperate.

Bernie stumbled as Harper pulled her along. Her shoes clicked on the hard floor but didn't echo. Not a big warehouse then, she thought. Somewhere smaller. Probably with things inside to absorb the noise. She sniffed but couldn't work out any distinct smells. Maybe wood. Oil of some kind perhaps. Wherever she was, she wasn't about to sit down on a comfy sofa and have a cup of coffee.

Something creaked in front of her. A door opening? Harper's hand moved to her back and shoved Bernie forward.

'Stay in there until we're ready for you,' he said, whipping the pillowcase off her head.

Bernie gasped as she fell into the room, landing on her knees hard.

'Ow!'

The door shut behind her, cutting light into the room. It was pitch-black. Bernie lifted her hand to her face but she couldn't see it. Everything in her wanted to scream but she wasn't going to give Ben Harper the satisfaction. Her knees hurt like crazy as she stretched out in front of her, trying to feel what was there. The floor was gritty on her fingers. The air was musty. Some kind of unused storeroom? Her fingers touched a wall. The surface was rough. Brick, most likely. Bernie listened carefully but couldn't hear anything other than her own laboured breathing. If she couldn't hear anything in this black cell, it was unlikely anyone would hear her crying for help.

Slowly, she stood up, wincing at the pain in her knees. She was glad she'd worn trousers today so her skin was somewhat protected. She followed the wall up with her hands, stretching her arms above her head until she reached the ceiling. Over two metres high then. Width and length would be harder to work out. She didn't particularly want to move from this spot, not knowing if there was anything in the room she could fall over. It would mean crawling but her knees hurt so much.

A stabbing pain in Bernie's left side made her wince. Her scar, long healed and faded, was warning her a panic attack was imminent. Bernie slid down the wall until she sat on the floor. She slowed her breathing in an effort to stop the panic consuming her. Resting her head in her hands, Bernie waited for everything to subside.

After a few minutes, Bernie was aware that her heart rate had slowed down, her breathing quieter. It was then she heard it. Something scraping on the floor. And then someone or something else breathing. A rasp more than a proper breath. She wasn't alone.

'Hello? Is someone there?' Bernie's voice was swallowed by the darkness. She waited for a reply, hoping it was a person and not an animal.

'Bernadette, is that you?'

Bernie clasped her hand to her mouth to stifle her sudden sob. Now she understood the photos Jade had shown her. They weren't about her daughter. It was her grandmother.

CHAPTER 51

Then

Bernie woke up to the sound of a bouncing ball. She eased out of bed and looked through the blind slats to see who was on the netball court. It was Zac Ambrose and Carlton Jones. They were playing basketball, diving round each other, trying to take the ball. Bernie knew what was coming next. Zac tried to shoot into the netball goal but it was too small for the basketball and got stuck.

Bernie got dressed quickly. She didn't want the goals ruined. She took a netball with her. She didn't mind them practising with that.

'Hey, boys,' she called out to them as she approached. 'I don't mind you playing on the court but please don't try to shoot into the goals. They're only suitable for netball-size balls.'

Zac was trying to knock the ball down. He stopped and glared at her. Carlton Jones sucked his teeth. For the first time in ages, Bernie was vulnerable. No uniform and padded vest to protect her. No baton. No pepper spray. No radio. She'd forgotten to put her wire on. If the boys turned on her now, no one would know. She tried to lighten the mood.

'Bit early for you guys. Thought you'd want to spend

your Sunday morning in bed.' Bernie was tempted to mention that Carlton had been up early on Saturday too but knew that was unwise. She looked up at the bright blue sky, the sun already blazing. 'Still, nice morning to play basketball.'

Neither teenage boy spoke or moved.

'OK. Well, as I said, happy for you to bounce the ball around but stay away from the netball goals please. The girls won't thank you if you break the nets. If you want to borrow this ball to shoot, then you can. I'll leave it on the side for you.'

She started to walk away.

'Wanna play?' said one of the boys.

Bernie turned back and saw Zac had got the basketball down. He bounced it a few times.

'Sure. Just let me find my trainers.'

Bernie darted back to her little flat to put on her hidden microphone and trainers. There was always the chance that Zac and Carlton might give something away. She jogged back to the netball court, trying to warm up her body a little. These boys were not going to go easy on her.

'One on one?' she asked Zac.

He grinned. 'Danny would like to play that with you. But I think we should include Carlton. Take it in turns to win the ball and pass to the free player. You know what I mean?'

Bernie nodded. 'Yep. I'll try to win it from you first.'

Zac laughed. 'Like to see you try.'

Bernie walked up to him as he bounced the basketball and she knocked it out of his hands straight away.

'Hey. I wasn't ready.'

'Got to be faster than that, Zac.'

She ran and bounced the ball a few times before throwing it to

Carlton. Laughing as he caught it, he dived round Zac, bouncing the ball and then sent it back to Bernie.

As she bounced, she said, 'I was goalkeeper in my netball team. It was my job to get the ball and protect the goal. Got to use my height somehow.'

She curved the ball over his head back to Carlton. He laughed again.

'She's playing you big time, Zac. You don't stand a chance.'

The game soon descended into piggy in the middle as Zac couldn't get the ball off either of them.

'OK. You win,' he said to Bernie. 'But I'll get you next time, Libby. It's too early in the morning for me.'

'Well, I did say you were up early but I guess you're heading to the beach soon.'

'What?'

Bernie had to play this carefully. 'Danny said you're all going to the beach today. Have a picnic. Which one are you going to?'

Carlton threw the ball to Zac. He bounced it a few times.

'Not sure yet. Gotta check the trains. Maybe Brighton.'

'Brighton's nice. Pebbly though. I prefer sandy beaches. Although you don't want to get sand in your sandwiches.'

Zac flinched a little before speaking. 'Nah. Which is why Brighton's better. You see Leesa recently?'

Bernie nodded. 'Saw her on Friday. She's a bit better. Not sure she'll be well enough to go to Brighton though. Bit of a long way when you're feeling rough. Mind you, sea air might do her some good. Not long before you get your GCSE results now. I hope she's not worried about that.'

'Leesa? Nah, no worries there. Top of the class. Me and Carlton though—'

'Hey, speak for yourself, bro. I'm in second set for Maths.'

'OK. So, Carlton's gonna do well enough in Maths to be an accountant—'

'I don't wanna be an accountant, bro, despite what boxer man might say.'

Boxer man? Bernie thought. Who's that?

'No, Carlton, it's good to know how to handle money. All the top people need accountants,' Zac replied.

Top people? What was going on here?

'And what about you, Zac?' asked Bernie, wondering if he had any aspirations outside selling drugs.

Zac dropped his head. 'You'll laugh.'

'No, I won't.'

Zac shrugged. 'Don't really mind what I do as long as I earn enough to live. But I'd like to find a nice girl, settle down and have a family.'

'He means Leesa,' Carlton interrupted. 'You just need to get in there. Do the dirty.'

'Shut up.'

Bernie tried not to show disgust at what Carlton had said. She didn't think Leesa was keen on Zac but she didn't want to dash his hopes.

'Get to know her as a friend first before trying anything else. That's the best approach and you'd do well to remember that too, Carlton. Well, I'd better let you boys get on. I guess you've got a picnic to sort out, sandwiches to make. I hope you're not expecting Jade to do it all for you.'

Carlton gave Zac a look she couldn't quite read.

'Nah. Wouldn't expect my mum to do anything like that. She's got Joshua to look after. Danny and I look after ourselves.'

CHAPTER 52

Then

Bernie sat at the back of the church. Her phone was hidden under her bag that she kept on her lap. It was on silent but vibrate was working. Leesa had texted to say she would go to the meet but would leave late. Bernie hoped her team would be on time so that Leesa wouldn't be caught with the drugs. That was the last thing they needed.

Leesa's father was preaching and the air was punctuated with lots of 'amens' but Bernie wasn't taking in anything he said. From her position at the back, she had a good view of the congregation. It was packed, even though it was the holidays. Not many people could afford to go away. She saw some of the children and teenagers with their parents, including Joshua with Jade. Church was family for the residents on the estate. Bernie thought about Pops and Granny. She missed them both, even her grandmother which was saying something. She normally ate a meal with them and her mother once a week. It was an anchor in her routine that kept her grounded. She hoped the operation would end today as she really wanted to see her family again. Especially Pops. He was the only one who seemed to love her unconditionally. When she was a child, the day always improved when Pops came home from work. Before that, it was about being good for Granny. She couldn't be naughty for Granny. Bernie sighed. She loved her grandmother but she was very strict. It was years before her own mother, just fifteen when she gave birth to Bernie, was brave enough to stand up for her daughter.

Bernie looked around. Her dual heritage skin was the lightest one there. Everyone else was black. For all she knew, her other grandparents could be here. Maybe even her father. She didn't often think about him, and her mother gave her little detail. But she had her father's surname – Noel – so she had something to go on if she did want to look him up. But not now.

Now, she had a job to do and someone to protect. She snuck another look at her phone. No messages. It was close to the meeting time and the police raid. She was restless. It was almost impossible to sit still. She wondered how much longer Leesa's father, Barnabas, would be with his sermon. Bernie wanted to get out of the church building. It was hot and most people were fanning themselves. But none of them had the pressure that Bernie felt.

Bernie's phone buzzed on her lap. She slid it out and looked. It was a text from Leesa.

Leaving now.

Sweat trickled down Bernie's back. She had to get out of the building. She was too jumpy to stay sitting in her seat. Adrenaline was pumping round her.

There was a change in tone of Barnabas's voice and she realised the sermon had ended. The pianist started to play and the choir stood up, along with the congregation. Bernie took her chance and left. Being in the end seat, close to the door, she didn't think anyone would notice.

DI Thornton had told Bernie to wait at the church until after the raid and that Leesa was to join her there. Bernie checked the time. It was five minutes until the raid. Leesa had been told to meet Danny at an empty flat on the estate. It wasn't far from the youth centre. That would be a better place to meet Leesa. She wouldn't have to run so far then. Bernie pulled out her phone. Her fingers hovered over the screen. She'd already stuffed up once though. She couldn't afford to do it again.

Bernie sat down on a wall under the shade of a tree. The minutes slowly ticked down until the time of the raid. She hated not knowing what was happening. Had Leesa managed to stay out of sight? Had the officers found Danny with the drugs? Would she finally get her life back and go home?

Bernie paused. She'd actually enjoyed the last few weeks with the kids at the youth centre – playing netball with the girls; recycling clothes to make new fashion items; getting to know the kids. None of them were bad really. Misguided perhaps. An inspirational person could guide them in the right direction. Could she do it? For real? Not be a police officer any more? Bernie's phone buzzed. A message from Leesa.

Something's wrong. Police have gone in but no Danny. I'm scared.

Bernie rubbed sweat from her forehead. Was it a setup? Did Thornton's informant have the real time of the deal? She texted back.

Change of plan. Meet me at the youth centre.

CHAPTER 53

Now

'Granny?'

'Oh Bernadette, it is you. Where are you? I can't see.'

'Don't worry. I'll find you. Are you sitting on anything?'

Bernie started to pat the floor in front of her. It was hard to work out where her grandmother's voice came from as there was a slight echo.

'No. I'm leaning up against a wall. You're in front of me, I think.'

'OK.'

Bernie eased herself forward, crawling on her hands and knees, wincing with the movement. She hoped she wouldn't have to run later because that would really hurt.

'Keep talking to me, Granny.'

'You're getting closer. I can hear you're nearer. Are you shuffling?'

'No. On hands and knees. Don't fancy falling over.'

'Don't blame you. Keep going.'

Bernie crept forward until her hand touched something.

'Is that you, Granny?'

'Yes. My foot. You'll have to come to me. I'm so stiff from being here that it's hard to move.'

'Oh God, Granny.'

'Language, Bernadette!'

'Sorry. How long have you been here?'

Bernie's grandmother sighed. 'No idea. I'd just finished watching the Sunday evening news and was about to go to bed when the doorbell rang. I opened it and there was this man with a police warrant card. I've seen yours enough times and it looked genuine to me. Said you'd been in an accident and could I go to the hospital?'

Bernie had reached her grandmother and put her arm around her shoulders. Susan Baxter was a small woman in comparison to her granddaughter but fierce in nature. If anyone could cope with being thrown into a pitch-black cell, it was her.

'I asked about Dougie,' Susan continued, 'and he said that Dougie was on his way but I was nearer. Oh Bernadette, I'm sorry, but I cursed your mother and Gary for being away on holiday. I was tired and wanted to go to bed. But you were hurt and needed me. So, I gathered my things together, got in the car and next thing I knew, I was in here. He must have used chloroform or something to knock me out. What's the time now?'

'I don't know exactly,' Bernie replied, 'but maybe around four p.m. on Monday. My phone and watch were taken. They picked me up from court. Said it was my car home to Wiltshire. Or rather, I assumed it was. Granny, I'm so sorry. I think you were taken because of me. I'm due back in court tomorrow as a defence witness. I expect they want me to take the blame for some of Jack Thornton's charges.'

'Don't you dare. You tell the truth, like Pops always taught you. You have been telling the truth, haven't you?'

Bernie hesitated.

'Oh Bernadette. I can guess which part you haven't mentioned.'

Bernie frowned. Granny knew nothing from her time on Operation Willow. Only Pops had gone to court when she gave evidence. Had he told her?

'I don't know what you mean.'

'Yes, you do. It's time you owned up to what you did.'

'What I did?'

'Yes. How you got that job in the special operation. You slept with someone to get that. An older officer.'

Bernie pulled her arm away from her grandmother's shoulders.

'What makes you think that?'

'I saw you. Early June that year. You were leaving a seedy-looking hotel in London. He was behind you and touched your back. You looked sad though.'

'Where were you?'

'In the little shop opposite. I'd got lost and stopped in there to ask for directions. It was after that I got my smartphone. Anyway, the next day, you came in after your shift and told us about your new role as a detective constable.'

'Granny, I didn't become a detective constable because I slept with someone. I had to pass an exam.'

'I know that. But you got the job on that special operation because of that man, didn't you?'

Bernie sighed. 'Yes and no. I got the job because he wanted to stop sleeping with me. End our affair. His wife had found out so he sent me to a covert operation where he wouldn't have to see me any more. I'm very ashamed of myself.'

'As you should be. It was adultery, Bernadette.'

Bernie sniffed. 'I know.'

Susan brushed Bernie's arm and found her hand. She took it and squeezed.

'I've always been tough on you, Bernadette, and it was wrong of me. I… I should have been kinder to you when you were growing up. Truth is, I resented you. I didn't particularly want children but Eric did. I agreed to having one and Denise was born. I wanted to go back to my job in the bank but Denise was a sickly child and I took so much time off, I had to leave. They were going to sack me otherwise. Anyway, she was better by the time she started at secondary so I got a job in a different bank. I was doing well and was quickly promoted to assistant manager. The manager was due to retire and I was a shoo-in for the position. But then Denise got pregnant with you and I had no choice but to give up my job. Again.

'You weren't an easy child but I understand now that I took my frustrations out on you. I was mean. And I think I only realised this on Friday when I had Mira. She's such a joy. I thought she wouldn't want to stay with me but she was adorable. And then I remembered that you'd been like that as a baby. But I think my bitterness and resentment affected you. You became sullen and difficult because I was. You mirrored me. And I'm so, so sorry, Bernadette,' Susan sobbed.

'I'm sorry too, Granny.'

Bernie put her arms around her grandmother and hugged her.

'It's a shame it's taken being locked in a pitch-black room for me to say those things to you,' said Susan. 'I'm very proud of you. Not just as a police officer but a mother too. I was too young to be a grandmother in my forties. But it seems right in my seventies.

That's if you'll have me.'

'Of course. You'll be a very special Great Granny. And Dougie told me that it looked like Mira had enjoyed herself. Well, as much as a nine-month-old baby can.'

'She waved goodbye to me. She's a clever girl, like her mother. So, the question is – how do we get out of here, Bernadette?'

CHAPTER 54

Now

It seemed like forever before the door opened and a sliver of light appeared. Bernie and Susan had inched their way round the room until they had found the doorframe. As it opened wider, Bernie lunged up and pushed hard against the person coming in. There was a clatter as what sounded like a tray hit the ground. Bernie grabbed Susan's arm and they ran out of the room.

The light was muted which Bernie was grateful for. A bright light after such darkness would have hurt their eyes. Despite being in her seventies, Susan was keeping reasonable pace with Bernie.

A large shutter door was ahead of them and they ran towards it. They were almost there when Bernie heard an unmistakable click – the safety catch on a gun being released. She stopped and Susan toppled into her.

'Why have you stopped?' her grandmother asked.

Bernie turned round slowly, raising her arms. 'Because they have a gun.'

Ben Harper was stood there, feet a shoulder width apart, both hands on the weapon to create a steady shot.

'Ah, Glock Seventeen,' she said. 'Standard police issue.'

'Seventeen M, actually.'

'Snazzy.'

Susan whispered, 'What does the M stand for?'

'Military,' Bernie whispered back.

'Oh. He means business then.'

'He does.'

'Shut the fuck up.' Ben glared at them both.

Bernie knew Ben could kill them in a matter of seconds so she tightened her lips together.

Ben waved the gun. 'Over there.'

Bernie walked slowly in the direction Ben was pointing. There were two chairs and she spotted restraints on the arms and front legs. She couldn't decide what was worse – being restrained in the light and seeing the bullet hurtling towards her, or crawling around in the pitch dark not knowing when her fate was coming. A Wiltshire armed officer had waxed lyrical to Bernie a year before about this Glock. She hadn't listened to most of it but had remembered what the M stood for and that it had a night sight. Ben Harper was ready to assassinate her regardless.

Bernie sat down and Susan followed. Jade stepped forward to tie them up. There was a brown stain down her top, smelling of coffee. Bernie yearned for a drink but it gave her satisfaction to know that Jade was probably scalded a bit. Her eyes locked with Jade's.

Jade's lips moved but no sound. 'Trust me,' she mouthed.

Bernie wasn't sure she could do that.

Having secured them, Jade stepped back.

'Right,' said Ben, 'that's better. More comfortable than that dirty concrete floor.' He pulled another chair over, swung it round so the back of it faced Bernie and Susan. He straddled the chair, the gun resting on the top of it, looking like he was in a gangster movie. Jade stood behind him.

'So, Detective Inspector Bernie Noel, you have done well for yourself,' Harper snarled. 'From a new DC to a DI in six years. Impressive.'

'It was actually four. I'm guessing you're still a DC.' Bernie was pushing her luck and knew it.

'You always were a smart arse. I got so sick of listening to your voice. I even started hearing it in my sleep. Yes, I'm still a DC but I've changed departments a few times. Got a lot of skills under my belt.'

Bernie nodded. 'Firearms training. Is that where you are now?'

Ben Harper chuckled. 'I'm surprised you haven't worked it out yet.'

Her mind ticked over. There weren't many police departments where you might have a gun. Or perhaps it wasn't police issue. Maybe it was an illegal gun, in which case he could be anywhere. Bernie pushed the gun idea to one side and tried to think as rationally as she could whilst tied up with an armed weapon aimed at her.

Harper had been part of Operation Willow and had listened to all her conversations. He was probably the one who had tipped off Danny Ambrose about her conversations with Leesa, not DI Jack Thornton as she had thought. Was Thornton innocent then? She shook her head slightly. She found that idea hard to believe. Focus on Harper, she told herself. What were his skills? Surveillance and covert operations. Firearms trained. Knowledge of gangs and drugs. No one had ever found him during Operation Willow so he was good at hiding. Bernie tipped her head forward as it dawned on her.

'You're in Witness Protection,' she said, lifting her head and staring straight at DC Ben Harper. 'You work with DS Colin Ferguson and I bet you're the officer who said you had to leave Carlton Jones alone as you had a family emergency. Except you didn't leave.' Bernie flicked her eyes up to Jade's to gauge her reaction. Carlton had been Zac's friend. 'You killed Carlton, dismembered parts of his body and then waited for Lewis Brown and Aaron Swan to turn up to dispose of him. How am I doing?'

'Pretty good, detective inspector. You've obviously learned some things about detection work over the past few years. What else?'

Bernie thought for a moment, trying to unravel the theories that were building in her mind. She and her team had thought there were two people involved in Carlton's death because there were two officers in the black Mercedes. But DS Ferguson and his colleague hadn't been involved. They did their job a bit too well.

'Something went wrong,' she said. 'I'm guessing Brown and Swan were late to the barn where Carlton's body was waiting. There was an argument and you shot Swan. Brown took off in the car with Jones's body in the boot. Ferguson arrived quicker than you thought and saw Brown's BMW hurtle out of the lane. They went after the BMW... no, wait, they didn't. Not straight away. Ferguson told me he checked the caravan first. You must have hidden somewhere. That's something you're good at. Then Ferguson and your other colleague went after Lewis Brown, giving you time to clean up and get away.'

An image of the crashed BMW came into her mind, seeing Brown's body in the driver's seat and then Jones's in the boot. 'You weren't expecting the crash, though, were you?'

Bernie paused. She could see herself driving to work for the first time after her maternity leave. Not far out from Marchant, winding round the bends until she saw the smashed car with PC Barton standing nearby. She gasped as she realised.

'No, Lewis Brown wasn't meant to crash,' she said. 'He was meant to deliver Carlton Jones's body to me.'

CHAPTER 55

Then

Bernie's thighs burned as she ran back to the estate and the youth centre. She wanted to get there before Leesa. With keys in her hand, Bernie rounded the corner to the centre and her flat. There was no sign of Leesa.

Opening her door, Bernie ran to her bedroom and threw her bag on the bed. She pulled out her phone and slipped it into her shorts back pocket. She then felt under her bed for the one thing she was told to bring but only use in an emergency – a police baton. She spoke aloud so DC Ben Harper would hear her.

'Something's wrong. Danny wasn't at the flat. Leesa's coming to the youth centre. I'm here already. And I have my baton.'

If anyone other than Leesa saw it, then her cover was blown. Bernie sat on the bed for a minute, allowing her breathing to calm down, her heart rate to slow. Thornton would be furious if she blew her cover now. It would ruin the whole operation, especially as Leesa had said that Danny wasn't at the flat. But surely that meant her cover was already gone. Danny had delivered the message to Leesa via Bernie. He knew. Bernie tightened her grip on the baton. If Danny was coming for her and Leesa, then she needed something to protect her. She wasn't going to be able to talk her way out of this.

There were shouts from outside. Bernie looked through her window and saw Leesa being chased by Zac, Carlton and Danny on the other side of the netball court. Shit. She was expecting Danny, not the other two.

'I have eyes on Danny and Zac Ambrose and Carlton Jones. They're chasing Leesa. Urgent assistance required at the youth centre now. I'm going in.'

Bernie hoped Harper was listening and would redirect the team already on the estate. She ran outside to find Leesa on the netball court, the boys edging towards her in a pincer movement.

Danny held his hands up as he approached her. 'Just wanna talk to you, Leesa. Why'd you run like that?'

Leesa was visibly shaking as Bernie closed in on the court. There was only one way in and out. It would be like entering the Roman Colosseum and even though she had a baton tucked in the back of her shorts, Bernie didn't feel like a gladiator. She needed back-up now. Standing at the entrance, Bernie braced herself. She'd try talking first.

'Hey guys, what's going on?' she asked in an attempted breezy manner, walking slowly in.

All eyes swung to her.

'That's what I was asking Leesa just now,' Danny said. 'Saw her running, looking scared. Was worried for her.'

'Right. Looked like you were chasing her to me.'

Danny shook his head and chuckled. 'Nah. You got that all wrong. We weren't chasing. Trying to catch up. She's a fast girl.'

'So why are you surrounding her?'

Danny's eyes hardened. 'Why are you asking so many fucking

questions, Libby?' He sauntered towards her. 'Always asking questions, Libby. Libby, Libby, Libby. Bloody stupid name. Is it even real?'

Bernie's heart raced at that comment but she tried to keep her composure. 'Of course it's real. It's from Elizabeth.'

Danny tipped back his head and roared with laughter before speaking. 'No, you stupid bitch. I know it's a real name. The question is – is it your real name?'

Zac and Carlton were moving towards her now, the focus off Leesa. Good, thought Bernie. That would give her a chance to escape and hopefully get some help. Even with a baton, it would be hard for Bernie to fight off three attackers. She reached her right hand back and found her police weapon. As soon as she pulled it out, it would be game over.

CHAPTER 56

Now

Bernie kept her eyes on Harper. She didn't dare look away from him. If he was going to fire the gun, she wanted to see it coming. To have one second to think of Dougie and Mira and the life they could have had.

'You know,' said Harper, 'I never understood the faith Thornton had in you. Why you even got the job in the first place.'

'It's because she slept with another officer,' Susan piped up.

'Granny!'

Ben laughed. 'Oh dear, Grandma. I don't think Bernie likes that. But it would explain it. You were meant to be incompetent at it though. Not enough training was all part of it. You were supposed to keep in the background and just focus on the girls. You weren't supposed to turn maverick. It was your stupidity that got Leesa killed. I'm sure Jade would agree with me on that.' Harper turned his head slightly towards Jade behind him but stared at Bernie. 'Isn't that right?'

'Yes,' said Jade but she gave a slight shake of her head.

'See? Her boy's in prison because of what you did. She hates you as much as I do.'

'But if Thornton goes to prison,' Bernie said, 'all his old cases will be reviewed. Including Danny's. He might get an appeal. Get out. So I don't understand why Jade is working with you.'

'Because she has another son she'd give her life for.'

Ah, thought Bernie. Joshua. Yes, Jade would do anything for him.

'Are you beginning to understand now, Bernie? Tomorrow, you'll play your part in court and accept all the mistakes you made during the operation. You'll make it clear that DCI Jack Thornton isn't a corrupt officer but a good one. That what happened was down to you.'

'Thornton's facing lots of charges, not just conspiracy to Leesa's murder.'

'I know. But cast doubt on one, you cast doubt on them all.'

'And if I don't play ball tomorrow?'

'Granny gets it.'

Susan laughed out loud. 'You silly man,' she said. 'Do you honestly think I have a good relationship with my granddaughter? I made her life hell growing up. She won't give two hoots if you kill me.'

'Maybe not. But I think she cares about Joshua.' Harper turned back to Bernie. 'You've really screwed up Jade's life. Her eldest in prison because of you. Her second son dead because of you. Are you really going to risk her youngest? Precious Joshua?'

Bernie looked at Jade who stared back, impassively. Was Joshua really in Jamaica? She thought about the two times that Jade had said to trust her. Bernie was tied up. Jade wasn't. She had to signal to Jade that she now trusted her.

'I won't risk Granny and Joshua. I'll do as you say.'

'Good. Now, if you don't mind, there's someone else who wants to hear you say that.' Harper took his left hand off the gun and slid a phone out of his jacket pocket. He looked at the phone and gun in his hands. Bernie realised his dilemma. He needed to open the phone with his right hand.

'Let me take that for you,' said Jade, sliding her hand over Ben's.

Bernie noticed an intimacy in it, as though Jade's hands were quite practised in sliding over Ben Harper's body. It worked as he released the gun. He then jabbed at the phone and a few seconds later, there was a ring tone on speakerphone that was quickly answered.

'Ben, I trust you have our guest.'

Bernie recognised Jack Thornton's voice immediately.

'I hope she's being cooperative.'

'She is, sir. She's agreed to the terms for tomorrow.'

'That's good to know. Judging by the echo, you have me on speaker so Bernadette can hear me. Anything you want to say to me, DI Noel?'

Bernie could think of plenty to say, most of them swear words, but decided not to be drawn.

'I guess not. You're doing the right thing, Bernadette. Leesa died because you didn't listen to me. You don't want any more blood on your hands.'

Bernie closed her eyes and willed herself not to speak. Thornton had blood on his hands from the three young men she'd seen in the last week. She wouldn't give him any more.

'I'd better go, Harper. Someone might hear me on the phone and dob me in. I'll see you in court tomorrow, Bernadette.'

Bernie opened her eyes as Harper ended the call.

'Good. That's all settled then.'

He pocketed the phone and reached back for the gun. He froze.

Jade was behind him, the muzzle on the back of his head.

'It's not settled,' Jade said. 'It's not settled until I have my youngest back safe and sound and my oldest out of prison.'

Harper slowly raised his hands. 'Come on, Jade. We talked about this. You can't have both. But we can make sure Danny has a good time in prison.'

'Put your fucking hands by your side. I'm not stupid, Ben.'

'Really?'

Harper lurched up and twisted round to grab the gun but Jade was too quick for him. The shots rang in Bernie's ears as one hit Harper's right shoulder and the next, his left knee. He sank to the ground, trying to hold on to the chair. His wounded knee hit the floor and he yelled in pain.

'Fuck, Jade. What are you doing?'

'Saving my sons.' She pointed the gun towards his groin. 'I'll fire down there if you're not careful. I'm disgusted by what I had to do to you. But never underestimate a woman, especially a mother, Ben. I'll do anything for my boys.'

Keeping the gun trained on Harper, Jade edged round him and moved back to Bernie. She pulled a small knife out of her left pocket and cut the plastic tie on Bernie's right wrist.

Bernie took the knife and cut the rest of her ties, before doing the same for Granny.

'I hope you have a plan, Jade,' Bernie said.

'Of course.'

Bernie had to walk past Harper to get out. He reached up with his left hand and grabbed her ankle.

'You won't get away with this, DI Noel,' he said. 'You'll have blood on your hands.'

Bernie shook her head. 'No, DC Harper. After what I've seen

in the last week, you're the one with blood on your hands. You're going to wish that Jade had killed you. Prison for a dirty cop is a bad, bad place.'

CHAPTER 57

Now

The car screeched as it pulled away from the car park, with Jade at the steering wheel.

'I've had it stashed there for a couple of days,' she explained as they drove away from the industrial area near the River Thames.

Bernie spotted the aggregate plant that she thought she'd heard on the way in and then there was a rumbling above. Lights in the dark sky indicated a plane coming in to land. She instantly knew where she was.

'We're near City London Airport, aren't we?' she asked.

'Yes. South of it. Not far from Greenwich.'

'We ought to call the police, Jade. Let them pick up Harper.'

'Do we have to? I'd rather let him bleed to death. You have no idea what I had to do to that man to keep him... satisfied.' Jade shuddered.

'I understand. But even so. Wouldn't you rather have your day in court? See him go down for what he's done?'

'Do you really think he killed Carlton?'

'I don't have proof but yes. The thing is though, Jade, Carlton had sexually assaulted quite a few women. He was the bus attacker I was looking for last year when Zac was killed. And he was going to get a new life for giving evidence against Thornton. I don't know how sympathetic a jury would be. But there's also Aaron Swan that he shot. It would be harder to prove anything for Lewis Brown. However, abducting an old lady and a police officer wouldn't look good.'

'Less of the old, thank you,' Susan said from the back seat.

'Sorry, Granny.'

'What are you really asking, Bernie?'

'I'm asking for my phone back.'

'Sorry, it got left behind. Your watch too. Don't worry. Once we're safe, I'll make the call.'

Bernie slumped in her seat. Jade had always been a determined woman. She studied the road signs as they weaved their way through heavy traffic, despite it being late, trying to work out where Jade was taking them. They cut through a lot of back roads but after a while, Bernie began to get her bearings. She'd been out of London for a few years but was recognising place names. They were heading south-west.

'Oh my God. We're going to Peckham, aren't we? Are you insane? I can't go back to Peckham ever,' Bernie said, her eyes widening with alarm.

'We are but it was only ever me you had to fear and I've got your back. And besides, I'm not taking you to the estate. There's a property somewhere else where you'll be safe. As I keep telling you – trust me. I've just shot a man twice in order to get you out.'

'You took a while to do it,' said Susan. 'Could have shot him as soon as you got the gun.'

Jade glanced back. 'I could but it was important that the call was made. Thornton thinks that Bernie is going to behave in court tomorrow. And of course, she's not.'

'I'm not? What about Joshua? I'm not willing to risk him.'

'Nah. Joshua's fine. As I said to you before, he's in Jamaica. Someone did take him out there for Thornton but the idiot white man knows nothing. I just offered double the amount being paid and he was released.' Jade smiled. 'Thornton did a stupid thing going up against me. Bernie, tell the truth in court, please.'

Bernie sighed. The adrenaline was starting to fade and she now realised how hungry she was and how much her breasts hurt. They were engorged with milk and aching. The thought of not feeding Mira sparked tears. She wiped them away quickly, not wanting Jade to see. As well as calling the police, she'd need to call Dougie. She should have been home hours ago and suspected that a search might be under way for her. At least she hoped so.

A while later, Jade turned into one of the leafier roads in Peckham. There were nice Victorian terraced houses but graffiti still adorned some of the walls and garage doors. Jade parked the car. Bernie noticed the permit holder signs but there was no permit on the car. She didn't think Jade lived here.

'Come on. Let's get you two inside. You must be desperate for a wee if nothing else.' Jade opened the door and jumped out, the door slamming behind her.

Bernie turned back to her grandmother. 'Are you OK, Granny?'

'I think so. A nice cup of tea might help. Do you trust this woman, Bernadette?'

Bernie looked at Jade who was now halfway up a garden path.

'I don't think we have much choice, Granny.' Bernie undid her seatbelt. 'Let's hope whoever lives here will be happy to see us.'

Grandmother and granddaughter got out of the car. Bernie put her arm around Susan and they followed Jade to the front door.

Bernie had no idea of the time but most of the road was in darkness so definitely after eleven p.m., maybe even midnight.

Bernie heard a bolt being pulled back. The door opened but the chain was still on. Jade was in front so Bernie couldn't see who was behind the door.

'Yes?' said a male voice.

'It's Jade. I need your help.'

'It's late.'

'Would Jesus turn away people cos it's late?'

Jesus? Who is Jade talking to, Bernie thought.

The door was pushed shut and Bernie heard the chain being removed. The door swung open wide and there, framed by light behind him, was Barnabas, Leesa's father. Gloria, her mother, appeared a second later.

'Barnabas, what's going on?' she asked. She stopped when she saw Bernie.

'We need your help,' Jade said. 'Urgently. I wouldn't ask if it wasn't important.'

'You've got a nerve asking us for help,' Gloria said. She looked back at Bernie. 'You too.'

Susan pushed past Bernie and Jade. 'Then perhaps I could ask for help instead. I was abducted last night. Hardly fed and watered and you don't want to know what I was given to use as a toilet. Please have mercy on an old lady.'

Gloria looked at Susan and nodded her head. 'Of course. You can all come in.'

As they stepped forward, Bernie whispered in Susan's ear, 'So, now you're old?'

Susan gave her granddaughter a wry smile. 'Well, it worked, didn't it.'

CHAPTER 58

Then

With a movement practised over and over again, Bernie removed her baton and flicked it to full length.

'Ah, so I was right,' said Danny. 'It's not your real name. You're a pig. I'll be honest, as pigs go, you're pretty attractive. I'd do you.' He edged nearer. 'Right now, in fact. I'm sure the boys would be happy to hold you down.'

Bernie glanced quickly at the other two. Carlton was grinning but Zac looked shocked. Leesa was behind them, frozen to the spot. Run, thought Bernie. Run! Freeze, not flight, seemed to be the only option for Leesa. For Bernie, though, it was fight. As she had always done throughout her life. In that moment, she was willing to do whatever it took to save Leesa. She tightened her grip on the baton. Where the hell was back-up?

Danny stepped closer with a menacing look. There'd be no more banter between them now. It was swelteringly hot and sweat poured down Bernie's face, blurring her vision a little. She wanted to wipe it away but she didn't dare move her left arm. Instead she raised her right and pulled it back a little, ready to swing.

Carlton came first. He was shorter than Bernie so she had the advantage. She swung the baton at him, catching his neck and shoulder. His hand went to his neck straight away so Bernie then rapped his knuckles.

'Shit. I think you've broken my hand, you pig.'

'Better a pig than a grass, eh?' Bernie hissed.

'You're talking shit.'

Carlton lurched towards her but staggered back as the baton narrowly missed his face.

'Stop,' Zac called out. 'It isn't worth it. We should go now. There must be others coming soon.'

Danny stared at his younger brother. 'Bro, what you talking about? We can outrun the police. I vote we have some fun until they get here.'

Bernie caught sight of Zac's worried face. He really didn't want to get caught by the police. She remembered his dream of having a family and being happy. There wasn't time to think more as Danny leapt forward to grab the end of the baton. Bernie twisted and kicked out with her leg, landing a blow on Danny's stomach. She'd been aiming a little lower but Danny had a longer body than she thought. He doubled over with a groan. Bernie brought the baton down on his back, knocking him to the floor.

She looked at Zac, the only one not wincing in pain.

'You still here,' she said.

He turned to run but collided with a still frozen Leesa. Both fell to the ground.

'Leesa, run,' Bernie shouted. 'Get up and get out.'

There was a roar and Bernie looked too late to see Danny coming at her. She swung her baton back as he lunged forward. Sun glinted on metal in his hand. Her baton failed to connect with him. It felt like the worst punch ever to her left side. She fell backwards, Danny landing on top of her.

'That's it. Stab the fucking pig!'

Bernie recognised Carlton's voice and Zac joined in too, laughing, now his brother had the upper hand. Warm blood trickled down her as Danny pulled out the knife – the worst thing he could do. He raised his hand for a second attack. Sirens filled the air.

'Fuck. Time to go, boys,' he said.

He jumped up. Bernie clasped her hand to her side in a useless effort to stem the blood. She tried to push up with her other arm to see if Leesa had got away. The teenager was still on the ground, probably winded by Zac falling on her.

'Leesa,' she called, as loudly as she could.

Danny turned back and ran to the teenage girl. 'This is what you get for grassing us up to the pigs.' He plunged the knife into Leesa's chest.

'No!' Bernie screamed. 'No!' She tried to get up to reach Leesa. There was nothing she wanted more in that moment than to stem the blood pumping out of Leesa's chest. But pain ripped through her, and her body was rapidly losing strength along with blood. The sun was hot on her face but coldness was creeping up her, covering her like a blanket of snow.

Sirens were all around her now. Footsteps. Voices. Hands on her, pressing down hard on her side.

Then a voice she recognised. 'It's all right, Bernie. We've got them.'

Her focus was going in and out but DI Jack Thornton was there, his broken nose unmistakeable.

'Leesa?' she whispered.

'Paramedics are with her. Air ambulance will be here in five minutes. We'll get you both to hospital asap.'

Bernie drifted as the paramedics worked on her, barely hearing what was being said. Her eyes flickered open as she was lifted and then moved. As she was wheeled past Leesa, she looked at the teenager, a bundle of people surrounding her. Blood fanned out around her, finding routes to trickle along the asphalt. At the edge of the blood pool, the netball from this morning, pushed by a sudden breeze, rolled through the pool, tracking blood with it. In that moment, Bernie knew. There would be no more netball for Leesa. There would be no more of anything.

CHAPTER 59

Now

A school photo of Leesa hung over the fireplace. Bernie stared at it. Leesa was smiling. She looked smart. Her tie was neat. Her hair braided. It was an image so at odds with how Bernie had last seen her. So alive. Tears flowed silently down her cheeks. She reached out to touch the photo but pulled back as she heard Gloria's voice.

'If you're happy to sleep on the sofa, then your grandmother can have the spare room.'

Bernie turned towards her, not bothering to hide her tears.

'Ah. You've found Leesa's photo. It was her final school one. We moved here after she died. We couldn't stay in our old house. It wasn't a home without her.'

'I'm so sorry to land on you like this. I had no idea Jade was bringing us here.' Bernie looked back at the photo. 'The last thing I want to do is stir up memories and hurt you.'

'Too late. The court case has already done that. Come, now. Sit down. You've obviously been through something bad since court this afternoon. You look a state, Lib... Bernie.' Gloria shook her head. 'Still not used to that.'

Bernie lowered her head. 'I know. I didn't like the deception.

Hated it in fact. I only ever wanted to—'

'Hush.' Gloria put her hand on Bernie's shoulder. 'We'll speak no more about it tonight. You need to rest. Although, I'm wondering if you might need a bath. You have a baby, don't you?'

Bernie frowned. 'How do you know?'

'I don't think it's tears that have made your shirt that wet.'

Bernie looked down at her stained white shirt. 'Oh heck. I hadn't even realised that I'd leaked. It's all been a bit traumatic. I should ring my partner. And work. I'm guessing an alert went out when I didn't arrive home. But I don't have my phone. It got left behind. Jade said she'd call the police but I'm not sure she has.'

'Oh dear. Jade's left already. You can ring on ours.' Gloria fetched a landline phone.

'Thanks.' Bernie cradled it in her hand. 'God, I can't remember Dougie's number. How stupid.'

'You're in shock. Why don't you just ring nine nine nine?'

'It's a sensitive case, Gloria. I need to make sure the right team attends the scene.'

'Do you know your work one then?'

'Yes. Of course. There might be someone there on the night shift.'

Bernie pressed the numbers and waited for someone to answer.

'MCIT. DS Allen speaking.'

'Kerry? Why are you at work? Why aren't you with Debs?'

'Bernie! Where the hell are you? I'm at work because Dougie reported you missing. Wait a minute. I'm putting you on speaker.'

'Who's there?'

'Everyone. We're all trying to find you. Dougie's here too.'

'What? Where's Mira?'

Bernie heard a chair screech back and footsteps running.

'Bernie? Don't worry. Anna and Paul have Mira.' It was Dougie.

'Yes. Oh God, I'm so sorry. I couldn't ring any earlier. Listen, you need to record what I'm about to say. I've got a long story to tell you.'

Bernie settled down on the sofa to sleep. Gloria had persuaded her to take a bath to help with her engorged breasts. The last thing she needed was mastitis. She'd left everything in the hands of her colleagues. Hannah Drake was going to deal directly with the Met. Bernie had described as best as possible where she and Susan had been taken and who they'd find there. Jade hadn't come back, which bothered her. She'd shot a police officer twice. It wasn't strictly self-defence but Bernie would do her best to help Jade.

Bernie shut her eyes but knew that Leesa's photo was on the wall in front of her. She'd spent so long trying to push the trauma away. If she'd stayed silent and not called out Leesa's name, maybe Danny wouldn't have gone back and stabbed her. And Leesa wouldn't just be a photo on the wall. She'd be twenty-two. Living her life. Bringing joy to her parents.

Bernie opened her eyes. Even in the dark, there was still enough light pollution outside to see the photo frame.

'Leesa, I know you're not here any more,' Bernie whispered, 'but I'm going to tell the truth at court. I'm going to tell them everything I know.'

CHAPTER 60

Now

TUESDAY

Bernie startled awake. Was that a doorbell she'd just heard? It wasn't hers. She blinked as she looked round the room, unsure where she was. Light escaped from behind curtains. There were voices. They sounded familiar. The door pushed open and Gloria came in. Now she knew where she was and what had happened.

'The police are here to see you,' Gloria said.

She'd barely moved out of the way when someone rushed into the room and drew Bernie into a hug.

'God, Bernie. I thought I'd lost you.'

'Dougie.'

Bernie buried her face in his shoulder and sobbed. After a while, Dougie pulled back and took her face in his hands. He kissed her before speaking.

'Right. No more tears now. You have a job to do today. I've brought you fresh clothes and we've got evidence bags for yesterday's. Your grandmother's too. Poor Granny, being dragged into this. Is she OK?'

'"She" is perfectly fine,' said a voice behind him. Susan was wearing a dressing gown that was far too big for her.

Dougie smiled. 'Good to see you again, Granny.'

Susan grinned back. The Scottish/Italian charm had won her over.

'My granddaughter did a good job of taking care of me. As did Jade, once we realised she was on our side.'

'Ah yes. Jade.' Dougie stood up. 'I'd like to introduce you to Detective Chief Inspector Charlotte Butler from the Met.'

A woman appeared from behind the door. In her forties, she was wearing a smart grey trouser suit.

'Good morning, Detective Inspector Noel. I'm from Serious Organised Crime. I've just come from the scene you described.'

'You found it then? Was Ben Harper there?'

'Yes.' Butler's look was grim.

'Alive?'

DCI Butler shook her head.

'Oh God, I should have called earlier. Got paramedics to him sooner but my phone was left behind and Jade still had the gun so.' Bernie shrugged.

'We found your phone and I presume your watch too. In the report you gave last night to Wiltshire Police, you stated that Harper was shot twice – in the shoulder and knee.'

'Yes,' said Bernie.

'That's right,' said Susan. 'I was there too.'

'Well, the body I've just seen also had a gunshot wound to the head. My guess is that Jade went back and finished him off.'

'God, no,' Bernie said. 'Why did she do that? I told her that we'd explain everything to the police. Thornton and Harper had her youngest son, Joshua, abducted. They were making her do stuff, to help take me. But she paid the abductors more money and got

Joshua back, which meant she helped us escape.'

'Hmm. And got her revenge at the same time by the looks of it. How well do you know Jade Ambrose, DI Noel?'

Bernie sat up on the sofa, keeping the duvet over her. 'Our paths have crossed a few times now over the last six years. Quite well, I suppose. Not enough to fully trust her though.'

Butler nodded. 'That's wise. I haven't met her but I think I know her a lot better than you. I've been reviewing Operation Willow and all the evidence. Your taped conversations were quite illuminating. All along we thought Danny Ambrose was the one running the gang and the drug deals. But he wasn't. It was his mother. Jack Thornton chose the wrong woman to scorn. So, let's get down to business. Breakfast, witness statements, trip to court. We have an appointment with the judge at nine thirty. Yesterday's events will either stop the trial or be a "straight to jail" for Thornton.'

Bernie was just finishing getting dressed when there was a knock on the lounge door.

'Come in.'

Gloria and Barnabas appeared.

'I'm so sorry again for all of this—'

Gloria held her hand up. 'It's no problem, Bernie. We have something to say to you, well, I have something to say. My husband is a better person at forgiving. He forgave you a long time ago. When you and Jade turned up last night, I wanted to slam the door in your faces. The two women who were connected to my daughter's murder – why should I help you? If your grandmother hadn't been there, I would have refused. But then I saw you looking at Leesa's photo, crying. You really cared about her. If Jack

Thornton is responsible in some way for Leesa's murder, then you must speak up and tell the court what you know. What happens to him is up to the jury. But what happens to you, right now, is up to me.'

Gloria stepped forward and took Bernie's hands in her own.

'I forgive you, Bernie. I absolve you of any guilt you might feel over Leesa's death.'

'Thank you. I'm not sure I can forgive myself though.'

Gloria sniffed. 'I can't help you with that one. But we release you from any guilt you have towards us. You are free. Now, in that knowledge' – Gloria leaned forward and whispered – 'go kick ass.'

CHAPTER 61

Now

The judge was wearing his robes, ready for the hearing, but had yet to put on his wig. Balding on top, his hair was shortly cropped at the sides. He reminded her a little of the super. He was reading Bernie's statement, having already gone through Susan's.

Bernie sat in front of his desk, along with DCI Butler. Neither the prosecution nor defence barristers knew they were there. Bernie had been ushered in through the back door that she'd left by the day before. She was still having trouble processing everything that had happened in the last twenty-four hours. She didn't really want to stand up in court again. She just wanted to be home with Dougie and Mira. Especially Mira. After missing another feed, her chest ached.

The judge placed the statement down on his desk.

'Well, DI Noel, I think it's fair to say you've been through the wars. Hmm. Witness intimidation is a very serious crime. If you were a jury member, then I would dismiss the jury right now and order a retrial. As a witness, I could have you removed and your testimony disregarded. Or, you could continue to give evidence today and be cross-examined by the prosecution. I got the sense, yesterday, that you were cautious with your replies. I'll remind you again, that you took an oath to tell the truth, the whole truth. Of course, if you do give evidence, you must not talk about what happened last night. That will be for another time.'

The judge paused for a moment.

'I probably shouldn't do this but I'm going to give you the choice, DI Noel. What do you want to do? Leave now and your evidence will be removed from the case, or, stand in the witness box this morning?'

Bernie bowed her head a little. She was exhausted. Going home was a definite option. But Gloria's words came back to her. She owed it to Leesa to stand up and tell the truth, the whole truth this time. Even if it risked her own reputation.

She looked up. 'I'll give evidence and without the curtain. I want to see Jack Thornton's face.'

Bernie looked across to the public gallery and saw some friendly faces. DCI Butler and Barnabas were there. Gloria had stayed at home to look after Susan. Dougie was waiting in the Witness Room. Although he'd already given his evidence, there was still the possibility of a retrial. Plus Bernie thought Dougie might not be able to contain himself, he was so angry with Jack Thornton. Bernie was pretty angry herself. She allowed her eyes to linger on the man she once called 'sir'. He looked at her and there was a faint glimmer of a smile. He clearly had no idea what had happened to Harper. Bernie was looking forward to wiping the smile off his face.

'Detective inspector,' said the prosecution barrister. 'My name is Christopher Mason. I'm sure you're well aware of what my job is.'

Bernie turned her attention back to him. She didn't know if

counsel had been told about her abduction. That was up to the judge. But there seemed little concern on the defence barrister's face, so she assumed not. Roger Howe-Turner was about to get a shock.

'Forgive me if I'm wrong,' Mason continued, 'but yesterday it felt to me as though the defence were leading you in a certain direction and you were reluctant to go there.'

Howe-Turner sprung to his feet. 'Objection. I did not lead the witness.'

'Sustained. Find another way to phrase your question, if indeed there is one,' said the judge.

Mason inclined his head. 'Of course, your honour. Detective inspector, you gave us a fairly detailed account of Operation Willow but I sensed you were holding back. Obviously, in a court of law, we can't rely on senses and feelings. We need evidence. So, rather than asking you lots of questions, I'm only going to ask you one. Is there anything that you would like to add to the testimony you gave yesterday?'

Bernie swallowed. She wanted to look across to Barnabas but didn't dare. And she certainly wasn't going to look at Thornton. Not until the end. Instead, she focused on the jury.

'Yes, I would like to add more detail. I spoke the truth yesterday but not the *whole* truth. I did so out of concern for my own reputation as a police officer. It's important for the court to know that I didn't join Operation Willow because I applied for it. I wasn't head-hunted because I was a talented young DC. I wasn't even chosen because I'm dual heritage. I was given the role because...'

Bernie looked down. She was relieved Dougie wasn't in court to hear this. But he did need to hear it and soon.

'I'm ashamed to say that I had an affair with a senior officer. He wanted to end it and he wanted me away from the police station.' Bernie closed her eyes. She'd said it. Shame stung her eyes with tears. She wiped them away with her hand. She looked back up and focused on the jury.

'I walked into that operation as a new DC with no training, no experience, no knowledge of what I would be asked to do. I was the last person who should have been in that role. And that's exactly what Jack Thornton wanted. He wanted naivety. He wanted someone who would listen to his orders. What he didn't want was someone who thought outside the box. Who picked up on things and ran with them. I might have been new to covert operations but I'd been a uniformed officer for nine years at that point. I couldn't ignore my gut and the feeling that things weren't right.

'There were five of us on the netball court the day Leesa was murdered. Only two of us are still alive – myself, and Danny Ambrose who murdered Leesa. Earlier that day, Carlton Jones made reference to "boxer man". Zac told him to be quiet. Last year, I spoke to Zac Ambrose's girlfriend after he'd died and she referred to a man who looked like a boxer. She went on to describe a man who fitted Jack Thornton's description. At the time, I didn't connect what Carlton said with Jack Thornton but I believe now that "boxer man" is Thornton. And if that's the case, how did Carlton know him?'

Howe-Turner bounced out of his chair again. 'Objection. The witness is surmising about a dead man and we only have her word that Carlton Jones even said that.'

Bernie pulled her focus away from the jury and looked at DCI Butler. The nod of her head was imperceptible but enough for Bernie to notice.

She turned back to the jury. 'Almost all of my conversations were recorded, including this one with Carlton Jones and Zac Ambrose. I'm sure it could be dug out of the evidence store.' She stared at Roger Howe-Turner. 'Would that be good enough?'

He huffed and sat back down.

'More than that, I followed Carlton Jones to a meeting he had with Jack Thornton. I didn't see them together but I met with Jack there just thirty minutes later. It was our regular rendezvous point. That led me to believe that Carlton was an informant. But the fact that Zac knew about boxer man as well...'

Bernie shook her head. 'As a police officer, I'm used to dealing with facts and solid evidence. And what I saw at the time suggested that Carlton Jones was the informant. But I've had a long time to think about this. Jack Thornton didn't need an informant because he was the one supplying the drugs. They all knew "boxer man". He gave the orders. He was, and still is, Jack Thornton.'

Christopher Mason smiled. 'Is there anything else you'd like to add?'

Bernie looked at Jack Thornton now. His head hung low. Carlton Jones hadn't been able to give evidence against Thornton while alive but he had in death. Bernie had done a good job as a defence witness casting doubt, but in the wrong direction for her former senior officer. But she knew it wouldn't be the last time they met in court. Fresh charges would soon be made.

'No,' Bernie replied. 'For now.'

CHAPTER 62

Now

When Bernie reached the Witness room, she wanted to throw herself into Dougie's arms but there was another policeman with him. She recognised his face instantly. She'd seen him enough times on the television. It was the Met Commissioner.

'Ah, here she is,' said Dougie.

The Met Commissioner, smart in his impeccable uniform, turned and held out his hand. Bernie took it.

'Well done, DI Noel. It couldn't have been easy in there.'

'It wasn't.'

Bernie pulled her hand back. She was sweaty. Why was the Commissioner here? Had he heard her evidence? Was she going to be reprimanded for her mistakes in Operation Willow? Or for sleeping with a married officer?

'You're probably wondering why I'm here.'

'Yes, sir.'

'I want to apologise for your treatment by one of my officers. DC Harper's actions weren't just criminal but unforgiveable. I believe you've already met DCI Butler. She'll be reporting to me directly on this case. We will get to the bottom of this, you have my word.'

Bernie nodded. 'Thank you, sir. That means a lot to me. And thank you for all your help so far. I know Chief Constable Drake appreciated the time you gave her last week.'

The Commissioner flushed a little. 'I think I need to apologise to her too. On reflection, a ten-minute phone call wasn't enough. Had I given her more time, none of this might have happened.'

Bernie frowned. A phone call? Hannah Drake had told her it was a face-to-face, all-day meeting. If she hadn't been at Scotland Yard the previous Thursday, where had she been?

'Well, I won't hold you up,' said the Commissioner. 'I know you have a little one waiting at home for you. I thought it was important to see you in person though, DI Noel. I'm sure DCI Butler will be in touch with you soon. Safe journey back.'

He shook Bernie's hand and then Dougie's before leaving. Once gone, Dougie put his arms around Bernie and kissed the top of her head.

'Shall we go home?' he asked.

'Yes please.'

Mira clung to Bernie's neck, crying.

'It's OK, baby, Mama's home now. Do you want some milk?'

It was the middle of the afternoon and early for her nighttime feed but it was probably the only thing that would calm her down. Bernie settled on the sofa and Mira latched on as soon as she could. Bernie sighed with relief. It brought her comfort as much as Mira.

She wondered how her grandmother was. They'd offered for her to come back with them but she'd refused. Barnabas and Gloria had said she could stay with them until Bernie's parents got back from their holiday.

Dougie brought her a glass of water. He sat down next to her and stroked his daughter's foot. He looked exhausted.

'Do you want to go to bed?' Bernie asked.

'Only if you're coming.' He winked.

'Honestly. I'm not sure this one would let me anyway.'

'Yeah. I think she'll be in our bed tonight.'

Bernie looked down at her baby girl. 'When Harper was pointing a gun at me—'

'Bernie, you don't have to talk about this now.'

'I know but I want to say. I didn't have my life flash before me. Instead, I thought of all the things I'd miss with you and Mira.' She looked up at Dougie. 'Of the life I wouldn't have.'

'Oh Bernie.' Dougie shuffled closer to her and put his arm around her shoulders. 'I was going insane last night. Kerry was this close to throwing me out of MCIT.' He leaned his head against hers. 'I knew Thornton was capable of a lot of things but to have you and Granny abducted, well it shows how worried he is about the verdict. The prosecution case is strong against him. And DCI Butler said you did really well and were very brave.'

Bernie bit her lip. She'd never told Dougie everything. She was aware of his thoughts on adultery due to his cheating ex-wife. There was never going to be a good time to tell him so she might as well get it over and done with.

'Dougie, I need to tell you what happened. Not just with Leesa but how I got the job in the first place.'

Keeping her eyes fixed on her daughter's head, Bernie poured out everything. By the time she finished, Mira was asleep, grasping Bernie's finger with her little hand.

'Thank you for telling me,' Dougie said. 'I see now why you struggled to say anything before. Louise and I were... different.

And it was brave of you to say some of that in court.'

'I'm worried about losing my job though.'

'Don't be. If anyone should lose their job, it's the officer you had an affair with. He was senior to you and should have known better. He threw you under a bus when he sent you to Thornton.' He yawned.

'Oh Dougie, you really should go for a nap.'

'Only if you come too. This little one will sleep well between us.'

Bernie climbed the stairs carefully so not to disturb Mira. Dougie pulled the curtains to shut out the fading light. The sudden darkness hit Bernie and she started to tremble.

'Dougie, I can't be in the dark. I just can't. I need a bit of light.'

'Sure. I'll put the landing light on.'

He was back a few seconds later and put his arms around her. 'It's OK. You're safe now. I'll take Mira and you slip into bed. Then I'll give her to you.'

Bernie did as Dougie said, her body relieved at being in her own bed. Mira stirred as she was placed next to Bernie but she settled with her mother's hand. Dougie slid in the other side, his hand reaching Bernie's.

Bernie drifted but images were playing around in her mind. Carlton and Zac playing basketball. Leesa on the ground, not moving. Carlton's body on her front doorstep. Her tired brain pushed back with a thought. No, he was in the car... but he was meant to be on the doorstep. Bernie's eyes flickered open. Jack Thornton knew where she lived. Would they ever be safe from him?

CHAPTER 63

Now

WEDNESDAY

'I should really send you home, Bernie. You've been through a terrible ordeal.' Chief Constable Hannah Drake leaned forward in her chair. 'And I definitely shouldn't let you rejoin the case.'

'But...' Bernie looked hopefully at the most senior officer in Wiltshire Police.

Hannah Drake sighed. 'But, as long as we allow DCI Butler to do her job in London in regard to your abduction, the CPS has said you can continue dealing with the deaths of Carlton Jones, Lewis Brown and Aaron Swan. It will probably mean two trials and I'm going to strongly advise you not to give evidence if we find a connection between Thornton and the young men's deaths. The best charge we can hope for is conspiracy to murder. Ben Harper confessed to you his involvement so we know he was the one who pulled the trigger. But it's clearly Thornton pulling the strings. Find the evidence. One good piece of news is that DCI Butler and her team found a phone on Harper. They're going to share the data with us as soon as they have it. You said Harper called Thornton on that number so hopefully there'll be other times when he made contact.

'Right, go back to your team but please take it easy. You will have counselling sessions so don't even think about ducking out of those. Equally, we can arrange sessions for your grandmother too. She was held for longer. Just let me know. I'm going to a meeting this afternoon but please keep me in the loop. You can leave messages with my PA.'

Bernie stood up. 'Thank you, ma'am.'

As she reached the door, she turned back.

'One more thing, ma'am. I saw the Met Commissioner yesterday. I thanked him for all the help he gave you last week when you were at Scotland Yard.'

Bernie looked intently at the chief constable. She thought she saw Drake's mouth twitch.

'That was very considerate of you, Bernie. The Commissioner has been of significant help. It was a good day.'

Bernie smiled briefly and left the room. Hannah Drake had just reinforced her original lie. Bernie was determined to find out why.

Before Bernie reached MCIT, Jane Clackett found her and enveloped her in a huge but slightly uncomfortable hug. Jane wasn't a 'touchy feely' person.

'I am so glad to see you,' Jane said, stepping back. 'We've managed to keep it out of the press for now. God, Bernie. I'd have been a mess if you hadn't come back. Although, I would have a lot more chocolate. Want some?'

Bernie grinned. 'Thought you'd never ask. Need some energy today. Sleep has been in short supply over the last couple of nights.'

'I bet. Is Mira OK?'

'She was clingy last night but she happily waved goodbye to me this morning. So, she's not traumatised.'

Jane patted Bernie's arm. 'Unlike her mum. You can't fool me. I don't mean to worry you but you ought to step up security at your house.'

Bernie nodded. She'd spent most of the night thinking about that. 'I know. Dougie's looking at alarm companies today.'

Jane opened her office door. 'You might want to think about a panic alarm too that connects to headquarters. Although—' Jane stopped.

'If they're serious, they'll be in and out in minutes,' Bernie continued. 'We'll be dead by the time police arrive.'

Jane nodded grimly. She opened a desk drawer and took out a bar of chocolate.

'Here. Have it all. You bloody deserve it. And if there's anything I can do to help find evidence on Thornton, let me know. There might be some journalists who could spill the beans on him.'

'You could try Clive Bishop. For a local journalist he does seem to have amazing connections.'

'Hmm. Maybe.'

Bernie laughed. Jane and Clive did not get on well at all.

'I'd better get to MCIT. I have a team to thank.'

Bernie was barely through the door when Kerry launched herself at her.

'Don't you ever do that again.'

'What? Get abducted? It was hardly my fault.'

Kerry wiped her eyes. 'I know. But it was bloody awful not knowing where you were.'

'Thank you for looking for me and taking care of Dougie. I gather he was going a bit insane.'

'God, yes. Just a bit.'

'And how's Debs?'

Kerry gave a quick grin. 'All good. Everything's fine.'

'I'm so pleased. Now, where is everyone else?'

Bernie looked round the empty office.

'Coming in at nine this morning. It was a bit hard going doing a twenty-four-hour shift. I'll be honest, we've made little progress since Friday.'

'Well, we'll have a briefing when everyone else is in.'

Bernie went to her desk to put the chocolate away.

'What've you got there?' Kerry asked.

'Nothing gets past you, does it? Chocolate from Jane.'

'A whole bar? Wow. Now you can see how worried we all were.'

Bernie gave a quick smile. 'Nice to know you all care.'

'Care? We bloody love you. You should have seen us. We were a mess. Even the super lost the plot. Only the chief constable was calm enough to deal with it all. Without her, we wouldn't have made any progress at all. Helped that she knew exactly who to contact at the Met to get the ball rolling their end.'

Bernie slipped the chocolate into her drawer. It was heartwarming to know how much her team loved her.

'Right, let's work out where we're up to and where we need to go from here. Alice, will you scribe please?'

Bernie surveyed her team. If they were surprised about her being back in the office then they didn't show it. Matt had done a bakery run so everyone had something to eat. Even Leigh was eating a Danish pastry. It gave Bernie an air of normalcy, which was much needed.

'Let's start with what I know,' said Bernie. 'We don't need to look for the person who murdered Carlton Jones and Aaron Swan.

That was DC Ben Harper who abducted my grandmother and me. He's now dead. Jade Ambrose was also with us and she shot Harper twice but he was alive when we escaped. It's thought Jade went back to finish him off but that's for the Met to deal with. DCI Charlotte Butler is heading up that enquiry.

'Our job now is to see if there's a link between Jack Thornton and the murder of Carlton Jones, who was due to testify against Thornton. It'll be harder for Aaron Swan. That might have been "a heat of the moment" thing from Harper. It's looking likely that Lewis Brown's death was a tragic accident. He probably thought it was Harper in the car chasing him. I'm guessing he'd witnessed Swan's murder and didn't want to end up the same way. Sadly, he did.

'Look, we know what Carlton Jones was capable of. He should have been tried for his assaults and what he did to Leigh.'

Bernie glanced across to the local crime investigator. If anyone had an inkling of how Bernie was feeling, it was her. Thankfully, her abduction had lasted minutes not hours. Leigh was twisting her rings. Bernie knew to take the attention off her.

'But we need to find out exactly what happened to him and who's responsible. So, let's start with Dennis Pinner. Was his house checked?'

Mick raised his hand. 'Yes, ma'am. Alice and I did a thorough search. There was nothing to indicate that anyone had been living there recently. It smelt quite musty when we went in. The fridge was empty but still switched on. A few items in the freezer. Some clothes appeared to be taken as there were empty hangers but not all of them. Same with toiletries. Couldn't find any suitcases. So, at first glance, it would suggest that they've gone away.'

'At first glance?' Bernie asked.

Mick grinned. 'I managed to get into a locked desk drawer and found their passports. If they have gone away, it's not on those passports. There was also a USB stick that was stuck to the back of the locked drawer. It's with Tom. Hoping he might have some info today.'

'Good work, Mick and Alice. How about Helen Brown and her sister, the former Mrs Pinner?'

'I've been looking at that, ma'am,' Leigh said. 'Managed to track them to the Eurostar at St Pancras. They boarded with Irish passports. Got out in Paris but lost them from that point. We've informed Interpol saying that they're vulnerable witnesses who require protection but' – Leigh raised her hands – 'they can't be forced to come back.'

Bernie rubbed her forehead. She had to find the link that connected Thornton to Carlton Jones's murder.

'Ma'am.'

Bernie looked up. It was Matt.

'Yes?'

'There is someone who might be able to shed more light on this – the officer from Witness Protection. Colin Ferguson?'

'Yes, Matt. You're right. I can think of a few questions to ask him. Starting with how he missed that Ben Harper was a corrupt officer.'

CHAPTER 64

Kerry and Matt sat on one side of the table, Colin Ferguson and a police rep on the other. Bernie watched them on a screen. Most people underestimated Kerry as a petite blonde but she was Bernie's secret weapon. She could fell a man a foot taller than her and tie people up in tangles in an interview. Bernie was relying on her to do just that with DS Colin Ferguson now.

'So, DS Ferguson, as I've already explained, you're here as a witness and can leave whenever you want to,' said Kerry. 'Are you happy to get started?'

Colin Ferguson nodded, his shock of white hair moving slightly.

'OK. When did DC Ben Harper join the Witness Protection Service?'

Bernie and Kerry had written the questions before the interview. The plan was to focus on Harper before turning to Ferguson's own dodgy behaviour that night.

'He joined six, seven months ago.'

'So not long then?'

'No.'

'How was he recruited?'

'We had a vacant post. He applied, along with others. After

spending time in covert operations, he had skills that some of the other applicants didn't have. He was perfect.'

Kerry glanced at Matt and he took over the questioning.

'Who decided he would look after Carlton Jones?'

Ferguson turned to Matt. 'Ben wasn't chosen specifically. It was my team that was selected to look after Carlton Jones.'

'And where had Carlton been staying before being at the barn?'

Ferguson narrowed his eyes, angrily. 'You know I can't give away that kind of information.'

'OK. Let's try this one – who chose the caravan at the barn?'

Ferguson rubbed his forehead. 'It was Ben. He was concerned that the previous address had been compromised. Said he knew a good place. We only needed it for a couple of nights.'

Kerry tapped her notebook with her pen. Time for her to take over.

'Why was Carlton out of prison anyway? He was on remand. Surely prison would have been the safest place for him.'

'Stupid boy was boasting about getting out and walking away scot-free. Didn't know when to keep his mouth shut.'

Bernie scoffed. That was Carlton all right. Too mouthy by halves.

'Were threats made to him?'

'Not just threats. He was beaten up. Cut a few times rather than stabbed. We had to get him out.'

Bernie thought about the cuts Nick White had referred to in the post-mortem. That would make sense.

'Going back to the caravan – did you check out the owner, Dennis Pinner?'

Ferguson rubbed his forehead again. A nervous tic? thought Bernie.

'No. Ben did that. Wish I had now. I've looked him up since.' Ferguson shook his head. 'Look, there are a number of people that we look after. I left Ben in charge of Jones. The protection side was only for a few days – a week at the most – and then Jones was going to be relocated.'

'So a possible sex offender was going to be released into a new and unsuspecting community.'

Ferguson stretched his arms up, as though bored by Kerry's questions.

'I don't decide who gets immunity and protection. That's down to the CPS. They wanted Jones to give evidence against Thornton. Blame them, not me.'

Kerry appeared to write that down. Matt took up the questioning.

'Was there any indication that Carlton Jones knew who Ben Harper was?'

'None that I noticed.'

'How was Carlton feeling about testifying?'

Ferguson shrugged. 'He didn't really say. But he did talk a lot, almost hyperactive, and I wondered if it was down to nerves.'

'Why did you allow Ben Harper to leave his post that night?'

Ferguson rubbed his forehead once more. Is he all right, thought Bernie. Is he unwell? The last thing she needed was him collapsing during the interview.

'Are you OK, DS Ferguson?' Kerry asked. 'You keep rubbing your head.'

Ah, thought Bernie, you've noticed too.

'I have a headache. I could do with some painkillers and water.'

'Of course,' Kerry said. 'We can pause for fifteen or twenty minutes. I'll get you something to drink and eat, along with some paracetamol.'

'Ibuprofen would be better, please.'

'Sure. I'll be back soon.'

Kerry left the room. Bernie went to meet her.

'Going well so far,' Bernie said.

'Really?' Kerry replied. 'I think he's answering the questions without really answering them. If you know what I mean.'

'I know exactly what you mean and that is what he's doing. And we know it. So, it's going well. Once his headache has gone, you'll be able to go in a bit heavier. But not too much. I trust you to find the balance.'

Bernie's phone buzzed in her pocket. She pulled it out and looked at the screen. She didn't recognise the number but it was from London. She answered.

'Hello?'

'Hello, DI Noel. It's DCI Charlotte Butler here. Are you free for a chat?'

'Yes, I've got time. I was watching an interview but it's paused for the moment.'

'Interview? You're at work?'

'Yes. Got three young dead men that I need to find answers for.'

'Personally, I think you're bonkers but each to their own. Could you do me a favour and take this call outside, please? Maybe in your car.'

Bernie frowned. It seemed a strange request but she'd honour it.

'Sure. Give me five minutes.'

CHAPTER 65

Bernie settled herself in her car. It wasn't particularly warm. Spring still hadn't completely sprung. She called Charlotte Butler.

'Hi, DI Noel. Thanks for calling back. And I apologise for the "cloak and dagger" approach. All will become clear. In some respects, I shouldn't be giving you some of this information but it might be pertinent to your case. We found two phones on Harper. One was a burner, the other was a personal phone.'

'The chief constable only mentioned one phone to me,' said Bernie.

'That's because I only told her about one phone – the burner, which surprise, surprise, had been wiped by the time we found it. His personal phone and smart watch have been very helpful though. Time of death was before midnight, meaning—'

'Meaning, Jade didn't do it. Sorry, I shouldn't have interrupted you.'

'It's good to see we're coming to the same conclusions. I have ballistics working overtime on the bullets. All three were still in Harper's body but early indications are that the third bullet was fired from a different gun but the same type.'

'The military-style Glock?'

'Yes.'

'Like the sort issued to the Met.'

'Exactly.'

Bernie had a good idea what that meant. 'So, potentially, another officer killed him. I can see now why you wanted this conversation away from headquarters.'

'Yes. I'm outside too. There's more. Harper texted someone on his personal phone after he was shot. Mistake number one. It said, "Been shot. Send help." Mistake number two – he'd texted a traceable phone. It belongs to a DS Colin Ferguson.'

Bernie widened her eyes in surprise. 'You're kidding. That's who we're interviewing but as a witness rather than suspect.'

'Keep him as a witness for now but see if you can get his phones. We're looking at his phone records now and combing CCTV for footage of him. We're triangulating mobile signals to see if we can place him at the scene that way.'

'That's a good point. We should do the same here for the night our three men died. His story's hanging by a thread. I'll get our Digital guy on to it.'

'DI Noel—'

'Please, call me Bernie.'

'Bernie, I've been doing some digging and I've discovered that Chief Constable Drake and DCI Jack Thornton used to—'

'Work together. I know.'

'Bit more than that. They were in a relationship. In fact, they were together during your undercover operation.'

'Thornton and Drake were together? That makes no sense. She told me Thornton sexually harassed female officers and she tried to stop it.'

'That's bullshit. A female detective told me she'd complained to Drake about Thornton and was told to put up with it or move teams. Needless to say, she moved. You need to be very careful, Bernie. I'm not sure where Hannah Drake's loyalties lie. Keep this to yourself for now. But if you find anything that ties the chief constable with Harper, Ferguson, and Thornton, then let me know asap.'

Bernie closed her eyes. Headquarters had always felt safe to her. Now, it seemed she was about to walk into a lion's den. 'What about Thornton's phone?'

'It was found yesterday. My officers searched while you were in court.'

'Wiped?'

'Actually, no. But the only number on it relates to Harper's burner. That was probably his only contact. All phone calls. No texts.'

'So, nothing useable.'

'Possibly not but leave that for me to worry about. Focus on your case for now. Having said that, I've been checking on court today and the barristers are due to start summing up. Thornton was supposed to take the stand but refused to do so last minute. I think he's discovered that his phone is missing. He's rattled. We'll get him, Bernie. We'll get them all.'

CHAPTER 66

Bernie stayed in her car for a few more minutes. Her first thought was to tell Kerry what DCI Butler had said. She hated keeping anything from her right-hand woman but for Kerry's own safety, she had to, especially with Debs pregnant. Bernie had seen what these bent coppers were willing to do.

There was a reason for asking Ferguson for his work and personal phones, though, and it related to the night Carlton Jones, Aaron Swan and Lewis Brown had died. Where was Ferguson really when Harper phoned him to say he needed to leave his post because of an emergency? Who did Ferguson call after Lewis Brown crashed? And who was the other officer in the car with Ferguson? His earlier refusal to name him was suspicious. Bernie thought for a moment and then hit her forehead as she realised. It was Harper who was driving and he knew where to find Brown in the BMW because he'd given him the route. Things were slotting into place but they needed the evidence. She wrote some notes on her phone and messaged them to Kerry.

'How's your headache, now?' Matt asked DS Colin Ferguson.

Ferguson grimaced. 'Still hurts a bit but I can feel it's lifting.'

'Are you OK to carry on then?'

'Yes. Let's get on with it.'

Matt made a point of looking at his notebook but Bernie was fully aware that he knew which question they'd paused on. He looked up.

'Why did you allow Ben Harper to leave his post that night?'

'As I told DI Noel last time,' Ferguson looked briefly up at the camera. 'The officer on shift, who I can now name as DC Ben Harper, had called to say that his child was ill and had to go to hospital. It was an emergency. I said he could go. Carlton Jones had a tracker on him and the caravan could be locked. Even if he had escaped, we'd have found him.'

'But someone else could have found him too,' Kerry said. 'It was a huge risk.'

Ferguson sighed noisily. 'It was. And one I'll pay for. It was my operation.'

'And what happened after the phone call from Harper?' Kerry asked.

'I called another member of my team to come and pick me up—'

'Name, please,' Kerry interjected. She gave Ferguson a hard stare.

'As I told DI Noel, I'm not prepared to give away that name at present.'

'Why?'

'My officers deal with some very serious cases. It's important to keep them as safe as the witnesses.'

'As safe as Carlton Jones?'

Nice one, thought Bernie.

Ferguson shook his head. 'Until I'm authorised by the Met Commissioner to name the other officer, I won't be doing so.'

Kerry looked at Matt. He continued the questioning.

'What happened when you arrived at the barn?'

Ferguson leaned back in his chair and folded his arms.

He's shutting down, Bernie thought. Great.

'I've been through this already with DI Noel and DCS Wilson. We were almost at the turning for the barn when we saw a white BMW pulling out at speed. We drove to the barn. Carlton was missing and another young man was dead in the caravan. We went after the BMW and managed to catch up with it. It crashed. I checked the driver for a pulse and couldn't feel one. I found a mutilated body in the boot which I believed to be Carlton. I called my boss and was told to leave the scene. Which, with hindsight, was the wrong thing to do. I'm sorry. I truly am.' Ferguson huffed.

'OK,' said Kerry. 'Thank you for going through it all again. Just one more request of you and then we'll be done. As you're not willing to name your colleague, we'll need your phone to corroborate your whereabouts and the phone calls made that night.'

Ferguson looked at the police rep who nodded. Ferguson reached into his pocket and pulled out a phone. Bernie recognised it as a work mobile. So did Kerry.

'Your personal one too, please.'

Ferguson froze. 'Why?'

'Just to help corroborate your movements.'

Slowly, he pulled out another phone. As he did so, Matt stood up and opened the door to the interview room. Tom came in with two Faraday evidence bags and the phones were immediately placed inside and sealed. It was too late to wipe the phones. Mistake number three, thought Bernie.

CHAPTER 67

'Where did we get to with the timeline for the Mercedes?' Bernie asked her team.

Embarrassed faces looked back at her.

'Sorry, ma'am,' said Alice. 'We did start to look at it but then we got drawn into something else.'

'Such as?'

'The Pinners. Chief Constable Drake thought we should be looking more at them and where they'd gone.'

Bernie pondered for a minute. Hannah Drake had been quick to take over the case from her. Had she deliberately misdirected Bernie's team?

'Well, get back on it. I want to know exactly where that car has been since the night of Carlton Jones's murder.'

'Every day since or just that night?' Mick asked.

'Every. Single. Day. Mick, you help Alice and Leigh with that. Kerry, Matt and I will go through the data on Dennis Pinner's USB stick. I hope you've all got some food with you as we're working through until we find answers.'

Matt opened up the files Tom had sent and Bernie and Kerry sat either side of him.

'Right, ma'am. Luckily for us, Dennis Pinner was a methodical record keeper. There are lots of spreadsheets detailing drug deals and car sales. It appears that Dennis was either a supplier or worked for one. See, in this column here we have the name of the drug gang. Then we have the different drugs sold with weight and price.'

Matt flicked through some different tabs on the program. 'These go back ten years. Whoever's been running this business earned a lot of money.'

'What's the most recent transaction?' Bernie asked.

Matt found the relevant page. 'Last month. February fourteenth. Labelled "Valentine's Special". If the gangs collected in the morning then it could be out on the streets by nightfall.'

'How many gang members do you know who get up early in the morning?' Bernie laughed.

'Well, there must have been some because,' said Matt, clicking on a row of figures, 'they cleared about seven hundred and fifty thousand pounds that day with twenty-four gangs.'

'Wow. Now we know why Dennis Pinner held on to those outbuildings and barns,' said Kerry. 'Great place to store it all. The cars too. Although, they probably weren't there for very long.'

'No,' said Matt. 'Change of licence plate and straight back out.'

'The question is – can we tie any of this to Thornton, Harper or Ferguson?' Bernie drummed her fingers on Matt's desk. 'Mick?'

'Yes, ma'am.'

'You found this USB stick hidden behind a desk drawer?'

'Yes. It was taped there.'

Things were ticking in Bernie's mind. Things she didn't even want to consider but DCI Charlotte Butler had already sown the seed.

'Was the chief constable meant to do the search with you?' she asked.

'Yes,' said Alice. 'But she got dragged into a meeting. She did call us, though, to find out if we'd discovered anything. At that point, we hadn't. Mick found the USB after the call.'

'And did you tell the chief constable about it?'

'No,' said Mick. 'We told Kerry and she said to log it and give it to Tom to look at. Then we heard you'd gone missing and all hell broke loose.'

'OK.' Bernie stood up. 'I'm going to pop down and see Tom. Everyone, carry on with what you're doing. I don't want to load pressure on you all but we need some results today.'

Digital Forensics was in the basement of headquarters. Bernie often wondered about Tom's sanity being stuck down there without natural light but he was a friendly guy and, more importantly, amazing at his job.

'Hi, Tom.'

'Oh hi, DI Noel. I'm just working on these phones DS Allen sent me.'

'Got anything interesting?'

'The police work phone is fairly standard.'

'What phone calls were there on Sunday night a week ago? Especially going into Monday morning.'

The phone was connected to Tom's PC. 'Here's the log of ingoing and outgoing calls. There's an incoming one just after midnight. It's from another police mobile that was registered to DC Ben Harper.'

Bernie nodded.

'You were expecting that?' Tom asked.

'Yes. It tallies with what we've been told.'

'OK. Next call is outgoing at two forty-six a.m. Lasts a couple of minutes. Also to a police mobile but I need authorisation to get access.'

'It was to his boss – whoever that is – so would make sense as probably a high-ranking officer. But wait, there isn't an outgoing call after Harper rang?'

'No. Would there be?'

'We've been told a phone call was made to a colleague.'

'Not on this phone. Let's try the other one.'

Tom connected Ferguson's personal mobile. He tapped in a number code and the phone sprang to life. He went straight to the call directory.

'No. A call wasn't made on this phone either. So, what does that mean?'

Bernie leaned against Tom's desk. 'It means either Ferguson drove himself to Clench that night or, the colleague who drove was already with him.'

'In the middle of the night?' Tom asked.

Bernie raised her eyebrows.

'Oh. Let's see if we can find out who.'

Tom opened photos and searched for any people who regularly appeared. Apart from Ferguson himself, there was no one else. A scroll through his photos suggested a nature lover or maybe he was looking for safe places.

'You know, I've been doing this job long enough to know that the juicy stuff is normally hidden in an innocuous file. Give me a few minutes.'

'No problem. Mind if I wait?'

'Sure. Grab a chair.'

Bernie pulled out her phone and texted Charlotte Butler.

Got phones and searching now. Btw, was Harper married with a child?

A few seconds later, a response came in.

Good work on phones. Yes, married but separated with one child. Saw wife yesterday. She's OK.

And the child? Ferguson's saying that Harper's excuse for leaving was that his child was ill and in hospital.

Unlikely. Wife said she hadn't had contact with Harper for three weeks. Said he was on a case.

OK. Thanks.

'Tom, before you go down a rabbit hole, can you check his text messages for Monday night this week.'

'Of course.' He flipped back to texts. 'Here you are. There's one here that came in just after twenty-three hundred hours. It says, "Been shot. Send help." Is that from Harper?'

'Yes. Look at his phone calls.'

Tom switched back to the call log. 'Yes. He made a call to the other police mobile a minute after the text message. The one he rang early hours of Monday morning.'

'The one we'll need to get authorisation for?'

'That's the one. Shall I keep searching for any hidden photos?'

'Yes please.'

Bernie tapped her phone against her chin. Charlotte Butler's earlier comment was weighing on her.

'Oh shit. Sorry, ma'am. Think I've found it.'

Bernie looked at Tom's screen. A photo of a sleeping, naked woman was there. Long dark hair, streaked with grey. He flicked through more intimate photos until there was one of Ferguson and the woman having sex.

'I think they might be stills from a video,' said Tom.

'That doesn't reassure me. And please, don't search for the video. We have enough here to prove a relationship.'

'But it looks like—'

'I know who it looks like. Can you check for a date stamp on this? I'm guessing last Thursday.'

'Really?'

Tom clicked on the photo to find the data.

'God, you're right. How did you know that?'

'A hunch. She told me she was in London. But clearly not at Scotland Yard.'

'Ma'am, this is serious. What do we do?'

'Well, this stays between you and me for now. There's a Met officer who's going to be interested in this info but we need to triangulate Ferguson's phone and this other number to find out where they were when Carlton Jones and Ben Harper were killed. In the meantime, I'm going to confirm the owner of the mystery phone. Although, I think it's pretty obvious.'

Bernie left Tom working and headed upstairs past MCIT. She knocked on an office door.

'Come in.'

Claire, the PA, smiled as she saw Bernie.

'I'm so sorry, DI Noel, but the Chief Constable is out at a meeting.'

'Damn. I've got a very important update on the case and she

asked me to keep her in the loop. When will she be back?'

'Not until after four p.m. some time. She's with the Police and Crime Commissioner.' Bernie tapped her fingers against her leg. 'It's really important. Maybe I could send her a text message. Do you have her mobile number please?'

'Oh, I'm not supposed to give that out. I could send her a message.'

Bernie shook her head. 'Sorry, Claire, this stuff is very confidential.' Bernie sighed. 'I really need her input now otherwise... I'm going to have to let a murderer go free.'

'Can't DCS Wilson help you?'

'No. I've already asked him and only the chief constable can action this. That's how serious it is, Claire.'

'Right. Well, I'll probably get told off but I'll give you the number.' Claire scribbled something down on a post-it note. 'Here you are.'

'Thanks, Claire. Don't worry. I'll take any flak for this.'

Bernie left the office and looked at the number in front of her.

'Bingo,' she said.

CHAPTER 68

'My God, are you absolutely sure?'

Bernie had never seen the super this flustered before.

'I'm sure. DS Ferguson called the chief constable after Lewis Brown crashed his car and again after Harper texted saying he'd been shot. We were both there when she claimed to have no idea about Carlton Jones being held in Wiltshire. And she and Ferguson are in a relationship. She was with him last Thursday when she told us she was with the Met Commissioner.'

'You have proof of that?'

Bernie thought about what she'd seen and heard. 'Oh yes. The Commissioner told me himself that he only had a ten-minute phone call with Drake. There are photos on Ferguson's mobile that have the date stamp for last Thursday. You should have seen his face when Kerry asked him for his personal phone. He knew then that we'd find them.'

'Where is he now?'

'Still here. Not sure why but I'm wondering if he's been instructed to do so by the chief.'

'Or he's hoping she's going to bail him out. Do you have enough to arrest him?'

'Almost. I've left Tom to look at phone data to see where both Ferguson and the chief were when Carlton Jones and Ben Harper were murdered.'

'You think one of them killed Harper or ordered his murder?' Wilson wiped his face. 'Oh God.' He leaned back in his chair. 'I wish the deputy chief constable wasn't on holiday right now. And the assistant chief is off sick.'

'Sorry, sir, this is a lot to process. I'm not sure we're going to find all the evidence today. Dennis Pinner was a meticulous record keeper and I think there's going to be plenty in there.'

'We just need enough to hold them for the moment. Do you think you can get it, Bernie?'

'I'll try my best, sir.'

'Let me know when you do and I'll text the chief constable. I do have her number. Can't believe she made such a big mistake with her phone.'

'She didn't sir, it was Ferguson.'

Bernie called her team together.

'OK, I know you'll hate me for saying this but this case has moved up a massive level and there are things I can't tell you.'

Mick groaned.

'I know, sorry. But it's essential now that we gather as much detailed evidence as we can. Where are we up to with the Mercedes timeline?' Bernie asked.

Mick looked at Alice, who in turn, looked at Leigh.

'Is one of you going to tell me?'

'Well.' Leigh was hesitant. She was the most junior officer in the room. Bernie wondered why the other two weren't speaking up.

'So, we ran the registration plate and nothing showed up for the

Sunday night. But we did find it on Monday morning around ten o'clock. It was on the M4 heading towards London. It then stayed there.' Leigh was flushed and twisting one of her rings.

Bernie turned to Mick as she wanted to take the heat off Leigh. 'What conclusions do you draw from that, Mick?'

Mick swallowed. 'The car was already in the area. Possibly even at the barn where Jones was killed.'

'Have you checked for when it did arrive?'

'Started to look at that. It wasn't Sunday.'

'Look at Friday and Saturday.'

'Yes, ma'am. Now?'

'Yes, now please, Mick.'

DC Parris scuttled off to his desk to put in the request.

'Kerry and Matt, what about Pinner's records?'

Matt scratched his head. 'There's a lot going on in there. Think we're going to need a specialist fraud officer to look at it. There's years' worth of financial stuff to go through, plus messages. He's saved everything by the looks of it. Not sure if he did it as insurance in case anything happened to him, or if he left it for someone else to find.'

Bernie had her views on that but opted not to say anything.

'Tom told me it wasn't even password protected or encrypted,' Matt continued, 'which I find very odd.'

'I agree, Matt. I'll ask the super for a specialist for the finances but you and Kerry can search through the messages.'

Bernie turned her attention back to Alice and Leigh. 'You say the car stayed in London. Do you know if Forensics looked at it? I'm assuming the chief constable ordered that after I left on Friday.'

Their blank faces said it all.

'It's not been examined then. Mick, while you're there, check for this Monday night, please.'

'On it.'

Bernie rubbed her face. It seemed unbelievable that so much hadn't been done in her absence but those photos on Ferguson's phone suggested the misdirection in the case was deliberate. It was time to get in touch with DCI Charlotte Butler.

'I'm just going to get some fresh air for a few minutes,' she told her team.

'You OK?' Kerry asked, looking concerned.

'Yeah, I'm fine. There's a lot to process here and I need a clear head. I'll be back soon.'

In the safety of her car, Bernie called Charlotte Butler.

'Hi, Bernie. What can I do for you? I'm driving but I'm on hands free.'

'OK. I'll be quick. We've found some interesting things that we need to share with you. Can I have your email address please?'

'You can show me in person. Currently on route to you. Satnav says an hour and a half. You still got Ferguson?'

'Yes.'

'Keep him. And where's the chief constable?'

'At a meeting with the Wiltshire Police Commissioner.'

'See if you can get her back. I've got some dynamite evidence. Between us, Bernie, we're going to blow them out of the water.'

CHAPTER 69

Bernie came back to an enlivened team.

Mick stood up as soon as she came back in. 'Ma'am. We've got some ANPR hits. The Mercedes arrived in Wiltshire on the Friday before Carlton's murder. After going back to London on the Monday, there's nothing until Monday this week, the day you were in court. It's caught on Monday night, around twenty-three thirty hours, in the vicinity of where you were held hostage.'

Bernie smiled. It was starting to come together. 'Great work. See if there are any photos. Mind you, at that time of night, it might be hard to see who's driving.'

'I don't know,' said Leigh. 'Ferguson has quite distinctive hair.'

'Unless he's wearing a hat,' Mick replied. 'I'll get onto it, ma'am.'

Kerry waved Bernie over. 'Got some interesting WhatsApp chats between Pinner and an unknown person from a couple of months ago. But reading between the lines, I think it's Harper. Pinner is asked to provide a safe place for a "live package". I think that's Jones. He's also asked for a safe courier to transport the "live package".'

'So, if Aaron Swan was told that, he would have expected a living person, not a dead one. And Lewis was expecting it to be a normal stolen-car job,' said Bernie.

'Exactly. And that might be where it all kicked off with Swan and Harper.'

'Anything with Ferguson?'

'Nothing obvious. Maybe Harper was the only one to deal with Pinner. But it sounds as though Ferguson has a lot to answer for with the car.'

Bernie nodded. 'His phone calls too. I'm going to see the super. I think we might need to formally arrest Ferguson but I want his blessing first.'

Chief Superintendent Detective Wilson looked grave. Bernie had related everything they had on Ferguson plus the information from Charlotte Butler.

'When's the DCI arriving?'

Bernie checked her watch. 'About an hour.'

'And she didn't say what she has?'

'No. But it's dynamite.'

Wilson shook his head. 'Oh Bernie. It was bad enough with DCI Thornton but this...' He shook his head again. 'I'll text Hannah Drake. I might have to make some other calls too. Really it ought to be the police commissioner but she's with him right now. Maybe we should wait and see what DCI Butler has.'

Bernie could see Wilson was nervous. She nodded.

'I agree. Let's see what this explosive evidence is first.'

While she waited for DCI Butler to appear, Bernie and Kerry worked on the interview questions for DS Colin Ferguson. Perverting the course of justice was the easiest charge they could arrest him for. This wasn't about a confidential operation any more. Ferguson was deliberately misleading them.

The rest of the team were busy at their desks, heads down, gathering the evidence required to back up the questions. Now was a good time for Bernie to discreetly let Kerry know what was going on.

Bernie kept her voice low. 'Kerry, there might be another detective in with you when you interview Ferguson.'

Kerry looked puzzled. 'I'm guessing it's not someone from this team.'

'No. Not even Wiltshire. The Met. DCI Charlotte Butler who's investigating my abduction and Harper's murder.'

Kerry's eyes flickered with curiosity. 'He's involved in that too?'

'Possibly. She'll be here soon. I don't know what evidence she has though. Hopefully, she'll share before the interview. We'll state what we have. I know there isn't much from Pinner's stuff yet but the car details, the evidence on his phones and his general flimsy account of that night should be enough to pin Ferguson down. Even if the CPS aren't convinced initially, then we will hopfully get him suspended and a full investigation. He won't get away with this.'

DCI Charlotte Butler shook hands with the super.

'Thank you for accommodating me, sir.'

'I'd like to see your evidence first.'

Butler nodded. 'Of course. Give me a minute to set up my laptop.'

Bernie looked at Wilson. She understood his reticence. She didn't want to believe it either. Kerry seemed unfazed but she didn't know about the chief constable.

'Here we go. This is CCTV footage from a building a few doors down from the building where you were kept, Bernie. It's quite a new camera so I suspect Harper and Ferguson didn't know it was there. Now, here, just coming up to sixteen hundred hours, we see the car you were in arriving. We have the previous day's footage too when your grandmother was abducted.'

Bernie shivered. She would never have forgiven herself if something had happened to Granny.

'But that's all to do with Harper and Thornton. Harper we can't do anything with but I plan to arrest Thornton after the trial result. The jury's gone out by the way. Might get a result by the end of the week. Anyway, it's Ferguson who we have right now. And it's him we're going to get.'

Charlotte Butler fast-forwarded the tape until the evening. 'This is you and the others escaping and then' – she pressed fast-forward again and then paused – 'here is a Mercedes pulling up and what appears to be Ferguson getting out of the car.'

Bernie looked at the image. His white hair was unmistakeable. He clearly didn't know about the camera as otherwise he would have worn a hat or balaclava. She watched as the video played. Ferguson went in. Then there was a slight flash from inside the building. The shot being fired, perhaps. Moments later, he reappeared, placing something in his pocket. The gun maybe?

'As I explained to Bernie earlier, we know that the third bullet that killed Harper was fired from a different gun. We have him at the scene around time of death as shown on Harper's smart watch. I know you have Ferguson's phones and I'd like to see what you have there before we go into interview. But one of the things we've been looking at is the phone call Ferguson made after receiving Harper's text. I'm sorry to say that the mobile he called was here at headquarters.'

Bernie and Wilson glanced at each other. Butler noticed.

'I see the two of you know this already,' she said.

'But I don't,' said Kerry. 'What's going on?'

Bernie looked at Wilson and he nodded.

'The phone belongs to Chief Constable Hannah Drake,' Bernie said. 'We have evidence that she's in a relationship with Ferguson and previously with Thornton. You were here that night, Kerry. Do you remember her taking a call on her mobile?'

Kerry thought for a minute. 'Yes, I do. It was sometime around eleven o'clock. It was starting to get a bit crazy by then. She took the call in the briefing room. Said something like, "You have my permission to do whatever you need to do to get a good result." I remember looking at her and she mouthed, "The Met" to me.'

'Did you see her take any other calls or make them on her mobile that night?' Charlotte Butler asked.

'No. She was very calm throughout the whole thing. She kept telling me that we'd get Bernie back. I thought she was trying to reassure me but now... oh God, she knew about Bernie's abduction. She was in on it from the beginning, wasn't she?' Kerry's fists clenched.

Bernie rested her hand on Kerry's shoulder. 'It's looking that way. Pretty brazen of her to take the call like that.'

'It would have looked worse if she'd been secretive about it,' said Butler. 'So, Kerry, I guess you're interviewing with me. If you want to handle the stuff relating to Carlton Jones and I'll deal with Harper's murder. Let's start with you arresting for perverting the course of justice and go through your questions. Then, I'll rearrest for murder and continue the questioning. Hopefully, at some point, the chief constable will make an appearance. And that's when the explosion will happen.'

CHAPTER 70

Ferguson had looked slightly stunned when Kerry had arrested him. But sitting opposite her and Butler, he now seemed resigned to his fate. Bernie expected him to go 'no comment'. He kept glancing at DCI Butler. Did he recognise her from the Met?

Wilson sat next to Bernie as they watched the screen. He'd sent a text to Hannah Drake explaining they were formally arresting DS Ferguson. A wise woman would have run at that point but Bernie suspected the chief constable would want to know if Ferguson was going to rat on her. And she was right. Drake had replied saying she would get there as soon as possible.

'I know we've been through this all already,' said Kerry. 'But there are some things that just aren't ringing true for us. Let's start with the Mercedes you were in during the chase with Lewis Brown. You live in London, correct?'

Ferguson narrowed his eyes. 'Yes.'

'And were you in London when you received the call from Harper?'

Ferguson hesitated and looked at the lawyer the police rep had recommended. He shook his head.

'No comment.'

'Really? It would be easy to say where you were when you got the call from DC Ben Harper. The one that you previously told us about. The one where he said he had to leave his post because his child was sick. It's there, on your phone log. We know you answered it.' Kerry leaned forward. 'But I tell you what isn't there, on either your work phone or personal one, is the call or text that you said you made to a colleague asking to be picked up. Why's that?'

Ferguson lowered his head. 'No comment.'

'Do you want to know what else isn't there? Any ANPR pings for the Mercedes that night. In fact, the Mercedes you were in arrived in Wiltshire on Friday night and didn't head back to London until Monday morning. Can you explain that please?'

Bernie loved the way Kerry asked questions. Presenting facts that couldn't be explained away.

'No comment.'

'Well, it seems to me that whoever drove the Mercedes was already in Wiltshire when Harper made the call to you. We've heard from Harper's estranged wife that his child wasn't ill. So, was Ben Harper lying to you?'

'No comment.'

'Or are you lying to me?'

There was a pause before Ferguson said, 'No comment.'

'We know that Harper did call you. But it had nothing to do with his child. I think he was telling you he had done the job – killed Carlton Jones. Is that what he said?'

'No comment.'

'You know, it's strange. The Mercedes was in Wiltshire. Your phone was in Wiltshire according to triangulation. But you live in London.' Kerry shrugged. 'Help me out here, DS Ferguson.'

'No comment.' Ferguson had knitted his fingers together and

was squeezing his hands.

'He's struggling,' Bernie said to Wilson.

'He is.'

Kerry looked at her notebook. 'OK. Maybe I can jog your memory of that Sunday night/Monday morning a bit more. We've got a fabulous Digital Forensics officer here and he's been working very hard on your phones since you gave them to us this morning. According to your phones, work and personal, you were in Wiltshire from Friday night. And on Sunday, when DC Harper called you, you were both in the same location. You were both at the barn. Harper made the call to set up the alibi.'

Ferguson lifted his head and Kerry stared straight into his eyes.

'You were there when Carlton Jones was murdered.'

'No comment.'

'You were there when he was dismembered.'

'No comment.'

'You were there when Aaron Swan and Lewis Brown turned up.'

'No comment.'

'You were there when an argument broke out and Aaron Swan was shot.'

'No comment.'

'It was Harper driving the Mercedes when you chased Brown. He knew where Brown was heading to because he'd given Brown the address.'

Ferguson hesitated.

'Come on,' said Bernie. 'This is your chance to put the blame on Harper. He's dead.'

There was a knock on the viewing room door. Wilson stood up to answer and found Hannah Drake outside.

'Has the interview started?' she asked, coming into the room.

'Yes,' said Wilson. 'No comment so far. Here, have my chair. I'll fetch another.'

Bernie squirmed at the thought of being left alone with Drake. She no longer trusted the most senior officer in Wiltshire Police. She turned back to the screen. Ferguson was still silent.

'DS Ferguson, can you confirm that DC Ben Harper was driving the Mercedes that chased Lewis Brown in a white BMW?' Kerry's voice was firm.

There was a nod from Ferguson.

'For the recording, DS Ferguson nodded his head, confirming that DC Harper was the driver. Did DC Harper cause the BMW to crash?'

'No. The car lost control and he smashed into the tree.'

The lawyer placed his hand on Ferguson's arm. 'You don't have to say anything, remember?'

The chief constable tensed in her chair next to Bernie. She nearly jumped out of her skin when Wilson crashed into the room with another chair.

'Sorry,' he said. 'Bit hard to carry a chair and open the door.' He sat down on the other side of the chief constable, hemming her in. She wouldn't be leaving the room in a hurry.

Ferguson nodded his head. 'I know but it's been haunting me.' He looked at Kerry. 'I had nothing to do with the murders. That was Harper. He was the one in touch with Jack Thornton, carrying out his wishes.'

'And what exactly were his wishes for Carlton Jones?'

'Carlton was due to give evidence against Thornton, evidence that would have definitely sent him to prison. So Thornton wanted him gone. But he also wanted to send a message to DI Noel.'

'What kind of message?'

'Carlton's body was supposed to be dumped in front of her house. Brown had the directions on his phone. Harper took it after the crash.' Ferguson's knuckles turned white as he squeezed his hands tighter. 'The message was to tell DI Noel to behave when she gave evidence for the defence.'

'Interesting,' Kerry said. 'DI Noel didn't even know she was going to be giving evidence at court until later on the Monday.'

'The letter was held back deliberately until we knew she was back from maternity leave.'

'You made a phone call to someone after the crash. Who was it?'

Ferguson's talkative mood stopped. 'No comment.'

'You said before it was your boss. Was it Thornton?'

'No comment.'

Kerry looked at DCI Charlotte Butler. Time to change things up.

'DS Ferguson,' said Charlotte, 'I'm DCI Butler from the Met. Wiltshire Police have kindly let me in on their interview as our investigations cross paths. DS Allen has already arrested you on suspicion of perverting the course of justice. I'm going to rearrest you on suspicion of the murder of DC Ben Harper. I'll caution you again. You do not have to say anything. But, it may harm your defence if you do not mention when questioned something you later rely on in court. Anything you do say may be given in evidence. Do you understand?'

Ferguson's face paled. 'Yes.'

'Where were you on Monday evening around eleven p.m.? Monday of this week for clarification.' Butler's voice was clipped, very different from Kerry's Manchester accent.

Ferguson shuffled in his seat. Bernie could see he was about to clam up.

'No comment.'

'Oh. You were so chatty with DS Allen. Let's try another, bearing in mind that your phones have been analysed. Did DC Harper text you around eleven p.m.?'

'No comment.'

'Well, we know he did. It said, "Been shot. Send help." And then you rang your "boss" again. It's there in your call log. Was it Thornton?'

Hannah Drake looked at her watch.

'You all right, ma'am?' Bernie asked.

'Yes but I might have to go soon. I have an appointment this evening.'

'Oh. OK. But this is starting to get good. We might finally be able to nail Jack Thornton.'

Bernie turned back to the screen. Ferguson had dropped his head again.

'No comment.'

'Well, whoever you spoke to must have said something because the next thing that happens is this.'

She turned her laptop round and played the CCTV footage. Ferguson raised his eyebrows and his hands crept up to his mouth when he saw himself enter the building where Harper was found dead. Then the slight flash and him leaving.

'That's you, isn't it? I mean, if you're going to shoot someone dead, you really ought to disguise yourself better. That white hair gets you noticed.'

Ferguson shook his head.

'Why are you shaking your head?'

Ferguson shrugged.

'The person you rang – "the boss" – it's not your actual boss at Witness Protection because I've spoken to him. He's very concerned about this. What originally looked like a massive cock-up, now looks like corruption and conspiracy, dragging the department down. It's easy to blame it all on Harper because he's dead. And you killed him. Did you ring Jack Thornton?'

'No.' Ferguson trembled.

'Of course you didn't,' said Butler. 'Because Jack Thornton is in Belmarsh Prison in London. The person you called is in Wiltshire.'

Hannah Drake stood up suddenly, her chair tipping backwards with a crash on the floor.

'So sorry,' she said. 'I really do need to go now to make this appointment.'

Wilson stood up too. 'Are you sure, ma'am? I have a feeling that DCI Butler has almost finished.' He pointed back to the screen.

DCI Butler pulled the laptop back round and closed it. 'We've given you a lot to think about so I'm going to suggest a fifteen-minute break and you can discuss things with your lawyer. Do you think that's a good plan, DS Allen?'

'Yes. I think that's a good idea. Give DS Ferguson a chance to think about how amazing our Digital Forensics officer is. He can find *anything* on a phone. Especially hidden files.'

Hannah Drake lunged for the door but smacked straight into DCS Wilson. Bernie came up behind her.

'I think you ought to wait to speak to DCI Butler first before you go, ma'am. She's come all the way from London to see you,' said Bernie.

Hannah Drake spun round to face her. 'Oh, you're so bloody smug, aren't you? God, Bernie, I gave you one job to do – get Jack Thornton.'

'But why? He was your lover and partner in crime. Does he

know you're betraying him, like you've betrayed all your fellow police officers? You wanted it all for yourself, didn't you? Plus you have a new lover.'

Hannah Drake looked at DS Ferguson on the screen and shook her head. 'Men – they're so bloody incompetent, aren't they? I suppose you're going to arrest me now.'

Bernie shook her head. 'I'd love to, ma'am but I think it would be better to let someone else handle this. Like a Met officer.' She nodded towards the now open door where DCI Charlotte Butler was standing.

'Chief Constable Hannah Drake, I arrest you on suspicion of conspiracy to commit murder and abduction. You do not have to say anything. But, it may harm your defence if you do not mention when questioned something you later rely on in court. Anything you do say may be given in evidence. Do you understand?'

'Of course, I do.'

Drake stuck her arms out. Butler stepped forward and cuffed her. Wilson took his jacket off and placed it over her hands.

'Oh for God's sake. I don't need your chivalry,' she spat out.

'Fine.' He removed his jacket. 'Then all of your officers can see you cuffed as you're taken away. Do you need transport to London, DCI Butler?'

'Yes, please. I just need to confirm which station. Perhaps you could make the call to the CPS for Ferguson please, Bernie.'

'No problem.'

Hannah Drake gave Bernie a look of pure hatred as she was led away.

Jade's words echoed in Bernie's ears – never underestimate a woman.

Bernie reached into her pocket and drew out her phone. She'd switched it to silent during the interview. There were a few messages from her team about different things they'd discovered which would help with the case. But it was the one from Dougie that stood out.

When are you coming home? Got a baby screaming blue murder here to be fed.

Bernie saw the time was almost half past seven. It was only now she felt the ache. Kerry appeared.

'Have you seen the time? Go home. We can deal with the CPS,' she said. 'Mira needs you.'

'I agree,' Wilson said. 'In fact I don't want to see you in until Monday.'

'Monday? But that's four days away.'

'Bernie, we managed without you for nine months. We can deal with four days.'

Half an hour later, Bernie was settled on the sofa, feeding Mira. Dougie sat down next to her, a delicious smell emanating from the kitchen.

'What have you conjured up for dinner?' she asked.

'Chicken in white wine and cream, with rice. I've been thinking.'

'Sounds dangerous.'

'Well, it has been, these last ten days. Very dangerous for you. Maybe we have the parental leave wrong. Mira needs you more than me. I need you.'

Bernie placed her hand on his cheek. 'Oh Dougie. I'm sorry. You've been through hell too.'

He nodded. 'I really thought I'd lost you. That Thornton had you killed.'

'Let's talk tomorrow about what we do. I'm off work until Monday. I'd just like a normal night tonight.'

'Of course.' Dougie kissed the top of her head. 'I'll check on dinner.'

Bernie looked down at Mira. She opened her eyes and beamed at her mother.

CHAPTER 71

Monday

'I can't believe it was only two weeks ago, Bernie, that we were sat here on your first day back. So much has happened. I can honestly say I've had more excitement and trauma with you in these last few years than I've had in my whole career.'

Bernie smiled. 'Sorry, sir.'

The super looked exhausted. 'Don't be. I wouldn't change a thing. Now, one of the things we discussed two weeks ago was you getting home in time to feed Mira. I know there's been some exceptional circumstances but you haven't been able to leave on time. The job doesn't warrant it. I spoke to the assistant chief constable over the weekend. He's taking over for Hannah Drake at the moment. He agrees with me that you need extended compassionate leave. Not sick leave, I hasten to add. That raises complications with HR.'

'I'm not sure what to think about this, sir. On the one hand I'll love being home with Dougie and Mira. On the other, I've really enjoyed being back at work. Except for the kidnapping bit. How long are we talking here? A couple of weeks?'

'No. Ten weeks. It will take you to the end of parental leave.'

'Ten? I don't need that much.'

'Actually, Bernie, I think you do. I'd like you to attend trauma counselling during this time. One a week. The first appointment is on Wednesday.'

'Has Dougie put you up to this?'

They'd had some heated 'discussions' over the weekend about work.

'No. He doesn't know. You're a bloody good officer. I want you to stay that way. You can work this morning and then do a handover to Kerry. She'll be Acting DI while you're away.'

Wilson stood up and held out his hand.

Bernie was confused but stood up as well and shook Wilson's hand. It felt odd. It wasn't something he normally did. Was he… no, Bernie blinked that thought away. He wasn't saying goodbye. Was he?

Everyone was at their desks in MCIT, even Leigh. Bernie thought she might have gone back to Gable Cross in Swindon.

'Good to see you're still with us, Leigh.'

'Thanks, ma'am. The super's asked me to stay on the case for a while longer.'

'Good. We like having you here.'

Bernie looked up and caught Kerry's eye. She gave a broad smile.

'So, who's going to update me on the last four days?' Bernie asked.

'I will,' Kerry said. 'Although feel free to chip in if I forget anything. After you left on Wednesday, I went back to Ferguson and informed him that Hannah Drake had been arrested. At that point, he started singing like a canary. He'd only recently joined Thornton's organised crime group. Because going by Pinner's files, that's what they were. Drake lured him in. Before he knew it, he was in deep. Not surprisingly, he blamed Harper for Jones's and Swan's deaths but I think he was genuine. He told us where to find the other missing limbs so we have them. The idea was to lead you in a merry dance until it was time to reveal Carlton's identification. Anyway, fishing season has now opened and everyone's happy.'

Bernie laughed. It was good to keep the anglers on side.

'And what about our former chief?' she asked.

'You'll have to ask DCI Butler about her,' Kerry replied. 'But from what I've heard, she's currently enjoying remand in a solitary cell in an undisclosed prison.'

'Good.' Bernie thought about everything Hannah Drake had done over the past two weeks. She was glad Drake was on remand and not out on bail.

'What about the email from Honduras, sarge?' said Mick.

'Oh yes. That was a surprise,' Kerry said. 'Came in on Saturday evening as we were getting ready to leave. It was from the Honduran police with a signed statement attached. Guess who it was from?'

'The Pinners? Helen Brown or her sister?' Bernie said.

'No. Jade Ambrose, giving a very detailed report of everything she's been involved in. And I mean, everything. Put it this way, she can't come back to the UK now. She'd be arrested on the spot. And not just for shooting Ben Harper. But for all the drug dealing she's been involved in. A few things she said in her statement have helped us understand Pinner's records.'

'Let me guess, we don't have an extradition agreement with Honduras.'

'No, we don't. And it seems she's been preparing for this for a few years. She's now a citizen. Looks like she diverted her money there.'

'But she's left Danny behind.'

'Has she? If Thornton's found guilty, then Danny could go for an appeal.'

Bernie shook her head. Never underestimate a woman. Jade's words again.

'And if he gets out, he'll go to Honduras. She's got guts. But she always puts her boys first. I can't fault her for that,' Bernie said. 'I'm guessing the Pinners have done something similar and gone to a country without an extradition treaty too. Cambodia would be my first guess. Well, I'm sure there's a lot more that's going to come out over the next few weeks but I won't be here. I've been told by the super to take a break. Quite a long one. Ten weeks to be precise. But I'll be leaving you in Kerry's capable hands. We need to do a handover before I go.'

'Of course. We'll miss you,' said Kerry.

'Don't say that. You'll set me off.' Bernie wiped her eyes. She didn't want to leave again but knew it was for the best.

Each of her team stood up and hugged her, with Leigh giving her a tight squeeze.

'I might not be here when you get back but I hope we can still catch up,' Leigh said. .

'Of course. Thank you, Leigh. Right, Kerry. Let's get this handover sorted.'

Bernie pressed her key fob to open her car. Her phone was buzzing in her pocket. She drew it out and answered.

'DI Noel.'

'Hi, Bernie, it's Charlotte. I'm about to go inside the Old Bailey. Jury's back. I'll text you the verdict as soon as I can but it might be a while. Regardless of what happens, I'll be arresting Jack Thornton on suspicion of conspiracy to murder and abduction straight after the result.'

Bernie opened her car door, her hand a little unsteady.

'OK. I'm about to go home. I've been put on compassionate leave.'

'Good. I told DCS Wilson that you need time off. You'll have to go through another trial and I want you in tip-top shape for it. Your grandmother too. Shame we can't get Jade Ambrose back here but she's provided us with a lot of information.'

'She wants Danny out.'

'Of course she does. I'd better go in. I'll text soon.'

Bernie sat in her car for a minute, wondering whether to wait there for the verdict. No. She wanted to be home with Dougie and Mira. Despite her misgivings about such a long break, the three of them needed that time together.

Mira jumped up and down in Dougie's arms when Bernie walked into their little lounge.

'Oh. You're home early,' Dougie said, passing Mira over.

'Compassionate leave for ten weeks.'

'Wow. Ten?'

'Takes us up to the end of parental leave. And there are ten counselling sessions. One a week.'

Dougie put his arm around her shoulders and kissed her on her cheek. 'I think that's a good thing. And we can go on holiday for some of that time. Go to Scotland. Maybe take Granny with us. She's going to need help too.'

'I know.' Bernie paused. 'Jury's back in. DCI Butler's going to text me the verdict but she has to arrest Thornton first for conspiracy to murder and abduction. I'll have to go through another trial.

This nightmare isn't over.'

'Oh Bernie. You're the bravest woman I know.'

'Have to be. I live with you.'

Dougie smirked. 'Very true.'

Bernie felt a buzz in her pocket. 'I think that's a text.'

'OK. Let's sit down and we'll look at it together.'

Bernie put Mira on her playmat and surrounded her with toys. She pulled out her phone and sat down on the sofa next to Dougie.

'Ready?' he asked.

Bernie nodded and opened the text.

Guilty. On all charges.

Dear reader,

I want to say a huge thank you for choosing to read *Rewind*. If you enjoyed it, and want to keep up to date with all my latest releases, just sign up at the following link. Your email address will never be shared and you can unsubscribe at any time.

kluver.co.uk

I hope you loved *Rewind* and if you did, I would be very grateful if you could write a review. I'd love to hear what you think, and it makes such a difference helping new readers to discover one of my books for the first time.

I couldn't leave Bernie pregnant for ever, nor could I not tell her full back story. *Rewind* has lived in my head for a long time so I'm glad I've finally been able to share it with you. There's so much going on in this book – gangs, drugs, corrupt police officers – but none of these are the main theme for *Rewind*. I wanted forgiveness to be at the heart of this story. Bernie has suffered from guilt and PTSD for a long time. I'd like to think that Gloria's forgiveness could help start the healing process.

I love hearing from my readers – you can get in touch on my author Facebook page, through X, Instagram or my website.

Thanks,
Joy

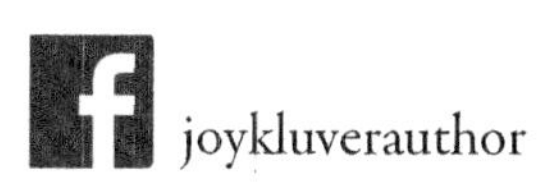

www.kluver.co.uk

ACKNOWLEDGEMENTS

Self-publishing is not easy and don't let anyone tell you it is. There's a whole host of people who've helped me with all of this. Firstly, Rebecca Bradley – without your guidance and support at the beginning, I'm not sure I'd have started down this path. I'll be forever grateful for the time you gave up to help me. Likewise, Vicki Goldman and Biba Pearce for your advice on so many things.

Sara Starbuck – my star editor! Thank you for being my cheerleader again and helping *Rewind* to be as good as possible. Thanks to Elaini Caruso for her sharp eyes with both copy editing and proof reading. To Michael Watermeyer – I'll never understand how you took my blurb and created the perfect cover. Not only did you capture the atmosphere but you also gave Bernie a face.

Even though I'm self-publishing this book, I've still had great support from my agent, Anne Williams. Thank you for everything you do.

As always, I try to keep the police procedural side of things fairly realistic. Thanks to former Met Chief Superintendent Raj Singh Kohli, I hope I've managed to achieve this again. Any mistakes are my own. Thanks also to Graham Bartlett for introducing us and also for the police procedural writing courses. I've learned so much from Graham's courses and the information is often fed back into the stories.

Thank you to Karen Bate, my first beta reader for all my novels. If I don't get a thumbs up from Karen, then I know it's not a good book. Such a relief to find you enjoyed *Rewind*! And to Ace Coggins, my second beta reader. Thank you so much for the time you gave up to read *Rewind*. I'm so grateful for the support you've given me as a reader.

Thank you to Anne Coates for being my tour guide round Peckham. I really enjoyed it and it helped me to get a good sense of the place. I created a fictional housing estate for the story but I've tried to add a few touches of the real Peckham. And I apologise to the people living in the small hamlet of Clench in Wiltshire. Google Streetview gave me the barns and the old caravan and it was too good an opportunity to pass up.

Huge thanks to the authors who gave their time to read and quote for *Rewind*. Reading takes up precious writing time so I'm very grateful to Alice Hunter, Heather Critchlow, Alex Khan, Joanna Wallace, Rod Reynolds, Victoria Goldman, Rebecca Bradley, Lucy Martin, A.A. Chaudhuri, Sarah Clarke, Victoria Dowd and Jacqueline Sutherland.

A special thank you to the SW London Authors group for all your support, especially Lucy Martin, Sarah Clarke, Jacqueline Sutherland, A.A. Chaudhuri, Emma Rae, Victoria Dowd and Anita Chapman, for listening to my tales of woe over coffee and then telling me to just write the book and publish it. The same goes for the West London Authors group, especially Emma Curtis.

To the wonderful bloggers who said yes to taking part in the tour – Jacob Collins, Jen Lucas, Mandie Griffiths, Karen Coles, Mags Naylor, Yvonne Bastian, Emma Welton, Joanne Robertson and Susan Heads. I can't tell you how relieved I was when you agreed to take part!

Huge thanks to Sarah McAlister and the Friends of West Barnes Library for continuing to support our author events and for your encouragement to me. And to our new writing group at the library.

To all my church friends and my neighbours who have encouraged me along the way.

To my family – my mother who showed real belief in this book. My kids, who once again put up with my mind being elsewhere. And to my husband, Phil, who has very patiently waited for a book to be dedicated to him.

And finally, to my readers. Without you, I wouldn't have considered taking the step to write and self-publish *Rewind*. So many of your reviews were calling for book four in the series and I couldn't ignore that. I hope you enjoyed it.

Printed in Great Britain
by Amazon